THE OTHER
JUDAS

VICKI CLARKE

prologue

When was the last time you felt inspired? Truly inspired? Blessed am I among men for I have lived with inspiration personified. He was a man, yes, but He was much more. He was our direction, the wind in our sails. He was our joy. We wanted His designs and purposes to be our own. He was different than any man this earth has ever known. He was the fresh scent of spring. His ideology piqued our intellect like the air of an early crisp morn. His compassion pulled us along like the strong current made by a wave. He was a man of authority and worthy of emulation. He was our king.

He had always been king, for true kingship is born both of royal lineage and appointment by Adonai, yet He was not always recognized as such. The intellects of our time, to their eternal disgrace, were blind to His right to the throne. It was the public masses, people like you and me, to whom this recognition fell. It was we, His subjects, who saw His virtuous nature and desired to live under His protection, to be sustained by His bounty and to live in the hope of His dreams and aspirations. We were the ones who paid Him homage. He was our blessed Jesus.

chapter one

My name is Judas. Not the notorious Judas Iscariot, that poor deceived soul, but I was also one of Jesus's inner twelve. I am 'the other Judas,' as I am called by my fellow apostles. I am the unassuming one, the one who worked quietly and diligently to make our blessed Lord a king.

I was not always a man of political ambition. What did I care of kings and king making? Of course, I believed in the prophet's writings for I am a devout Israelite. The scriptures foretold of a coming king who would restore Israel's lost glory. Our deliverer was promised by Adonai. But four years ago, I was not searching for a promise. I was content with my life as it was.

Before I met Jesus I was a merchant, like my father and his father before him. For generations my family had lived in Nain, a town in Galilee. My friends and colleagues called me trustworthy because I would not sell people what they did not want. My father, however, called me shrewd because I knew how to sell people what they did not need. Man's necessity was not my concern but his desires were what filled my pockets with money.

I have always felt that Adonai's great gift to me is my ability to read people. My clues to their thoughts are many and, when I was a merchant, my memory concerning what motivated them to buy was impeccable. I could see the deepening folds in an old man's wrinkled forehead as he justified spending money on a new plow when he had a sturdy one at home, the spark in a woman's eye when her desire for a gold bracelet was kindled or the nudge between a husband and wife that told me whom I needed to convince. With one client I played on his yearning for fashion, another his thrill at goading his neighbour and still another, the coin to be saved. I had no qualms about using my gift to my advantage. As a result, I lived quite well.

Father would regularly boast that my intuitive sense of what people held valuable was from his side of the family—then he would quickly add that my emotional side was from my mother. My wife used to tease me that if rain from heaven flowed as often as the tears from my eyes, Israel would never have to worry about drought again. Although being moved by the beauty of my world has caused me embarrassment at times, it does make it easy to love life. I appreciate the simplest things, the crafts my clients sought and sold, a sunset, a child's laugh, and the caress from the hand of my dear wife, Rachel.

It has been ten years since she has died. I believe the harshest blow she was dealt in life was not living long enough to see her first grandchild. My wife died unexpectedly of a severe fever when I was thirty-eight. Three months later Caleb was born. I comfort myself that at least Rachel had known the hope of Caleb's arrival. When she heard that our son Jonathan and his wife, Tabitha, were expecting, Rachel immediately started sewing for the new baby. I think her natural exuberance was increased because children were a rare blessing in our family. While all of my brothers have six or seven children, we have two. Jonathan was born a year after Rachel and I were married. Our daughter, Mara, arrived seven years later. We waited twelve years for another child and when finally there was a promise of another baby, we were to be his grandparents. Months before Rachel died, she and Mara created a colourful stack of new bedding and tunics in the corner of our living space.

My home was typical of many in the towns of Galilee. It had one room made of brick, not clay like the poor nor hewn stone like the rich. I did afford myself the luxury of an upper chamber on the roof for hot nights. This was enough for the four of us.

I was certainly not the richest man in Nain, but that was never my aspiration. We were happy to live without want—and our needs were not extravagant.

My life changed when I was forty-four: I had found a husband for

Mara, and Jonathan, trained as a merchant, was expecting his third child. Rachel's death had cut me adrift; my life had lost its purpose, day-to-day events had become rote.

Life, I find, has events that pull us in an unexpected direction as strongly as an ass pulls a cart off one path onto another. These happenings are not due to our decisions—although they will most certainly demand us to make decisions in the future. They are everyday affairs which suddenly become a point of divergence in our lives. If life were like a river, these points would be the deltas where one tributary pours into a river flowing in a different direction. It is the thoughtless brush of your hand across your brow which detects the initial sore of leprosy or the familiar voice behind you on the path that you turn to, only to see beyond your friend dust rising from the Roman legions as they march towards your town. For me it was a seemingly inconsequential conversation four years ago that changed everything.

"You must come back with me next week, Judas. He is to speak again!" James nearly shouted at me in his enthusiasm.

James was a potter. Back from a recent trip selling his pots and jars in Nazareth where he had attended a Sabbath service in the town. He was most adamant in telling me about a local man who had read from the scriptures and taught that day.

"What could possibly be so different in what this man has to say?" I wondered aloud, amused by his excitement.

"It's not just what he says, it's who he is, how he carries himself and how he makes you feel. He's amazing, Judas. Please, you have to come," he pleaded.

I had known James since we were children. He was not the type to heedlessly pursue frivolous ventures. Although he often argued a bit too aggressively for my liking, I respected his opinion for he held firm convictions and acted on them. Because of our friendship (and his insistence), I agreed to readjust my schedule for an upcoming business trip to make the village of Nazareth, a two days' walk north of Nain, my first stop. James immediately declared himself my much needed and loyal traveling companion.

Travel was a necessity in my business. I bought copper pots and earthenware jars from Azariah the potter, intricate bracelets and rings from Daniel the goldsmith, blankets from Anna and small farm implements from a local carpenter named Elkanah. Twice a year, after visiting my rural suppliers, I would take my loaded cart to towns and cities and set up my booth in the marketplace. A month ago I had finished collecting my merchandise, now it was time to sell.

James and I set out early mid-week to walk the dusty path to Nazareth. The days were long as we trudged beside my donkey, giving him an occasional tug of encouragement as he pulled my loaded cart. I appreciated the company, our light conversations helped to keep my mind distracted from my weary feet.

Seeing the homes of Nazareth in the distance at the end of the second day, we hastened our steps—eager to shed the days grime and rest at Jacob's house.

I would hardly call Jacob a friend. He was the type of person who bolstered his esteem by cutting down the character of those around him. I learned soon after meeting him to broach conversations gingerly and avoid anything controversial; he was quick with his judgments and was, I might add, often wrong. I tolerated him solely because he was a fellow merchant and was therefore invaluable when it came to selling goods and finding new suppliers.

It was late when we arrived. Making good use of the last light from the setting sun, we bedded the donkey and briefly refreshed ourselves before preparing for the Sabbath. We performed the evening's rituals with Jacob and his family, celebrating the *shabbat*, our Sabbath meal, and then sat down to visit with our host.

"I, for one, am anxious to hear Jesus speak tomorrow," James blurted out at the first opportunity he found to steer the conversation in his direction. I had neglected to warn him about Jacob.

"Oh, is that why you are here so early, Judas? I was not expecting you for another three weeks," Jacob inclined an eyebrow at me.

"Yes, after James was here last week and heard Jesus speak, he convinced me to change my travel plans so I could hear Jesus as well," I said, chuckling in an attempt to divert Jacob's incipient sarcasm. "Who is this man that he can command such enthusiasm from a stoic like James?" I asked, giving James a good-natured jab in the ribs, desperately hoping to keep the talk light.

"Actually, he's a carpenter," Jacob answered.

"Truly? Why have you never spoken of him before?" I queried. "I could have been selling his creations across the countryside."

"Because he's not very good," Jacob stated matter-of-factly.

James and I stared at him in silence. Jacob eagerly explained.

"His father Joseph was a good carpenter. He tried to teach Jesus the craft but Jesus could never master it like his father. When Joseph died about sixteen years ago Jesus took on the responsibility of caring for the family. A few local families took pity on them and employed him to do some woodworking. They were mostly widows and poorer people who could afford no one better and so he has managed to make enough for his mother, brothers and sister to eke out a meagre existence over the years. Now he has finally found a husband to care for his sister, and his brother, James, is making a profit as a carpenter and actually advancing the family name, so Jesus has selfishly decided to pursue personal interests."

He sniffed, shook his head disdainfully and, making no attempt to hide the contempt in his voice, continued, "And to think, for thirty years he has said nary a word about holy matters and now no one can keep his mouth from flapping. Well, from the ruckus he's created I guess he has at least found something that he is moderately good at."

I sat dumbfounded then glanced at James. His body was rigid, his lips pursed and his eyes narrowed as he glowered at Jacob.

Fearful of a clash between James's opinions and Jacob's temper, I cleared my throat, stretched and quickly said, "I'm exhausted. How about you, James?"

Before James could answer I turned to Jacob and said, "I presume we are sleeping on the roof tonight."

Jacob nodded, seemingly unaware of the offense James had taken to his comments. I rose, curtly nudged James to stand, ushered him out of the room and showed him to our sleeping quarters.

Long after we were settled for the night, I lay on my mat wondering at the diverse assessment these two men had made about Jesus. Such a disparity of opinion piqued my curiosity and I determined to find out for myself who this man really was.

chapter two

We rose early the next morning, dressed and made our way through the busy streets to a large building where people were assembling for the Sabbath service. Jacob glanced about, scowling.

"More and more visitors every Sabbath. Soon they'll push us out of our own building!"

Indeed, a very large crowd of people milled about waiting for the meeting to begin. Many wore traveling clothes and I recognized some from the villages I frequented on business. Curiosity gnawed at me. Could this man really be that extraordinary? Obviously, word had spread quickly to the surrounding area that he was speaking here today. Why were people excited to tell their friends and family about him? What was it about him that compelled men to walk miles and readjust their lives simply to hear his words? Jacob was clearly right, Jesus had found something that he was good at.

Near the south end of the gathering I heard excited voices begin chattering louder than the drone around me. Like a rock striking still water a ripple of murmurs spread through the crowd. Jesus had arrived. I struggled to catch a glimpse of him but, given how many were of the same mind, soon gave up. The doors of the building opened and the throng of men entered ceremoniously.

The service began. We sang our traditional songs and received the customary blessings from the rabbi. Jesus sat about ten rows ahead of me and a little to the left. I glanced in his direction. From where I was sitting he looked like any other man. He wore a turban on his head. His skin was the same olive colour and his jet black beard was oiled just like everyone else's in the room. He wore his robes in the same fashion and even his tunic was the same shade of blue favoured by many.

Just as the thought fluttered across my mind that I might be wasting my time, Jesus rose, ascended the platform and turned to face his audience. All credence to my last thought vanished.

Jesus looked at the men assembled before him, his gaze focusing everyone's attention upon him. It was as if he knew that we had come for the sole purpose of seeing him. Yet there was no pride or arrogance in his look, only gratitude for our efforts in having endured long roads and strange beds to be here. Although he was not overly tall and was but of average build, he had a regal bearing about him—as if he was sure of who he was and why he was there; confident that what he had to give we were in desperate need to receive. It seemed like he had nothing to prove and everything to share.

Again, he looked about the room but this time more intentionally, purposefully.

Oh, those eyes!

They were as bright as the sun on a cloudless day and shone with an intensity I had never seen. They were the windows of his soul and transformed his very countenance. They were deep brown yet they shone like polished copper—as if brilliance was being contained behind tinted glass.

As he looked at each man in turn, the thought came to me that he could see straight through their very being to their hearts, like an arrow driving with such force that nothing could deter or misdirect it.

Truly, the realization terrified me. *When he looks at me,* I thought, *there will be no hiding, no facades. I will be naked. He will see who I truly am. My flawed, sin-filled nature will be laid bare.* Panic spread from the pit of my stomach to my throat. I had no thought of how others around me reacted, I only knew that I felt an overwhelming urgency to flee and hide.

Run! my inner voice screamed.

I fidgeted, restless for a means of escape.

And then Jesus looked at me. Our eyes met. His eyes bore into my soul. I knew he understood me beyond how I knew myself. He could see my failures and doubts, my missed opportunities and regretful moments. He could see it all and I was powerless to stop him.

Ashamed, yet unable to turn my face away, I stared back at him. His eyes were not full of disgust or contempt as I expected. While my heart bled black filth, his eyes drew me in, held me. I felt embraced by a holy love, safe.

All this with but a look!

Two men on either side of Jesus unrolled the scroll of parchment containing the Torah and held it for him to read. As he spoke he reminded me of a writer reading his own words; it was as if he knew fully the intentions behind each phrase. When he expounded on the passage, he spoke of Adonai's voracious love, his profound protection and his undeniable presence. Jesus's words exploded with truth. As a man used to the mundane and mediocre, accustomed to cynicism and life's daily grind, Jesus's passion was to me like sweet cool water on dry, crusty, cracked ground.

Oh, but my soul drank it in deeply!

All too soon he was finished speaking and I knew my life would never be the same.

The next morning I began contriving ways to meet Jesus.

I have never thought myself an impetuous man but then I had never before met a man like Jesus. I had to speak with him. Never had I known the feelings that he had stirred within me and I was not content to let them be. It was all I could think of, all I knew, as if I had delighted in but a sip of exquisite wine that awakened my taste buds, a splash of sensation across my palate that left me savouring the thought of another taste.

James too was anxious for a chance to meet Jesus so we concocted a plan. James went to all the locations we suspected idle talk and gossip to be rampant. He was to glean information about where Jesus lived, who his close friends were, the establishments he frequented and any possible future travel plans. I went to the marketplace to pepper merchants and buyers with nonchalant inquiries; discreetly gathering information for personal gain was my true gift and in this new venture I intended to use my talent to the fullest.

At lunch, James and I met under a large yellow canopy at the edge of the marketplace to share our findings. We had done well. We had learned the location of Jesus's home and knew the names of some friends with whom he spent a considerable amount of time.

The houses of the first three people on our list were all empty, as was Jesus's home, but we were not easily discouraged. One of the merchants had mentioned the name of a widow for whom Jesus often did work so, after obtaining directions to her house, we set off again.

When we turned the corner to her street there was no doubt that we had found Jesus. Packed in the yard, clamouring about the house, were no less than fifty people. We walked up to the edge of the group to add ourselves to their number. I was afraid of this. I did not want to be merely one of the group observing from the back, I wanted to experience Jesus again.

I swayed, looked, went up on the tips of my toes and pondered what to do next. Then I heard two people chatting.

"He's leaving in a day, you know," said one.

"No! Where is he going?" asked the other.

"To Capernaum, I think," answered the first.

"That's more than a ten day walk. What does he want up there?" whined the second. "We can't afford to be patient any more. If we want to see Jesus we will have to get closer."

With a groan the man jutted out his elbows and tried to squeeze between two women in front of him.

I turned to James, whispering, "Let's go. I have another idea."

I explained the details of my plan to James as we walked back to Jacob's house. There we packed our belongings, thanked our host and went to the market.

Because I was on a business trip, my plan was easily accomplished.

I brought my cart to the edge of the market and began unloading its contents. James and I, each with an armful of goods, descended upon the booths selling everything at whatever price we could. Some items I was able to barter well on, others I knew could have sold for a fairer price had I the time to dicker. We went back to the cart five or six times to gather more armloads of supplies. Finally we sold the donkey and cart. All things considered, we made out quite well.

Next we bought enough food to last us for a few days. Then, while we still had an hour or two of the day's sunlight, we left Nazareth and headed north towards Capernaum. We walked until the full moon replaced the sun then lay down for a restless sleep beside the road. Traveling at night was dangerous, but in order for my scheme to work it was imperative that we stay ahead of Jesus.

I could almost hear the giggles of my wife Rachel ringing in my head. She used to tease me about taking two weeks to prepare for a short trip—what would she think of me now?

Before the sun crested the horizon we started walking again.

"How far did you say those rocks were?" asked James, breaking the stillness of the morning.

"Halfway between Nazareth and a small village called Kilia." I answered. "We should reach them in about two more hours." I had traveled this road numerous times and I knew precisely where we needed to go.

"It's strange," I continued, "to be seeking the place that I usually want to avoid."

"And the reason we seek it," added James, "is the same as the reason you fear it."

"Indeed," I finished lamely, "very strange."

Our desired destination was a large outcropping of rocks which crowded the road on either side. Normally I was leery of walking through the area, knowing it was an ideal place for thieves to hide. Now I desired the concealment the rocks would provide.

Just as I had predicted, we came upon the formation two hours later.

We explored the area together, searching for an optimum lookout as well as to convince ourselves that we were alone. Finally, we found the perfect location. We decided to hide behind a particularly large jagged rock that looked like a giant tooth. Boulders and rock ledges serrated the rock face a few feet below us. From our vantage point we could see down the road yet remain out of sight. We lay in a hollowed section of the formation's top slab, peering around the rock. It proved to be uncomfortable and hot, particularly in the afternoon when even the 'rock-tooth' would cease providing its shady protection, yet it was the surest place to watch for activity without being seen. We nestled into our hiding spot and waited.

Little happened for the remainder of the morning. We saw various manner of people pass by but not the one we sought. At noon we had a bite to eat.

"Do you think we should chance another night outside of a village, especially here?" asked James, toying with his bread. "If we left now we could probably make it to Kilia before dark."

"I know we already tempted fate sleeping on the roadside last night," I replied. "But this is a good hiding spot and we haven't seen anyone suspicious."

"I'm glad you think so," said James with a smile, looking relieved. "I would hate to lose this chance to meet Jesus. It's just that we would be such a treasure for a band of robbers and there are only the two of us."

"No one knows we are here," I reassured him. "And I think it's worth the risk even if thieves happen upon us and steal it all."

"Me, too," grinned James.

"But," I suggested, "perhaps we could be more vigilant. Why don't we take turns? You keep watch now and through the evening for Jesus. I will try to sleep during the afternoon and watch for danger tonight. That way we'll also be sure not to miss Jesus if he is traveling early in the morning."

James nodded and quickly finished his grapes and bread before scrambling up the rocks in order to perch again under the hot sun. I, meanwhile, rested in the shade of one of the lower craggy ledges.

In the late evening, with stars twinkling above, I took my shift behind the giant 'rock-tooth.' The night was thankfully uneventful. At dawn, after sharing breakfast with James, I lay down and James took my place to watch and wait again.

I don't know how long I slept but the sun was halfway up in the sky when James jostled me awake.

"He's coming! He's coming!" he whispered hoarsely, voice strained with excitement, trying not to yell.

I clambered up the rocks to peer over the ridge. Yes, there he was in the centre of about twenty men who grouped behind and beside him. Billows of dust blew across the road. They had no obvious order, three or four men walked abreast as the road allowed, chattering amongst themselves.

We gathered our supplies to run down the sloping scree above them, emerging on the road a fair distance north of them. The idea was to appear as fellow travelers, as if coincidence had us on the same road traveling in the same direction. Once in place, we slowed our pace to a snail's crawl and waited to be overtaken by the group.

We said not a word, straining to hear any indication that they were gaining on our position. I tingled with anticipation.

After a time, we heard the low drone of voices and the faint sound of conversation. Finally, I could make out a few words here and there.

Then came a shout.

"Yo, friends! Would you mind some company?" I could not be sure but I thought it was the same voice that I had heard speaking at the synagogue. Jesus, I believed, had called out a greeting to us.

My stomach tightened, my heart exploded into my throat, my hands went as cold as metal and my mouth felt like desert sand. We turned slowly and waited for the group of men. When they were near enough for us to speak, I lowered my eyes to the ground to convey my belief that their leader was a man of significance.

"It would be an honour," I said.

"Well," Jesus replied, and I realized that it had indeed been him who had called to us, "join us then! It seems to me that you have had a hard day and night. Please, let me help you with your load."

Giving no explanation as to how he had seen through our ruse, he reached out and stripped me and James of our packs. Shouldering my bag himself, he turned to the companion on his left and handed him James's belongings, asking, "Andrew, would you mind carrying this man's pack? He has endured a long night."

"Of course, Lord," said Andrew readily, with no apparent resentment at being asked to help.

"It is not necessary!" I blurted.

"It is a small thing and we want to do it," Jesus countered.

I was silent for a moment.

"I am Judas and this is my friend James," I said, motioning to myself and presenting James, who stood beside me.

"It is a pleasure to meet you both," Jesus replied. Relief washed over me and I realized that my eyes were still downcast. I slowly chanced a look at Jesus's face.

His smile was generous and true, making me feel like he was happy we were there. His gaze was a quiet, gentle breath of air gifting rest to my soul and putting me at ease. I had no need for pretensions. I felt I could be fully myself, like my first day home after too long a journey. It was the joy of relaxing in a place of belonging.

"Come then, Judas and James! Let us see if we can make a few more miles before the day is spent."

James and I happily fell into step beside Jesus.

"Judas," Jesus said, turning to me. His voice carried well and I knew the others listened as intently as I did. I thought his eyes looked almost mischievous. "I have a story that you may appreciate. There was once a merchant who diligently scoured the countryside for various valuable antiquities. On one of his journeys, he happened upon a pearl of incredible wealth. His find excited him beyond anything he had known and he knew that he must have it. Nothing else mattered compared to acquiring the gem. The pearl was costly, but the merchant cared not. He began selling his goods and saving his money. His determination was undaunted in his quest to obtain the pearl. I tell you the truth, Judas, that merchant was honoured because he knew true value and pursued, with strength, his worthy goal."[1]

I stared, awestruck at how his story mirrored our experiences of the past few days. How did he know of my sacrifices and risks? But more than that, immeasurably more, was the halting thought that he cared! I glanced at the men walking with us. They looked entranced by the interesting story but completely bewildered, as if they had not an inkling of what he was talking about.

"It seems it is time for some introductions," Jesus continued. "You already know that this man is Andrew." Jesus gestured to the man carrying James's pack. Then Jesus began a litany of names, adding a little phrase or story that conjured in my mind living images of each man's personality. I found that it was with amazing ease that I was able to remember the people around me.

"Tell us about yourself, Judas," Jesus said after he had introduced us to everyone.

"Well, I am a merchant," I began.

"Truly? Just like in the story?" It was Matthew who commented. Jesus had described him as a veritable scribe who always paid attention to detail.

I looked at Jesus with a small smile, trying to ignore Matthew's comment without seeming rude.

"I sell mostly pots, blankets and farming tools," I continued.

It seemed like I talked for most of the afternoon—telling them about my life and family while men from the group asked various questions which made me feel like they were genuinely interested in who I was. Jesus's questions and observations, though, were different. When talking about merchandise he commented that my wares seemed to meet the needs of everyday people, people who were the very salt of the earth. When I spoke of my family, he asked what game my grandsons most enjoyed playing with me. His questions seemed not so much to gather information as to endear me to his traveling companions, encourage me and promote fast friendships, building unity in our small group.

Later that evening when we made camp, I tried to remember what

Jesus and the others asked James, but forgive me, I do not remember their queries. So overwhelmed was I by my own feelings of welcome and acceptance that it was all I could focus on during our first meeting. I do not feel too guilty, however, because just before we ate supper with our new companions, James took me aside and said, "Have you ever seen the like, Judas? Jesus is a wonder! I just hope you did not feel too put out with all the attention that I received."

After a supper of pooled culinary resources both in food and cooking talent, we settled down to relax around the campfire. In only one afternoon I felt a part of Jesus's entourage. The night was not too dark; the moon lent its light to the glow of the fire. A few stars shone brightly enough in the dusky sky to peek and wink at us. The fire in turn, spit and crackled and sent up its own version of sparks of light.

Reuben and Jesse, two men Jesus had introduced to me, were deep in discussion behind me. What had started as a simple talk to pass the time fast became a heated debate and began to attract the attention of everyone close by. They were arguing the possible outcome of a disagreement which was to have been put before the magistrate that day back in Nazareth, a dispute that involved each of their brothers.

It seemed that Reuben's brother, Leban, had built a house, complete with a brick wall around the perimeter of his property. To secure the wall he had fashioned cables which extended beyond his property to the surrounding land. This land had not been owned by anyone at the time and so his method of strengthening his wall was of no consequence to anyone but himself.

A number of years later Jesse's brother, Asher, bought the property beside Leban. He began to excavate his property and, upon discovering the cables secured on his side of the wall, cut them—never bothering to tell his new neighbour of his actions.

More years passed and eventually the movement of dirt on Asher's property necessary to building his home, coupled with the lack of extra support previously provided by the cables, began to take its toll on the wall. The wall was now beginning to fall onto Leban's property and was actually endangering his home. A dispute ensued about who was responsible for the cost of repairing and girding the wall before it collapsed and took part of Leban's house with it. The magistrate was to decide if the man who had secured the wall outside of his property, or the one who had destroyed the cables without a word of warning, would have to pay. Reuben and Jesse were now aggressively discussing the merits of each brother's case.

Suddenly, in angry desperation to prove himself right, Jesse triumphantly bellowed, "Let's ask Jesus who he thinks should pay for the wall!"

All the men around the fire ceased their conversations, their eyes turning to Jesus. Based on the argument I had just inadvertently overheard, I guessed that the properties in question were held by men of high esteem who unashamedly took many opportunities to sway public opinion to their side. Given that this had happened in Jesus's home town, I had little doubt that he had heard the merits of the case debated more than once.

"I would prefer a world without walls," Jesus began. "Here we have barriers of separation that are used to define possession. In the world I would have, people would not be so concerned with personal property as with human dignity."

He took a breath and gazed towards heaven with a sigh of contentment. He looked as though he was seeing a vision of the world as he wanted it to be, not as it was. Every great king has plans for his kingdom, for the direction it should take, what it should aspire to and be remembered for. The purity of the vision is essential, for if it is too realistic it will be marred and miss the mark. Jesus continued, instilling in us but the merest a glimpse of his dream.

"My kingdom would have strongholds to be sure, but they would not be made of brick or mortar. Compassion and mercy would be laid side by side and these would be bound together with grace. These would be its protection and within it men would walk humbly, respectfully and meekly with their Adonai. Truth would be applauded and no record of wrongs kept. People would know how high and wide and deep God's love is for them and their hearts would be changed forever."

A wise man once said that men do not follow dreams, they follow men who have dreams.[2] I believe this to be true. As I listened to Jesus's dream, I decided that he was a man worth following. His dream was one of beautiful promise, a new beginning.

chapter three

Our number swelled substantially during the next three days. I enjoyed chatting with those around me as I walked. Some people told me that they had joined the group because they had heard of Jesus and could not believe their good fortune at meeting him along the road while others joined because of Jesus's warmth and friendliness. Some, it seemed to me, were there simply because they thought the group was the place to be and it was obviously gaining popularity. The road we were on was well traversed.

On Friday at midday we neared the town of Lyn which was a few days south of our final destination. The shabbat would soon be upon us so I knew that we would be spending the next two nights there.

The village was only big enough to have one public guest chamber. The rest of us would become a blessing to the villagers who would no doubt warmly welcome, bed and feed us. Local hospitality was more than etiquette, guests were seen as having been sent by Adonai, to entertain was therefore a holy act.

I had often frequented this town on previous business trips so knew some of the residents quite well. Anna was a weaver and one of my suppliers. Her unique yarns and threads as well as exquisite blankets were always the first to be sold from my wagon.

When I had visited her a number of months ago, she had not been able to sell me many blankets because she was recovering from a sickness which had left her bedridden for many weeks. As we approached the town, I wondered how she was managing.

Whenever I collected her products I gave her a fair commission but she could have made a great deal more money had she traveled the region herself. That however was impossible for she was quite crippled.

One evening many years ago she had told me her story. When she was eight years old, as a joke, some children had spooked four mules and sent them stampeding through the town. One of the animals had knocked her over and she had broken several bones in her upper back. Her family was told that her spine would heal given time and bed rest. However, because she could still walk, family necessity dictated that the luxury of rest would not be hers. Her parents soon had her sowing and delivering items—telling her that the pain was understandable and that if she worked but a little harder it would soon be forgotten. That was not to be. Her back healed poorly. Now, at age forty-five, she had a hunched back with a large visible knot on her left shoulder blade. She hobbled about because her left leg dragged; it was impossible for her to stand straight. She knew pain as a constant companion.

Yet she was kind. Whenever I came to the village, she would house me and provide every meal. She lived with and cared for her frail mother. Rebecca, a young woman whom she employed, also lived with her. Rebecca too had a story to tell.

She was born with one leg shorter and weaker than the other. Rebecca walked with a crutch which I had asked a carpenter from Nain to make. As a child she was teased incessantly and consequently rarely looked a single person in the face and barely spoke a word. The town was not that large so Anna had known of Rebecca's hardships and had always felt a kinship with her. When Rebecca was ten, Anna asked her to train as an apprentice. That was six years ago. The two had been inseparable ever since.

My thoughts about Anna and Rebecca were interrupted by a boisterous man speaking with Jesus. He was a recently added member of our entourage—a man of considerable wealth, judging by his clothes and servants, who had been telling Jesus of his understanding of the legality of Levitical property for the better part of an hour. Jesus had been listening, adding perspective and, at times, challenging the man's opinions.

As I watched the man expound upon his ideas, his arms flailing about, I noticed beyond him in the distance two women walking through the ditch picking up odd shaped objects. A donkey grazed contentedly near by.

As we got closer I could see that they were collecting scattered blankets from the ground and piling them onto a slab of wood. It looked as if the donkey, having decided it was time for lunch, had walked into an adjacent field to graze, tilting his pack and dumping his load of blankets throughout the sloped ditch in his quest for grass.

Jesus noticed them as well and placed his hand gently on the man's arm, saying, "Excuse me but would you allow me just a moment?" Then he turned and began walking towards the women.

The affluent man stared at Jesus's back with a look of disgust. I heard one of his servants behind me snicker and whisper to the other, "I wonder how he feels being placed second to a couple of women."

The man, oblivious to his servant's comment, huffed, gave a slight shrug and said to no one in particular, "I guess my understanding of the scriptures was a bit too intimidating for Jesus."

Then, motioning to one of his servants, he instructed him, "Hurry to the village and secure the guest chamber. With all these people I want to be sure to get the best room."

Most of the men who had been traveling down the path with Jesus continued into the village eager to turn strangers into new friends and find good lodgings.

I looked intently at the closest woman in the ditch and then at the other one. I recognized Anna and Rebecca. I hurried into the ditch quickly catching up to Jesus, almost tripping once or twice on the stubbled ground in my haste and calling, "Anna! Rebecca!"

Anna looked up, a smile spreading across her face in recognition as I reached her.

"Oh, Judas! It blesses my heart to see you," she exclaimed.

Rebecca gave me a slight nod, smiled shyly then quickly looked away, turning again to the scattered blankets. Andrew and James joined Jesus and me at Anna's side.

"I noticed this veritable village walking down the road," Anna continued with a laugh, "but I never suspected to see you running from its ranks. You seem to have acquired quite a following."

"Hah! I could never command such a force, good woman," I countered. "As you know I can barely convince the wine in my cup to pour down my throat." It was a personal joke between us that I would usually spill my drink at least once every visit.

"Alas, no," I continued, "I would gladly leave the leading to the master. Please allow me to introduce Jesus," I held my hand towards Jesus.

"Jesus, this is Anna and Rebecca," I said, continuing the introductions. "When it comes to blanket weaving, greater artists you will be hard pressed to find."

"Hello, Anna. Hello, Rebecca," Jesus smiled. "May I help you?" He held Anna's gaze for a moment. She rubbed her hands together nervously and cleared her throat looking as if she was trying to assess this 'leader' who wanted to help two crippled women.

"Th-Thank you," she stammered then turned to continue cleaning up the mess.

"What happened, Anna," I asked as we brought the blankets to the slab of wood. "I did not know that you even owned a donkey."

"I don't," she replied. "That was probably the problem. I was in need of some money for food and I wasn't sure when I would be seeing you again. My neighbour offered me his donkey and skiff to go to Titrane to sell some blankets. Rebecca and I left just after sun-up and have fought with that beast all day," she jutted her thumb accusingly at the munching donkey as she continued. "By lunch time we gave up, turned around and headed home. We had almost made it back when he decided he was hungry and meandered into that field, dumping everything along the way. We had unhitched the skiff because whenever we approached him with a few blankets he would slowly plod away. I think he enjoyed toying with the cripples chasing after him!"

It did not take long, with six people working, to finish our task.

There were only about three hours left before sunset and the beginning of the Sabbath when James and Andrew caught the donkey and held it while I hitched the skiff to the donkey's yoke. My back was to Jesus but I heard him say, "Anna, may I help you with your pain?"

Turning, I saw Jesus gently take Anna's left hand in his and place his right hand upon her back. His hand rested softly on the humped knot of her shoulder blade. As he pressed slowly and steadily, the hump deflated like a full wine skin being gradually poured out. He continued to push with his right hand on her back while steadying her with his left, standing her straight.

When first he touched her, Anna furled her brow questioning his odd behaviour. But then her eyes grew wide with terror, then wonder, and a gasp escaped her lips. Her hand in his quivered then shook uncontrollably. Her eyes, welling with tears, jerked to me, to the others standing awestruck around her and then to Jesus. There her eyes stopped. She stared at him, seemed to gain strength from him. Her eyes searched his face and she became, calm as if she trusted him to make all things right.

"My Lord," she said over and over again crumpling in a heap at his feet as if it were her only way to show the gratitude that she felt.

I heard a shuffle of feet behind me. Rebecca, her mouth agape, hobbled with her crutch to where Jesus stood beside Anna. Rebecca strained to touch Anna's now smooth back.

Jesus reached down and took Rebecca's hand.

"You too, my daughter," he said. Rebecca began to weep.

I saw a second sandal appear beneath the hem of her robe as her short leg lengthened to that of her good one. Tears rolled down her face while her body, shaking with sobs, straightened as her leg gained strength. She let go of her crutch and it thumped on the ground. Jesus placed his hand under her chin to gently raise her head and spoke barely above a whisper.

"You are whole. Your hurts are gone. There is no reason to feel ashamed. Come and live in the sun."

"Praise you, Jesus!" was all she said. Then she too fell to the ground.

I felt as though I had just intruded on someone's heart. Like I had witnessed the healing of a soul's pain and not only a physical restoration. We were standing on hallowed ground. I looked at Jesus. His eyes were wet with tears, full of joy, as if he knew that Anna's and Rebecca's past pains were ended.

I stood, unsure of what to do or say. I had never witnessed a miracle before.

"May we stay with you tonight, Anna?" Jesus asked innocently. It was as if he had not just changed her world.

Anna could not believe the question she had just been asked.

"Yes, Oh, yes! What an honour to have you for shabbat!" she answered excitedly, standing again. Then she stopped, her face changing slightly as if she had come to a realization. "My Lord," she began slowly, "You are obviously a great man. I am sure I can arrange for someone more prominent in our town to serve as your host."

Then partly to herself and partly to Rebecca she said, "Eleazar would be able to give a stylish reception. I can talk to him." Turning back to Jesus she added apologetically, "It's just that I have so little and you deserve so much."

"My dear woman," Jesus said, "I do not seek what you think. A heart that reveres Adonai and yields to His plans sets a high table by my standards. For tonight, some bread and a bit of broth would be a feast."

"That I can supply," said Anna, looking relieved. "Although the broth may be a bit watery since I did not get my blankets to market."

"Let's be off then," announced Jesus, with a laugh. "It will be a race against the sun."

Luckily, Anna's house was on the edge of the village so we were able to unload her belongings and have our Sabbath supper before the blue sky gave way to streaks of pink and purple.

Anna danced in every activity she did, her ordinary chores completed with abandon. It was like she had been bound to a yoke pulling a plow through hard, crusty land. Jesus had cut the harness and set her free to run and frolic. She seemed to revel in the joy, a joy so alive that she could not contain it in her heart. It was like it seeped into her arms, legs, feet and hands—her body pulsed with it. This is what Jesus had given her.

Rebecca seemed barely to realize that her legs were now the same length. It did not look like she cared that she could move easily about the house. But I could tell that her spirit was free. She behaved like a captive who had been kept in a dark hole for years and was now basking in the sun, her face turned to heaven bathing in the warmth. She seemed to immerse herself in it. It was as if Jesus had found the key to her cell, swung open the door and held out his hand to invite her into the light.

I believe she loved him for the invitation.

She seemed to hang on every word he said, serving him diligently and with great reverence. She sat at his feet, eager to see the world the way he saw it.

Anna was determined to give Jesus her best. The three women had been sleeping in the upper room because of the recent hot nights. Now, she insisted that we sleep in the coolness of the room. Wanting to honour Jesus in any way she could, Anna pulled out her best blankets for us to sleep on, ones that would have fetched the highest price at market, and laid out mats that she said were family heirlooms tucked away and never used. Jesus graciously accepted all of her gifts. I do not think that he wanted to deprive her of her gratitude

At last we crawled into our beds. I lay on my mat but could not fall asleep, my mind wondering at the implications of the day's events. Hours into the night I heard others in the room stirring. I knew that I was not the only one sorting through what I had seen.

This Jesus had the commanding presence of mighty King David, the righteous heart of King Josiah and the loyalty to Adonai of King Hezekiah. But he also had the healing powers of the great prophets of old, men like Elijah and Elisha. What could this mean? What amazing wonders was he destined to accomplish?

Israel needed such a man. A man who could lead our nation to restore its past glory. Jesus's kingdom would be a land of healing. Would it be a place without pain? He obviously had the ear of Adonai, an ambassador of Adonai, himself!

I could not fathom my great fortune. I knew Jesus and could be alive when he established his reign. I could help make it happen. Jesus could be our king!

My mind churned these thoughts endlessly throughout the night. When I fell asleep, I dreamed of stately buildings, royal courts and crowns of precious jewels.

I awoke early in the morning sleepier than when I had gone to bed. It did not take me long to prepare for the Sabbath service.

Every Sabbath the people in the town where Anna and Rebecca lived met in a plain structure large enough to hold the seventy or so men in the town while the women and children assembled outside of the building to listen quietly to the readings and teachings, straining to hear through open doors and windows.

About fifty people were already mingling in the courtyard when we arrived. They turned to greet the newcomers. One woman noticed Anna and exclaimed in surprise, "Anna, what has happened to you?"

"This man healed me!" Anna replied with glee, motioning to Jesus.

All eyes turned to Jesus.

"So this is the man who is responsible for blessing us with many visitors last night," smiled an older man who stood beside the woman who had noticed Anna.

As Anna began to recount her previous day's experience, everyone leaned in closer to hear, relishing the tantalizing account like seasoned gossips gathering juicy details in order to retell a good story. Anna did not disappoint and the story did not need embellishing. It was incredible; the proof, evident.

While more people entered the courtyard for the morning meeting, murmurs spread as friends provided newcomers with details about what was happening, excitement electrifying the group as the story was shared again. Someone spoke loudly, getting everyone's attention.

"Let's start our service. Perhaps this man Jesus will speak for us."

All present readily agreed. The men crowded into the building and Jesus took his place at the front. Every ear tuned to his voice. They were a people living in silence yearning for even the quietest of sounds.

Jesus's eyes were full of compassion as he looked out at the faces eager to hear his words. I had expected to see a man full of authority ready to instill his vision in the people, but his eyes were instead as soft and gentle as a doe's. They reminded me of my wife's eyes as she looked at our children. When our son Jonathan was a boy and scraped his knee he would run to her for comfort. She wiped his tears with the hem of her skirt and tenderly ease his pain with kindness, her sympathy more a healing balm than the ointment she put on his wound. Or when Mara had her feelings bruised by a friend's cutting words, my wife shared her daughter's heartache, longing to lessen Mara's suffering. These images of compassion filled my mind as I watched Jesus. It was as if he desired to ease our burdens, share our heartaches.

He spoke of comfort from inner pain, of peace and rest from weariness, his soothing words gave us direction towards a new way of living, encouraged us to trust in him and look to Adonai.

Following the service Jesus was swarmed by the villagers. Everyone who had an ailment rushed to him to be healed. He did not deny anyone who came to him. There was not a place left to stand in the building, yet when Jesus touched someone it was as though they were the only two in the room. He changed lives. It was like he brought people to live in the glory of the day instead of the worries of tomorrow. When men, women and children left, they looked alive. I believe they felt appreciated for who they were, what they had to offer. They seemed inspired toward godly designs and purposes. I wondered if they hoped, as I did, that Jesus would become their king; if they would delight in his lordship over them. I thought Jesus could ask these people for anything and they would seek to accomplish it. What he dreamed of, they would aspire to.

When we finally left the village the next day to continue to Capernaum, the town we left behind was clean, free of disease and pure. It was whole as I believe Adonai would have wanted it to be.

chapter four

hree days later we reached Andrew's home town of Capernaum. Jesus stayed with Andrew's brother, Peter, while James and I renewed old friendships visiting and spending nights with various people that I knew in the city.

James and I talked incessantly about the past week's events with everyone we met, our stories pouring freely from our lips like a river's rushing water with no barrier to hinder it.

Regretfully, neither of us were able to speak with Jesus for the rest of the week for the number of people he was attracting made that virtually impossible. So we joined the crowds that followed him.

We saw him heal a lame man. We saw the man jump and stomp about on his newly healed legs, hooting and giggling uncontrollably as he convinced himself that he could trust the renewed limbs.

We saw Jesus heal an old woman with cataracts. We saw her gaze in wonder at the crystal clear world around her like a baby discovering and examining the hands she has always had.

We saw him heal a boy who was mute and deaf. The boy began chattering to his friends and then burst into a joyous song obviously far beyond his musical abilities. We all laughed at his astonished face when he realized how off key his enthusiasm sounded.

I saw Jesus bring people to what they were meant to be. He granted dazzle to the mundane, colour to the drab and depth where before there were only height and length. I watched as he altered how people perceived their world. It was infectious. I wanted to see him do it again, to see him transform someone's world from being tolerable to being amazing, from merely functioning to truly living. It was joy to be where he was.

This is what brought me and, I believe, others to Jesus. He seemed sincere in his desire for our wholeness yet I wondered if his intentions were more far-reaching.

While I focused on the health he granted people, I could not help but notice that Jesus's miracles gave him great access the populace. I thought he was preparing to be a true king, wanting to know his subjects and to be known by them. The healings precipitated that knowledge. There is an aspect of leadership that is dictated strictly by the office the leader holds. But Jesus held no office. He had to earn and deserve the respect of others; he had to be a man worthy of emulation. That type of leadership is far better. How else can worthiness be understood and gained but by watching a man interact with his world, seeing how he treats those around him and observing his convictions live in action.

As people gathered to experience a miracle, Jesus built his following. When men serve a king they must trust in his wisdom and not question his authority. Sometimes this influence has to be imposed, dictated by force. With Jesus it emanated from him. Even the secret world around us, the one we have no control over, sickness as well as nature's mistakes and imperfections, obeyed his will.

Another group interested themselves in the intentions behind Jesus's miracles: teachers of the law. Within the Jewish nation these teachers wielded the greatest authority. Roman guards could bully, beat and kill, Caesar could command lands to be taken and lives ended, but our religious leaders were the guardians of our souls; they held our salvation. It was their rules and interpretations, their meetings with Adonai and their judgments that valued our worth, coloured our future and defined our past. Their statutes shaped how we saw ourselves and each other. If they deemed someone to be unclean that man was cast out. If they considered him holy, he was accepted and his life was good. Their decrees could hold you high or push you down. And not just you but also future generations as well.

The prophets of old who foretold of a coming messiah provided checks and proofs in their writings so that our people would not be deceived. One of the responsibilities of our religious community was to examine new leaders and their teachings against these scriptures.

I often saw many Pharisees and Sadducees huddled together while Jesus spoke, rubbing their chins, scratching their heads and nodding to one another. The majority of them, although they challenged Jesus vigorously, I believe were motivated by the pursuit of truth in discerning the veracity of Jesus's miracles and teachings. They spent the time and effort as scripture demanded, their diligence often unnoticed by the departing crowds.

Although many religious leaders were honourable, the position was vastly susceptible to abuse. First, any law decreed by the priests held the potential to become distorted, even though it may have initially been designed to show obedience to Adonai through strict adherence to Adonai's laws. For example, the Torah commanded that a calf not be cooked in its mother's milk.[1] In their attempt to show due diligence, some leaders added detail to this command to prohibit the preparation of meat in the same room that dairy foods are produced so that, even out of ignorance, no one could accidentally break Adonai's law. However, human nature, if given the choice, would rather define emotion through action than abandon it to an ambiguous concept. For instance, if I could prove my love to a woman by buying her flowers every week, I would sooner rely upon this tangible exercise than speculate whether or not she feels my love; defaulting to guaranteed particulars is far easier and reliable than attempting to live an opaque concept of love. So, too, with religion: it feels more secure to depend on regulations for piety than to wonder at the heart of Adonai. When considering a commandment such as 'keep the Sabbath holy,'[2] I would sooner be assured of righteousness by following rules: if I have a sore throat, I may swallow oil but may not gargle, or if my house is burning I may wear out as many cloths as possible but not carry anything in my hands save the holy scriptures, than wonder if I am being obedient to the nondescript command.[3]

Second, once these codes of conduct are established and accepted, those enforcing them can easily succumb to egotism—for the more fully a concept is defined the harsher and more quickly can justice be dispensed. Although the Pharisees and Sadduccees found the roots of their regulations in the law of Moses, hundreds of years of holding and administering justice had created a group easily susceptible to corruption. Just as a piece of fruit starts out sweet and delicious but with time ferments and eventually rots so, too, some of our religious leaders had taken Adonai's commandments and over time allowed personal ambition to destroy the health and nourishment the laws were intended to provide. As they interpreted and added to the commands, it became necessary to have measures and balances to assess, rank and impose standards. It seemed as if a bag of rocks was placed around each of our necks and our religious leaders decided if stones should be added or removed from the sack. The ability to burden or lighten a people's lot in life carries immense power. It is no wonder that some of our religious leaders were heady with it.

As with any esteemed person, vigilance is essential to guard against vanity. After a few years of being looked up to, asked advice of and sought after for favours, even those who begin with the best of intentions find it difficult to remain humble.

When it came to Jesus, those religious men who had failed to be assiduous against haughtiness seemed less concerned with how genuine Jesus was than they were with retaining power and prestige. In Capernaum, I noticed a group of about ten religious men, comprised of both Pharisees and Sadducees, who seemed intent on discrediting Jesus. James and I saw them at almost every assembly, it was hard not to for they wore flamboyant fabrics and shoved their way to the front of each gathering. We labeled them the 'naysayers.' They sneered and smirked after any miracle Jesus performed, huffing, sighing loudly or shaking their heads with exaggeration while whispering amongst themselves. During Jesus's teachings they asked him snide questions without any apparent desire to hear the answer, their intention only to make him look a fool. Sadly, the majority of Pharisees and Sadducees who sincerely considered Jesus's comments were often overpowered by this minority's flash and sarcasm. The naysayers reminded me of garlic. Just as a bowl of food steaming with fish, leeks, lemon and oil can be completely overpowered by too much garlic, a herb measuring the least in quantity, so too these few men overshadowed the noble intentions of the larger number of religious leaders.

As a merchant I had dealt with people like this from every vocation in life: fellow merchants, basket weavers, farmers, mothers, as well as religious leaders—individuals who, instead of weighing the merits of a case, would rely on the easier antics of personal attack and belittling.

From my perspective, Jesus's greatest adversaries were these naysayers from the religious community for they seemed to have the most at stake. They had experienced the wiles of power and were loathe to give it up. I was equally as confident that Jesus had assessed the identity of his enemies and anticipated coming battles, for I judged his coming rule to be a wise one. These battles would not be for possessions or lands but for the very lives of the people he sought to have and protect. Like a true king, Jesus wanted his people for himself, his passion for them was transparent.

I worried that the naysayers would soon declare war on this new upstart who could be king and that their subtle gestures would be replaced by a direct attack. As the same magnet will either attract or repel other magnets depending on its polarity so, too, humble people were drawn to Jesus but the arrogant were driven away with equal force.

During my third Sabbath in Capernaum while on my way to the local synagogue, I overheard an exchange between the two men walking ahead of me, a Pharisee and a man with a shriveled arm.

"How long have you been away, Timothy?" the Pharisee was asking, his decorative robes puffing out slightly as a light breeze caught the silky material. The cloth looked familiar and I recognized him as one of the naysayers pestering Jesus.

"At least a month," answered the man called Timothy. "My brother appreciated my help in planting his field. Thankfully you only need one good arm to scatter seed." He chuckled a little and extended his right arm towards the Pharisee. When I had first noticed Timothy, the sleeve of his tunic reached only to his elbow, yet it was apparent that his arm did not look normal. Now as he stretched his arm out I could see that the skin wrinkled and sagged about the bone which did not look entirely straight. Misaligned bone, not muscle, seemed to give the appendage its shape.

"You should try to sit near the front, Timothy," the Pharisee was saying. "Jesus, the man speaking at the synagogue today, has been healing people in Capernaum for the past three weeks. Perhaps he will see your twig of an arm and take pity on you." His comments sounded laced with contempt.

"There is no point," responded Timothy. "He can't heal me today anyway."

"Hmm. Yes, of course, it is the Sabbath," acknowledged the Pharisee, "however, if you make yourself known to him maybe you will have a better chance for healing tomorrow, that is if Adonai decides that you have atoned for your sins enough to be restored to health. Come, I'll help you get a seat near the front. Better to be obvious than risk going unnoticed."

When we arrived at the synagogue I saw the Pharisee usher Timothy into the building while I waited with the other men for the meeting to begin. About half an hour later the doors opened and I went in to find a seat. Because of my early arrival I was able to sit near the front. Timothy, I noticed, was in the first row.

When it was time to read the scriptures Jesus was invited to speak. He stood on a slight platform at the front of the building looking out over the assembly much as he had the first time I heard him. His gaze rested upon Timothy. I saw the familiar gentleness in Jesus's face. It was as if he had the ability to live the pain of another man's lifetime, knowing the sharp intensity of that pain before it had been dulled by the years. He looked as if he wanted to ease Timothy's hurt.

Then his eyes narrowed as he turned toward the Pharisee seated beside Timothy. I did not understand his anger but his wrath seemed to build like raging water churning and gaining momentum behind a dam. With a steady, even gait Jesus walked over to the two men. Staring directly at the Pharisee he asked, "Tell me, oh teacher of the commandments, is it lawful to help an ox who has fallen into a hole on the Sabbath?"

The Pharisee rose, adjusted his robes and cleared his throat.

"Adonai made man and beast," he began. "He told man to care for and tend his animals. In all likelihood the ox would be injured and in pain so yes, it is fitting that he should help the beast." The Pharisee ended his explanation forcefully, as though concerned that all could hear his words of wisdom and the instruction that he had been asked to bestow.

"I am sure that you would agree," returned Jesus, motioning to Timothy, "that a man is far more valuable to Adonai than an ox." Then, stepping towards Timothy, Jesus held out his hand and asked, "Would you like to be healed?"

"How dare you!" the Pharisee shouted, his voice full of authority and defiance. His stature was enough to make any of us cower—yet Jesus stood his ground, undaunted.

The Pharisee's conversation with Timothy in the courtyard flooded into my mind. I recognized it for the well-conceived trap to humiliate and discredit Jesus that it was. I looked to Jesus in desperation for some sign that he saw the treachery. The Pharisee, his trap sprung, looked like a hunter, club in hand, ready to administer a killing blow.

"How dare you," the Pharisee repeated, "blatantly disregard our laws, ways of life that have existed for generations. You may be able to fool the common man but I am a learned teacher and not so easily lead astray."

He turned to the congregation behind him and shook his head. With obvious disdain he addressed us, saying, "You should all be ashamed of yourselves. The ease with which this wolf can deceive you is a disgrace."

The floor was his and he made full use of his advantage, continuing in stride.

"For years I have studied the laws of Adonai and sat at the table of wise teachers. Adonai has asked me to guide his people and though I often weary in my efforts I will not shrink from my task. Adonai above has given us each our lot in life. Some he tells to be herders, others merchants, others leaders of the law, and others…" he paused to glare at Jesus, "…to be carpenters. Shame on you, deceiver! You lack satisfaction with what Adonai has given you and envy the gifts of others. These are grievous sins. Just ask Timothy. Since he was but a lad I have counseled him about envy. He covets wholeness instead of accepting his punishment for past wrongs."

A light spray of spittle escaped his lips with each charge.

Jesus moved with purpose to stand between Timothy and his accuser, calmly yet deliberately saying, "Your quarrel is with me not with this man."

The Pharisee's eyes widened and his head jerked back slightly as if surprised by Jesus's defense of Timothy. He recovered quickly.

"Fine! Why should I allow you to defy our laws unchallenged?"

"How is it, I wonder," asked Jesus slowly, "that you think Adonai decrees that the creation He has made in His own image should not be healed on the Sabbath yet an animal's pain should be alleviated no matter the day?"

It was an interesting question, one that I, and, judging by the shuffling and whispers I heard around me, others began to ponder. I believe it was only this Pharisee's arrogance and pride that kept him from giving any merit to the comment.

"I do not question the veracity of the scriptures," continued Jesus, "only self-serving opinions that exist at the expense of others."

"Do you profess to be wiser than our forefathers?" scoffed the Pharisee. "Do you think that you know the mind of Adonai?"

"I would hear the answer to my question," Jesus said more forcefully. "It is a sincere one. Why do you believe that Adonai would decree an animal to have higher standing than man only on the Sabbath? Can you answer the question? Is there any justification for your regulation?"

As they argued, the difference between the two men became starker: black gains boldness when placed against brilliant white, the line of definition sharpening as the two hues increase in intensity.

A louder murmur rippled through the congregation. The Pharisee, sensing that the opinions of the masses were swaying towards Jesus, answered flippantly, "How should I know? I, at least, do not presume to be smarter than those who originated the law."

"Timothy," the Pharisee continued, refocusing his strategy, "I beg you to show some reason and refuse this man's healing touch. If this self-appointed rabbi refuses to heed our laws, it falls upon you to stop this. Please, Timothy, do not heap sin upon yourself and become more guilty than your arm already proclaims you to be."

"Enough!" Jesus boomed, his jolting voice undeniable in authority. "Your accusations against Timothy will stop!"

The Pharisee closed his mouth as if his words were a rolling pebble hitting a stone wall. His eyes, however, remained defiant.

"I have no desire for Timothy to have a greater burden," Jesus continued. Then turning to the gathering he addressed us, saying, "Come to me, all who are weary and heavy laden, and I will give you rest. For my yoke is easy and my burden is light."[4]

Everyone in the room was silent, stunned by the implications of what Jesus had just said. It was a kingly sentiment. He was asking us to accept his lordship, asking that we accept him as leader. The invitation implied authority, an admission of his ability to grant what he was offering.

Jesus regarded us levelly and elaborated. "Burdens are not just physical. They encompass guilt, insecurity and inadequacy. Timothy's suffering has stemmed not so much from his arm as from the judgments daily heaped upon him. In the midst of what this world hands you, I want you to know freedom. You will find this freedom in me: freedom from guilt, accusation and condemnation. But you must not think that freedom means that it is free. It comes with great cost. Its cost is believing in me instead of yourselves. Its cost is being tied to and bound to me."

"Do you find it strange to think that bondage is required in order to be free? Think about a tree. A tree is bound to the ground yet it cannot be a tree if it is not held by the soil. Its bondage allows it to be a tree in its full beauty; a tree that reaches to the sky and houses birds in its outstretched limbs, giving shade and producing fruit. All this fullness happens only because of its bondage to the ground. The bondage allows complete wholeness. I want you to live in me. To be bound to me. Only then will you know what it truly means to be a man alive. Timothy, will you follow me? Trust me? Rely on me?"

"Blasphemy!" the Pharisee fairly leapt at Jesus. "We rely on Adonai, not some man. What proof do you have that we should put any credence in your lies?"

Jesus looked at Timothy and asked softly, "Would you like to be healed, Timothy?"

Timothy held his arm towards Jesus, his sleeve falling back to reveal his trembling, bent, deformed arm, as gnarled as a limb on an old olive tree. Jesus's hand rested on Timothy's shoulder and smoothed down his arm in a single gentle stroke. Before Jesus's touch was the imperfection of the world, behind it the perfection of Adonai. As Jesus's fingers moved from Timothy's shoulder to palm, the arm was made right. Timothy's eyes never left his arm. He saw fantasy turn to reality.[5]

As soon as his arm was healed, he turned it back and forth, examining it from all angles. Taut skin covered muscle encasing straight bone. Then he thrust his arm into the air and turned to face the audience of men.

His grin grew so wide I thought his face would break trying to contain it.

In the midst of Timothy's exuberance, the Pharisee loudly snapped the excess fabric of his robe and stomped from the building, his tantrum a distraction from the joy Jesus had bestowed. I feared that the naysayers' subsequent attacks would be more destructive because of this humiliation.

chapter five

the next morning I rose early. Before leaving the synagogue, Jesus had announced that he would be speaking at noon the following day a few miles outside of Capernaum. I was determined to find a place near the front of the gathering but I was confronted with a great crowd already milling about as I neared the meeting place.

My discouragement mounted. I had become one of many in an ever increasing crowd. I wanted more. I longed for the days three weeks earlier when I had traveled with Jesus and his band of followers had been controllably smaller. I wanted the camaraderie again, to build on the quick friendships that had begun between the men in Jesus's following; constant contact with the same people can accomplish great feats. I longed to be a member, not simply an observer of a higher order than I could attain on my own. Yet more than desiring this group with common purpose, I missed Jesus's focused attention. I wanted to again hear his personal ambitions and to feel encouraged in mine. I knew it was silly but I felt like a child wanting to call to his parents, 'Watch me, watch me.' Jesus's affirmation gave value and worth to what I was doing.

But, alas, I had not arrived early enough. Again I was simply one grain of sand on a beach. Sighing, I surveyed my surroundings and settled down to wait out the next few hours until Jesus arrived.

I found the meeting place well chosen. We waited in front of a tall shear rock face, almost semicircular in shape, which had at its centre a pile of huge stones. The half-circle was ideal for people to gather in, the boulders perfect for a man to stand and be seen by all gathered, and the shape of the cliff created a natural amphitheatre.

For no other reason but to pass the time, I began chatting with those around me. Many, I discovered, had been healed in the past few weeks and were eager to tell their stories, their excitement and exuberance as obvious as their outer cloaks. *Anyone hearing their tales,* I thought, *could not help but want to see the healing man with such power.* It was no wonder that the number of people seeking Jesus was growing quickly.

Time sped as I listened to the men and women around me and, despite my impatience, I actually enjoyed the strangers' conversation.

At last I saw Jesus coming. He made his way through the gathered group and took his place on the rocks, standing about shoulder height above us so it was easy for all to see. When he spoke, his words reverberated off the rocks and a small echo trailed his voice.

"I have spent much time in prayer," he began, "and I have come to a decision. Moses's father-in-law came to him after the Israelites' exodus from Egypt and told him that the great numbers of people would be better served if Moses took officers to help him with his work.[1] This was wise counsel. I find that my soul wishes to be with each of you but my body is rather restrictive and not at all cooperative."

He grinned, laughing with us.

"So, I too have decided to invite some men to help me. I will teach and council them. They will become my ambassadors, my representatives."

He paused briefly to allow the murmur from the men and women to subside.

"Do not believe that this will be a glamorous calling," he continued. "Their lives will not be easy. It will involve much traveling and many menial administrative tasks but the work must be done; for as the number of people grows daily, a governing body becomes a necessity. At times the work will seem overwhelming yet it will never be impossible. As I have said, I have been praying, praying for Adonai-sent men. I will ask twelve to join me. I promise these men that I will not forsake them. I pledge myself to them. They will know true loyalty. If you will accept this challenge come to the front and stand with me as I call your name."

How blessed those men will be, I thought. To eat with Jesus, learn about his kingdom daily, travel and talk with him on the road would be a boon of unequaled value.

He began his list of names. Andrew, the man I had met on our journey to Capernaum who had carried James's bag. Andrew's brother Peter, with whom Jesus had been staying the past two weeks. Four more men that I did not know were named. And also Matthew, the scribe who had traveled with us from Nazareth. Two others, Thomas and Simon...then he called my friend, James! And then I heard him speak my name!

"Judas, son of James of Nain."[2]

Me! It was my name!

The moment was surreal. Time stood stark still. Birds hung in the air like clouds on a windless day, shuffling feet moved noiselessly and the sun shone on me alone.

My heart pounded in my throat so loudly that my ears pulsed. Although they felt like wooden pegs, I willed my legs forward, the people around me separating to allow me to pass as they realized that it was my name that had been called. Jesus saw me winding my way through the crowd. He caught my eye and smiled. He looked glad that I had accepted his invitation, but I considered it my great fortune. He regarded with joy and gratitude my desire to be a part of his world.

Of the other men he appointed I only recalled one, Judas Iscariot, a man who shared my name. I do not remember what Jesus spoke about afterward, too mesmerized was I by the new direction my life was taking and the possibilities that awaited me. I hoped my family would be as excited.

The sun had begun to set when Jesus finally finished speaking to the people. We walked back to Capernaum and the twelve of us went with Jesus to Andrew's home for supper.

We sat in groups of three or four on various mats around the floor. As the steaming bowls of food were placed on the mats, talk and laughter flowed as freely as wine on a hot day. I formed my flat bread into a scoop and dipped it into the community bowl of broth in front of me then did the same with the fish. The meal was a typical one yet tasted delicious: perhaps because I had not eaten since the morning or perhaps because I so relished the people around me that I felt giddy with happiness.

When our meal was finished, Jesus stood and began the introductions. Everyone paid keen attention, aware that the men he introduced would be key players in advancing Jesus's kingdom.

Jesus described each man and told how he had come to follow him. We were as different as sky is to land, dust to water. Yet as Jesus spoke there appeared a common thread. We had each made some great sacrifice which demonstrated our commitment.

Jesus had called two brothers, James and John, who had left their father and a hired hand with the largest catch of fish the family of fishers had ever seen. A veritable "wealth of flapping fins" had padded their father's retirement fund alone since his two sons had literally jumped ship mid-pull of the nets. They forfeited the money from the catch for fear of being left behind when Jesus called them.[3]

Matthew had been a tax collector who stole unashamedly at every opportunity. He met Jesus and walked away without hesitation from a lifetime of ill gotten gain, trading the only life he had ever known for an uncertain future.[4]

Judas Iscariot had been a man of influence: well-respected and knowledgeable in the world of finance. He gave up comfort and reputation for dust and strange beds.

Each man had a story, each one a sacrifice.

Following the introductions, Jesus shared his plans for us, our concrete contributions to his kingdom, our daily tasks. Each job fit our personalities well yet pushed us beyond what we were comfortable with.

Judas would, of course, be our treasurer but he would also responsible for raising funds, an added duty with which he did not seem too pleased.

Simon, Bartholomew, my friend James and Thomas were to provide a type of policing force for Jesus. They were to aid Jesus in dealing with the growing number of people who sought healing. Jesus warned them that their jobs would be extremely difficult and reassured them that he would give them great support. Jesus promised to pray for each of us daily, but for these four men he pledged that his prayers would be particularly poignant. He cautioned them to consider the hearts of the people seeking a miracle instead of making decisions based on need or severity of injury. I found this a curious thing until I recalled my earlier impression that Jesus's miracles seemed to have a deeper purpose than mere physical health. Then, in the midst of his instruction, Jesus stopped to ask Adonai to grant the four men a godly sense of discernment tempered with compassion. Of the four men, Thomas was the most unsure of his ability to handle the job, but Jesus seemed to have confidence enough for both of them.

Jesus's closest confidants would be Peter, Andrew and two other brothers, James and John. These were to be his officers. They would meet more regularly and intimately with Jesus. I presumed that they would receive the most instruction and glean the deepest insights into Jesus's thoughts, for their opportunity was the greatest to learn Jesus's heart and intentions.

Matthew and Philip were to be scribes and reporters. They would spread the news of Jesus's arrival in the various towns and cities as well as record his teachings, creating a veritable campaign of information.

My responsibilities were the most mundane and practical of the duties Jesus assigned. I was to travel ahead of Jesus to secure accommodations and food for our troop as well as scout out meeting locations for the people who would hear Jesus. It was a logistically necessary job. While many people may have felt insulted by such a menial assignment, I warmed to it. The work suited me well and I resolved to do it with all diligence. I vowed to myself to hone lists of supplies, create itineraries, visit and inspect homes and beds to make sure all was ready for my master and new friends.

After Jesus finished sharing his vision of our part in his kingdom-building, we settled down to visit amongst ourselves and get to know each other. I had been sitting next to Peter so our conversation naturally turned to fishing as this was his primary vocation, as well as that of his brother, Andrew. By the end of the evening I had been invited to join Peter, Jesus and James, one of the other fishermen, for a boat ride the next morning to learn the art of fishing.

I am not overly fond of water and so was a little leery but I did not want to lose a chance to visit with Jesus without the crush of the ever increasing crowds.

We woke early to muted colour expanding across the sky; the sun barely crested the horizon. We walked to the shore and cast off in a boat of moderate size that could comfortably hold the four of us as well as any small amount of fish that might care to join us.

The water was calm and serene. All was quiet save the dipping of the oars and the occasional screech of a gull. I had, of course, been fishing before. When I was a boy, my father, grandfather and I went fishing now and then but I had not fished with "professional" fishermen before and I presumed that Jesus had not either.

I found it interesting that Jesus had chosen two sets of fishermen brothers to be in his inner circle. James and his brother John were enthusiastic youths I judged to be under the age of twenty, neither one even old enough to grow a full beard yet. Peter and Andrew were both at least ten years older than me, seasoned veterans of life who knew better than to take themselves seriously. The previous evening Peter and Andrew had everyone at the table laughing with their banter.

As he rowed, James entertained us with a story from his fishing exploits. "I remember," recounted James, "fishing with just a hook and a line from the shore. It was about three years ago. John, my father and I had been out all day with barely a fish to show for it, only enough for our supper. After we ate, I fashioned a line then threw it repeatedly into the water and pulled it back in just to pass the time."

His eyebrows rose slightly and his smile widened. "It was on my third throw that I felt a tug on the line. I presumed that I had snagged the hook on a rock so I gave it a good yank. Well, the jerk I received in return nearly toppled me head first into the water!"

He chuckled, his voice rising as he continued.

"I yelled for help and John came running. He stood on a boulder, peered into the water and hollered that he figured the fish must be this big!" James held out his hands on either side of his body with his elbows slightly bent.

"I gave a mighty heave and dragged the beast onto shore. Oh, he was quite a catch! I cut the line and I tell you no lie—that fish hopped up on its fins and walked right back into the lake!" James's wide eyes gazed at each of us in turn.

"Did you go after it?" Jesus asked eagerly.

"John did." James nodded. "Oh, was he wet! He bounded into the water trying desperately to scoop the fish back onto shore, but in the end the fish triumphed and swam back out to sea."

"I think I met that fish once," interjected Peter, the wrinkles in his weathered face deepening around his squinting eyes and toothy grin. "Did it have a flat head like a board with its eyes on top instead of the sides and a reddish stripe down its middle?" he asked.

"That sounds like the very fish!" answered James excitedly.

"It was only last year when Andrew and I met him. 'Destroyer,' we nicknamed him. But he must have grown since you saw him, for the beast we saw looked to be the size of an eight-year-old boy."

"What happened?" queried Jesus, his eyes sparkling with interest.

Peter leaned forward and placed one hand on each knee.

"We were net fishing from our boat. At first, as we pulled in the net, nothing seeming unusual … but then we saw him. More importantly, he saw us. Oh, the fight was on!" He slammed his fists together and pushed them back and forth against each other, rocking our boat with the effort. "First Andrew and I would pull on the ropes and almost get him into the boat. Then Destroyer would whip his tail in such a frenzy that we would have to let the net out in order not to lose him."

He paused for a moment, leaned back a bit and shook his head saying, "Do you know we fought with that beast for an entire afternoon?"

"Knowing you and your brother's determination, I expect you

feasted on fish for days after that catch." Jesus put in.

"I'm afraid not," answered Peter, sorrowfully. "We did, out of sheer stubbornness, manage to haul Destroyer into our boat. It was a small craft, probably half the size of this one. That is when the fish earned its name."

Again Peter leaned towards us.

"Destroyer flailed wildly, his tail thrashing everywhere," Peter's arms waved and flew about his head. "He walloped the back of our boat over and over. After five great 'whaps' the stern began to splinter, two more and the whole back end was in pieces. Then Destroyer slid out and swam away."

We were all quiet.

"The arrogant creature even gave one last swish of his tail," Peter added, "dousing Andrew and me with water before leaving us to our broken boat."

"How did you get back to shore?" I asked.

"We hung onto a piece of the wreckage and kicked our way to shore. By evening we made land and found our way home the next day. Father told us that he had heard of fish like that. They had to be speared and killed in the water before being brought into the boat."

There was silence again before Peter sighed and declared, "Well, men, we have finally reached our fishing spot! Let's get these nets into the water." He smiled broadly and turned towards James who helped him with the nets.

I looked at Jesus, pursing my lips and straining the muscles in my neck; I was less sure than ever of our expedition. He smiled warily back, slightly shrugging his shoulders as if empathizing with my discomfort.

Peter threw out the nets to demonstrate the proper technique then gathered them back so I could try. I made a couple of attempts, never quite able to convince the net to spread properly across the water. When I brought the nets in, I tried to draw the bottom ropes in first to create a scoop passing through the water as Peter had shown me, but to little avail. Then Jesus practiced.

For his part, Jesus took his instructions with good grace and chuckled at the ribbing he received for his efforts.

"Ho, we are to make the fish dry, not the men wet," Peter joked after Jesus made a particularly pathetic cast which resulted in a generous shower for everyone in the boat.

I gloried in the day, well-remembering my lament of only the previous morning of merely being one of a crowd. *What a difference just one day can make on a person's perception of the world,* I thought.

"What about you, Judas, have you any fishing stories to entertain us with?" asked Jesus after he finally had a successful cast and we settled into our seats to wait.

"Nothing as exciting as Peter and James's tales to be sure," I began. "I suppose my most interesting story is from when I was about fourteen and went fishing with my grandfather. We borrowed a neighbour's boat and went out for the day. I remember being excited because I could probably count on one hand the number of times I had been boating."

I drew in a large breath and smiled at the recollection.

"We were fishing with a hook and line and I caught a fair-sized fish. When grandfather netted it and took the hook out, his face lit up like a five-year-old boy who had just been handed a honeycomb dripping with honey. He said, 'Judas, I think this is a type of fish that always swims in large schools. I have heard that if you tie an inflated bag to its tail it will lead you to the rest of the school then you can hook fish after fish to your heart's content.' Well, I was up for an adventure so I filled a bucket of water in our boat in order to keep the fish alive, emptied out our water bag, blew it up with air and tightly corked it. Grandfather unraveled part of his belt and used it to construct a crude rope which he tied to the water bag and then, using the hook, attached it to the poor fish's tail. Then we let him go."

I shook my head and chortled, "We chased that water bag for the rest of the day. Whenever it stopped we got our hooks ready, but as soon as we dropped our lines into the water, the bag would start moving again and we would continue the chase. We did not catch a thing the whole day. In the evening grandfather conceded defeat, and said we should at least capture our water bag and have one fish for supper. I remember thinking that we were showing poor sportsmanship to eat the fish we had tormented all day but I was only fourteen and he was my grandfather so I helped him haul in the bag. We coiled in the rope but when we reached the end there was nothing there but a hunk of seaweed! I have no idea when our fish escaped or how long we had been merely chasing a bag caught in various currents!" I finished, my three companions laughing uproariously with me at my misfortune.

"I have had an experience with a water bag as well," offered Jesus, rubbing his sore cheeks.

"It was on a fishing trip with my uncle Zachariah when I was ten. Like you, Judas, we had borrowed a boat and I was thrilled because I had not been boating much. My uncle found a fishing spot that some local fishermen had said was well worth the row. We dropped anchor and began fishing. Unfortunately, it was not long before a storm began to brew. My uncle, not having much nautical experience, was immediately nervous. He frantically tried to pull up the anchor but it was stuck fast."

Jesus grinned, his whole face beaming as he recalled the scene.

"He decided that our only choice was to cut the line. My uncle, you must understand, is a very frugal man. My Aunt Elizabeth was always embarrassed to serve meals at her home because as long as a clay pot retained the slightest incline Uncle Zachariah believed it could be used as a bowl and so no new pots needed to be purchased to replace the broken ones. Their house was full of bits and pieces of broken pots.

"Anyway, Uncle Zachariah could not stand the idea of having to pay his friend who had loaned him the boat for the anchor so he happened upon an idea. He would inflate a water bag and attach it to the anchor's rope so that the next day when conditions were more favourable we could find the anchor and retrieve it.

"This we did and then began rowing into shore. We had rowed no small distance when we saw our water bag bouncing merrily beside our boat, obviously no longer attached to the anchor. Oh, my uncle's face," he stopped speaking and tried to control his laughter. "His mouth was so wide his chin almost touched his chest, his eyebrows so high I could not tell where they ended and his hairline began. Later, when I teased him about it he would laugh heartily and say that he just could not believe that such great ingenuity would go so unappreciated by Adonai. Oh, remembering the sight still brings me to tears."

We all joined in the laughter again. When the snickers finally subsided, Peter said, "So, men, let us bring in that net and see how we four professionals have fared today."

He drew the ropes in succession, pulling them smoothly towards the boat. Scowling a bit he grunted, "It does not look like there is much in here."

Then his face changed, his eyes growing wide in astonishment.

"Great heaven above!" Peter practically yelled, "It is Destroyer!"

All four of us leaned over the boat to stare into the net. The creature looked just like Peter's description, only a little smaller. Tail to nose it looked to be as tall as a five-year-old boy.

"We have to kill it first," Peter fairly screamed in excitement, grabbing an oar and leaning over the side of the boat. James, Jesus and I held tightly to the net, the fish thrashing to and fro and rocking the boat mercilessly. Without hesitation Peter began slamming Destroyer's head with the wooden paddle.

The boat pitched. Water sloshed over the edge.

I let go of the net to grip the hull of the boat, Jesus's and James's white knuckles loosened a bit on the net. Peter continued bashing the fish, oblivious to his boatmates concerns. Again the fish flipped and Peter, determined not to be bested again, yelled, "AAARRGGHH" and brought down the oar with a mighty blow. The whole boat pitched sideways, water poured in. Peter swayed heavily backward in a vain attempt to catch his balance and fell into the water, taking the boat, and us in it, with him.

Sounds reverberated in my ears: the hearty splash of the boat, the yelps of my companions as well as my own, muffled noises from various underwater theatrics. Water thrashed, boiled and thumped against the wood of the overturned boat as we tried to surface. I made a grab and clung to the hull, searching for Jesus, Peter and James. Jesus and James surfaced next, followed quickly by Peter who bobbed in the water, his mouth agape and his eyes bulging in disbelief. Truly, he looked more like a fish than the fish who had just bested him. I looked at Jesus. At first a smirk sneaked upon his lips then he snickered. Finally, unable to stifle it any longer, he bellowed a deep resonating laugh. It was infectious. Soon we were all roaring with laughter, even Peter.

Eventually, our sides aching and tears rolling down sore cheeks, we set about trying to right the boat. Peter and I grabbed the hull on one side while Jesus and James did the same on the opposite side. On the count of three we kicked, trying to lift the boat out of the water enough to flip it. However, after many failed attempts (as well as a few near-miss head injuries), we abandoned the plan and determined that our only course of action was to slowly kick ourselves to shallower water, boat in tow.

We kicked and swam with the sinking knowledge that we were making little progress as the sun made its way across the sky. As the day wore on exhaustion took its toll. Still in water too deep to stand we hung onto the side of the boat for took a well-deserved rest. I sucked great gulps of air into my burning lungs, tilted my head towards the sky, closed my eyes and drank in the sun, wishing the heat on my face could seep into my shivering body.

Over the past hours I had fleetingly wondered why Jesus did not miraculously right the boat. I reasoned with myself that Jesus did not perform such spectacles to convince, however, it seemed to me that our situation was fast becoming more desperate.

When I opened my eyes I gazed at the horizon and waited for my vision to adjust to the glare of the sun off the water. I thought I saw what could be a sail in the distance. I blinked and stared then asked hopefully, "Is that a boat?"

Everyone turned to look.

"Praise be, we are saved!" yelled Peter.

We began yelping, whooping, and hollering. Such a commotion, I am sure, has not been heard since David's triumph over Goliath. The boat in the distance turned, the sail growing as the vessel neared. As the mast increased in size my relief increased as well. Truth be told, I feared having to weather the night hanging onto our floating curse. As our rescuer approached and the vessel became clear, I turned to grin at Peter. Much to my surprise he wore a scowl upon his face. He muttered under his breath, "Oh, no! It had to be Andrew! Why did it have to be Andrew?"

I turned back to the approaching boat to see Andrew and my friend James on board. Andrew fairly gloated and his smile was smug.

Peter raised his hand towards Andrew sheepishly and said, "Nice to see you. How about a little help?"

"Ah, my dear brother. Wasn't the agreement," Andrew asked, feigning recollection of a distant memory, "that the next time I rescued you from the water you would have to shout to the heavens a little rhyme about your brother's superior skills on the sea?"

Peter's glare shot daggers at Andrew then he quickly turned his face to the sky and yelled, "In matters of seamanship, I do declare to my brother Andrew, none can compare."

Then he snapped, "Now give us a hand, will you?"

I peered around our swamped boat at Jesus. His smile was taut and his eyes looked watery: he might burst into unrestrained laughter at any moment.

We were hauled unceremoniously into Andrew's boat. Then, with ropes, a few added hands, and the advantage of being above the capsized vessel, we managed to right the overturned boat and head for shore.

Safely on dry land, Peter secured the two boats while Andrew started a campfire. We clustered around the fire's heat to cast off the chill of the water and heartily ate the supper Andrew had brought.

As the evening seeped away we assembled some blankets around the last of the heat from the glowing embers and waited for sleep to claim us.

The last thing I heard was Jesus's soft chuckle, "Peter, aren't you glad that I have made you a fisher of men?[5] They are a lot less slippery!"

chapter six

t he next six months were spent in Capernaum. I sent word back to Jonathon with a fellow merchant of my intentions to stay in this northern city at Andrew's home. I could only hope that this messenger would communicate not only my practical plans but also my enthusiasm about the new direction my life was taking.

Jesus preached each Sabbath and traveled to various regions in Galilee during the remainder of the week. I often went with Matthew and Philip to tell people where they could find Jesus and we scouted suitable meeting locations. Many villagers were willing to make small journeys, especially if they were guaranteed to see Jesus when they arrived.

It was on one of these treks, just after heading south toward the small village of Asteria, that I heard a familiar, "Hello!" behind us. Turning, I saw my son Jonathon running to catch up.

"Jonathon!" I called out, hurrying towards him. "What are you doing here? Is everything all right?"

Jonathon quickly closed the distance between us and reassured me, "Oh, yes, yes, everything is fine. I have just been chasing you for most of the morning and am glad to have found you!"

"How did you know where I was?" I asked.

"James told me. He was at Andrew's house. I came to Capernaum to sell some merchandise and hoped to see you as well."

Relieved that Jonathon was not bringing bad news, my smile broadened and I embraced him, kissing each cheek in a hearty greeting.

"Well, peace be on you!"

"And on you, Father," he returned with a smile of his own.

I introduced Jonathon to Matthew and Philip and we continued along the road to Asteria. Matthew and Philip walked ahead a few paces so that Jonathon and I could talk.

"How are Caleb and Abner?"

"Abner follows Caleb everywhere and is constantly tormenting his big brother," Jonathon laughed with a slight shake of his head. "For the most part, Caleb is quite patient for a seven-year-old, but every once in a while ..."

"Sounds like the big brother can give out his own torments!" I said, amused. "And how is my daughter-in-law feeling? She must be looking quite pregnant by now?"

"Yes, she does," he nodded. "She's a little tired but that's to be expected. Both boys love to feel her belly when the baby starts to move."

"And Mara and Josiah, how are they?"

"His crops are looking good so far and Mara certainly enjoys getting her hands dirty."

Turning to face the road, I nodded again, sighing with the satisfaction of knowing my family was well.

"And you?" Jonathon asked slowly. I sensed that we were broaching the true reason that he had run down the road to see me. "Tell me again about this cause that you are pursuing with such passion."

I stopped walking and turned to face him. "I believe that Jesus could be the future king of Israel. I believe we need him as our king."

Silence hung between us.

"What makes you so sure?" Jonathon finally asked.

I thought for a moment before replying. "His commitment to people is undeniable. He seems to genuinely want what is best for them. When he talks to Adonai, it is as if he actually knows Adonai's intentions and desires. He speaks with an authority I have not heard before.

"You and Mara each have your own lives now," I went on. "It feels good to be part of something that I believe to be important to our nation and our future." After a few seconds of quiet, I asked, "Were you worried that all sense had left me?"

"Mara was more worried than me," Jonathon responded, apologetically. "As soon as that merchant gave us word of your plans, she insisted that I make a trip to Capernaum. I told her that she was acting just like you—worrying too much."

"And what did she say to that?" I asked, chuckling.

"She said that I was just like Mother—not worrying enough!"

We both laughed.

"Well, please assure your sister that I have not succumbed to some enchantment and that I still have full use of all my faculties."

"I will," he said with a smile.

Jonathon came to Asteria and then returned with us to Capernaum. There he listened to, and met, Jesus. While Jonathon said he found Jesus's teachings interesting, it was certainly clear that he was not as committed to making Jesus's kingdom a reality as I was. I felt content that Jonathon did not disagree with Jesus's beliefs and Jonathon returned home at least devoid of the guilt that he had possibly abandoned his father to a madman.

During this sojourn Jesus spent a great deal of time with our group of twelve. He often snuck away for a leisurely evening walk with one or two of us to discuss the events of the day and share his friendship. Every morning he rose before the sun to find a quiet place of solitude where he could pray. He returned with strength to give of himself again, renewed in the soul he laid bare each new day.

Every few weeks Jesus and I took an evening to discuss the coming venues. These were my favourite times. Huddled around a fire we hammered out the nitty-gritty details of time and place and discussed the towns he planned to visit, how long he should stay, the numbers of people expected, the food and accommodations required. It all needed to be attended to. We even developed strategies like moving from small towns towards a larger city, building momentum as we went.

During these meetings Jesus often reminisced about that day's activities. It amazed me that he never tired of the people he met but seemed to be drawn to their whimsical uniqueness. With his voice laced in wonder he marveled at each circumstance:

"Did you see how high Ruth's mother swung her after Ruth was healed? I thought she would touch the sky."

"The relief in John's face when his son walked again was well worth our two week trek to get to that remote town."

"Oh, I thought I would never stop laughing when that dog started howling along with the song we were singing!"

Each person touched his spirit. The people knew it too. They sensed that they had an effect on Jesus which endeared him to them all the more. Imagine, the very man they sought wanted to seek and know them, too.

My frequent chats with Jesus were not the only fringe benefits to my duties. I also became close with many of Jesus's good friends. When we were on the road I traveled with our entourage until we were a few days away from our destination, then hurriedly traveled both day and night in order to arrive at the village before Jesus and the rest of the disciples. In some towns Jesus had friends with whom he regularly stayed. I usually lodged with these people to help them prepare for Jesus's arrival.

His friends quickly became my friends. He chose his companions well. Their hearts were sincere, their intentions pure. Of course, we shared a common purpose: to see Jesus made king—and this, too, hastened our friendships.

I had ample opportunity to become acquainted with these folk and they, in turn, had many chances to practice hospitality—for despite my strategizing with Jesus, he was maddeningly impetuous. Countless were the times I expected him to arrive within a day or two but his arrival was delayed for close to a week. He changed his plans on the edge of a coin. Once, with Judas's help, I had arranged a meal with a prominent businessman. Jesus had met someone in a tree and went to his home for dinner instead![1]

The twelve of us had our challenges, areas of our lives that we would just as soon not have to deal with. One of mine was having to balance Jesus's "live in the moment" approach with my need to have events unfold according to the predetermined plan. I often resented his lack of appreciation for the time and energy invested in helping to orchestrate his rise to power. Why could Jesus not understand that schedules must be adhered to and must time spent with influential people if he was to become a governing force?

My other challenge was dealing with disputes. I was the person people complained to when issues arose between hosts and guests. Oh, how I resented this imposition! My evening planning sessions with Jesus were often subverted when my presence was required to alleviate mere personality conflicts. Jesus reminded me repeatedly that the appreciation of man's diversity was tantamount to enjoying the beauty of Adonai's creation. I will freely admit, however, that applying his council was one of my greatest struggles in the midst of a fresh disagreement.

Judas Iscariot and I often talked together. We had to, for he held the money and I needed to spend it. The arrangement usually worked well. I realized that a public purse needed a treasurer and he generally accepted that I was not a frivolous spender. However, there were times I was annoyed at his aggressive questioning and persistent requests for me to justify my expenditures.

All my complaints, however, were easily overlooked and became mere distractions, like a buzzing fly to be swatted at now and then on an otherwise gorgeous day in the sun, when compared to the valuable time spent with Jesus and his followers.

One night, when all the disciples were together, Jesus announced that we were to depart for Jerusalem within the week. The journey would take a few months as Jesus wanted to make many stops along the way. I spent the next few hours recording Jesus's intended visits to sort out where I needed to concentrate my energies. Long after everyone in the house had gone to bed I worked and reworked schedules and made supply lists.

The next morning I scouted the trail and visited the first village on the itinerary. Then, returning to Capernaum three days before the

Sabbath, I acquired the food we would need to get us to Tiberias and inspected the tents, ensuring that any holes were mended to my satisfaction. After all my preparations I certainly appreciated the Sabbath's day of rest.

Early the next morning I met our assembled group with mingled apprehension and excitement. More than just the twelve were accompanying Jesus. About a hundred people had gathered at the city gates, half to travel with us and the other half seeing us off. It would be an unwieldy group to manage, but I was looking forward to the fellowship. After many hugs, kisses, well wishes and farewells, we left Capernaum and headed south.

I fell in beside Peter. During our stay in his hometown, I had discovered that I truly enjoyed his company. Like Jesus, he had worked in his family's business even though it was not his true passion. It seemed to me that he loved people, excelled in teaching and had a faith in Jesus and loyalty to him that exceeded the rest of ours. His confidence in Jesus's purpose was sure. Yet he was not conceited, readily admitting his mistakes and trying to learn from them.

Today as we traveled he asked about my days of preparation for our trip and what to expect along the way.

"The roads have been well-kept," I said. "We should have little trouble or incident on the way to Tiberias. That will be our first stop of considerable length."

"How long are we staying at Magdala before continuing to Tiberias?" Peter asked.

"Not long, I hope. The leper colony outside the village always makes me nervous," I confessed, then explained further. "When I was eight my cousin Mary developed leprosy. She had a sore on her forehead that extended up into her hairline." I pointed to my right eyebrow and traced it up my forehead.

"She was only ten," I continued, "and her parents were scared that they might have to take her to our priest. I can still remember the terror in their eyes when they talked to my parents about the emerging sore. I think they were hoping to be reassured that all was well and that they did not need to be concerned. But the sore was not normal looking. She had gotten a nasty cut from a low tree branch. The cut refused to heal properly and did not scab over. When the infection became deep and continued to ooze with pus, my aunt and uncle spoke to my parents."

"My father, however, confirmed their nightmare and told them that they needed to see the priest. When I heard my father's pronouncement I ran into our garden. I had played with Mary for as long as I could remember. She was more like a sister than a cousin. I couldn't believe it."

I paused, recalling the sight of Mary that day.

"I saw her sitting under a tree, shaking, sobs wrenching her body. I kept my distance—already afraid of her. I wanted to comfort her but was terrified to be too close. I called to her, lamely, 'I'm sure it will be fine. The priest will deem you well before you know it.' She did not look up. She only hugged herself, rocking slightly as if desperate to hold onto her heart, trying to prevent the panic from stealing it away."

I was quiet, caught again in that awful moment.

"What happened to her?" Peter asked hoarsely.

"She was immediately isolated. We were there when it happened. She whimpered 'No, please, no, again and again. But what could any of us do? For seven days we waited, giving her food through the slot in the door and listening to her cry. At the end of the week when the priest opened the door to inspect the sore, it had not spread. The relief we felt was overwhelming. It was not even a hardship when Mary had to have her head shaved and the door closed to the room again, for we thought the next week of isolation was only a formality. In seven more days we could eat and play together again. Her hair would grow back and life would return to normal.

"But when the priest at last opened the door, the infection had turned a reddish-white on her bald head and had grown towards her nose. Mary's hopeful smile vanished as she looked at the priest's ashen face and downcast eyes. Our priest was young at the time. I doubt he had ever had to condemn someone before, especially one so young. I felt sorry for him but he fulfilled his duty: he pointed his finger at Mary and announced, 'Unclean! Take off your clothes and proclaim yourself unclean.'"[2]

The memory of Mary made my heart beat faster. She had been ghastly white, her eyes livid with fear. She shrank as if her corpse were already decomposing and peeled off her clothes before our unbelieving eyes. Then she had whispered, "Unclean."

"Louder," the priest had coaxed, "it must be loud enough for all to hear." I remember him hugging himself, his hands rubbing his crisscrossed arms. He seemed more uncomfortable with his responsibility to castigate a little girl than his proximity to the dreaded disease.

"Unclean," she had returned, gulping air, tears streaking her cheeks.

"Louder," he had repeated softly.

"Unclean! Unclean!" she had sobbed back.

"I watched Mary walk alone that day," I continued telling Peter, omitting the details of her awful announcement. "She was naked, shivering. She eventually found a colony of lepers. I was glad she had somebody to live with."

We walked in silence for a good distance.

"Did you ever see her again?" Peter asked, cautious of disturbing my reverie yet genuinely curious.

"Only from a distance. Our families took turns leaving food outside the colony at a designated location. I pitied them but dreaded my turn to take the food. I was ashamed of my fear yet could not help feeling terrified that some day I would find a sore and have to go through what Mary did. Even though my parents assured me that all precautions had been taken to protect me, I remember meticulously inspecting my skin for days after each food delivery. I heard she died in her early twenties."

As I finished speaking, I heard someone moan, "Unclean, Unclean," as if a demon had escaped my past and was haunting me again.

There across the barren landscape walked two lepers. Their dirty white bandages trailed behind them in the wind. They looked like ghosts, ashen and forlorn. Terror reached its talons out and dug into my heart. I reassured myself of the distance between us and them. The gulf could not have been more real if a deep gorge existed with them on one cliff and us on the other. This gap was my protection. I cowered behind it.

I was not the only one gripped by fear. The dread seemed to creep through our group, thick and black, coating all it touched. We huddled together and quickened our steps, fleeing from the sight of them. All of us but one.

"Good day to you, friends!" Jesus called to the two ostracized lepers.

The greeting sounded unnatural and out of place. The lepers stopped, peering at Jesus. They looked skittish, more afraid of the man who dared speak to them than of the group of fifty healthy men who were terrified of them.

The lepers said not a word.

"Hello, friends," Jesus called again, his words hanging in the empty space between us and them.

Then Jesus took a step towards them.

A single step that reverberated through the silence like a bell's first tone on the crisp morning air.

Jesus took another step into the gulf of the abyss, then another. I felt like a man thrown into deep water who does not know how to swim. *What is he doing! my mind screamed, It cannot be! No! No! Someone stop him! He's gone mad!* Yet none of us moved. We were paralyzed with fear, afraid for Jesus but more so for ourselves.

Jesus closed the distance one footfall at a time, slow yet sure. It was not merely a physical distance: he was crossing a chasm of societal fear and cultural panic; it was a gap of protection and safety.

Jesus stopped in front of them. They looked so small next to him with their shoulders hunched and their eyes on the dust, huddled so close together they almost looked like one person. Their rigid bodies announced the utter unfamiliarity, the wrongness, of Jesus's actions.

He spoke to them. How long since they had stood a mere arm's span from a clean man? How long since one without blemish had spoken to them? Years? A decade? The lepers looked ill at ease and swayed slightly as they shifted their feet back and forth.

Then, Jesus touched them.

In the name of all we hold sacred, he reached out and touched their decaying bodies!

A unified gasp escaped the lips of every man in our group as pure life met the living dead, his disease-free hand in direct contact with breathing rot.

The lepers shrank under his touch as if it was a weight too heavy to bear. Jesus cupped his hands under their elbows and raised them up to stand tall.

Leading them off a little distance, he sat on some rocks while they talked together.

Our entourage stared, completely dumbfounded.

"Did he heal them?" Thomas asked in disbelief.

"Yes!" Peter responded, awe filling his voice.

We sat and waited for Jesus to return. Although we were convinced that we had seen a miraculous healing, no one was willing to walk over to the three men.

At last Jesus walked back to us.

"They will see the priest to perform the rituals so they can be pronounced clean. I want them to be completely exonerated of their uncleanness, fully reinstated to their families and community," Jesus informed us.

No one could think of a thing to say. What words can pass your lips after witnessing the impossible?

"Are we staying for the week until they are proclaimed clean?" Peter finally asked lamely, breaking the calm.

"No, hopefully we will be in Tiberius by then. Let's continue a few more miles before we make camp," Jesus responded.

Jesus walked apart from us, sensitive to our nervousness about what we had seen and, at this point, his very presence. As we walked, James and his brother John, the apostles who had known Jesus longer than the rest of us, told of other times they had seen Jesus heal lepers. I was heartened a bit by the knowledge that Jesus had not contracted the disease despite his previous exposure to lepers. Although I could not deny what I had just seen, I could not turn off a lifetime of prejudice.

Slowly we who had just experienced this type of healing for the first time were able to work through our torrent of emotions. I had joy for the peace these people would now have yet I was horrified at the proximity to the dreaded disease. The wonder of this incredible miracle conflicted with years of reinforced fear.

As we talked about other healings we had seen and the teachings of Jesus which had changed our lives, we helped one another process the events that had altered how we lived our lives. Gradually, through this sharing, our churning feelings calmed and our kinship grew.

chapter seven

Our journey south continued. Jesus spoke at various towns and healed many people but thankfully, although I was ashamed of myself to think it, no more lepers. We stayed some places a day or two, others a week. He led services on the Sabbath, telling stories and asking people to join him.

I continued with my work as well: preparing towns and people for the arrival of a king. I wanted it all to be perfect.

First, I determined Jesus's probable route of entry into a village. Then, after establishing a clean-up crew, we rid the road of debris and filled holes to make the way smooth. If time permitted I had the crews concentrate their efforts on the town itself, making streets and public areas as nice as possible in the time remaining.

It should be stressed that Jesus never demanded such tidiness. These actions were never done in fear of his rage, malcontent or shunning. To be sure, Jesus was the least pretentious man I had ever met. I did it because I knew Jesus to be a king. Kingship merits respect and regard. Like my old friend Anna pulling out her best blankets and mats for Jesus, giving my best was my way of showing honour and reverence. My desire was for Jesus to feel honoured. If a governor passed by a town, the roads would be made as inviting as possible to entice the dignitary to visit the place. How much more should be done for Jesus!

These menial activities also served a secondary purpose. As people inquired about what we were doing, I told them about Jesus and his arrival. Men, women and children were soon enlisted to help beautify the road and town, anticipation mounting as they prepared for this man of renown.

I divided my time between these activities and readying the homes in which Jesus would stay. I worked with the family to set their house in order. We dusted shelves, washed and dried linens, cleaned and polished each pot and bowl in the kitchen. I would open windows, air rooms, and have fresh flowers picked so the house would have a welcoming scent. Fresh, cool water awaited Jesus to soothe his feet after his journey. Food made with utmost care was prepared and ready. Then the family and I would wait so that Jesus would be sure to find us home, ready to greet him.

The townspeople's labour was always rewarded with Jesus's gratitude. Never arrogant, Jesus sincerely thanked them for their toil and acts of reverence as he greeted them.

Regretfully, however, while my intentions were noble to begin with, they did not remain so: like sweet milk gone bad when not tended properly, what began as righteousness soured when not kept in check.

Time after time I watched Jesus gush over the efforts of strangers. I began to feel less appreciated. He thanked me, to be sure, yet I often wondered if he understood the magnitude of my labour and contribution.

The affirmation I felt that Jesus denied, I looked to his disciples to supply. They did not disappoint. When my fellow apostles arrived they heaped praises on me for the welcome they had received or for the impressively level road. The gratitude of my friends slowly made my head swell like bread dough rising in the warm sun. Bruised by what I thought of as Jesus's rebuff, I would square my shoulders, bolstered and consoled by my friends' encouragement, and again pursue my work with zeal.

I was not always successful in convincing country folk to treat my lord as a king, but when a town did come together in welcoming him the results were outstanding. Jesus's traveling band felt appreciated and welcomed. The townsfolk in turn were easily endeared to Jesus's disciples. Mutual feelings fed upon one another like funds in a bank compounding with interest.

As my preparations continued from Magdala to Bethany, I often found myself thinking about what my new friends would say. Quite naturally their opinions gravitated to become a reflection upon my character. Their reaction was my sole source of self-esteem. As a result, my desire for perfection increased with each village and with it my work load, because it was impossible for anything to be completed to my expectations. Gradually, the efforts and contributions of others became a fruitless endeavour. I had to do it myself if there was any hope of it being done properly.

In the town of Salim, while correcting some road repairs that a young man had worked on for the better part of the afternoon, a Pharisee named Markus asked me to arrange a place for him near the front of the assembly when Jesus arrived. *Imagine, a Pharisee seeking me out to ask for my help! I should not be surprised,* I reasoned to myself, *it is only logical that my responsibilities should expand to introducing Jesus to prominent men such as Markus.*

Of course, I made the arrangements. I watched for Jesus atop the tallest building in town. When I saw the billowing dust on the road announcing his arrival, I ran to get Markus so he could walk out to personally meet Jesus, pre-empting the other villagers in the welcome.

That evening, after supping with us, Markus enthusiastically endorsed Jesus's efforts. The response during the remaining week in Salim exceeded our visit to any other town. There was no dissension or challenge by any religious scholars. The townspeople scoured the countryside to invite friends to hear Jesus. This, I was sure, was due to Markus's sanction. How much faster, I wondered, would our ministry flourish if every village mirrored this success?

I set about to make this happen, deciding to spend some time in each village meeting with the religious leaders. I knew that the campaign of information was primarily assigned to Matthew and Philip, yet they seemed to concentrate their efforts on common folk instead of esteemed men—a group which seemed to me to require more attention.

Because of his experience with dignitaries and men of wealth, I sought out Judas Iscariot in this venture. I valued his opinion and wanted to know his thoughts regarding my discernment in this matter. I hoped to entice him to join me.

"Even if the leaders do not believe in Jesus's message," I postulated to Judas during an evening walk, "surely they will soon see the importance of being where Jesus is. After all, image is everything in politics and the masses are with Jesus."

I paused. Judas gave me a knowing nod.

"How will the religious leaders ever be swayed by Jesus's arguments," I continued, more confident in my reasoning, "if they don't hear him as Markus did? Besides, even if the Pharisees do not accept Jesus's teachings, having them attend the meetings and greet him as he enters the city can only bolster Jesus's credibility in the eyes of the people."

"It sounds like a well-conceived plan," Judas conceded with a smile. "I would be happy to help, Judas. Anything that furthers Jesus's kingmaking seems to me to be reasonable and shrewd." I nodded in agreement, sighing slightly in relief. I was frustrated with having to fix people's feeble, haphazard attempts at clean-up in my pursuit of perfection. I longed for a new avenue upon which to focus my energies.

With Judas as my assiduous and like-minded companion, by the time Jesus reached the city of Alexandrium a group of respectable businessmen and influential leaders had been organized to meet with him. By Jericho, the head religious leader was at the city gate to greet Jesus when he arrived.

In this city we also assembled the rest of the people who welcomed Jesus by rank, meticulously placing the leading men of Jericho first, then other men of the city followed by women and finally children.

"At last Jesus is gaining the respect he deserves," I commented to Judas as we watched our handiwork from the roof of a nearby house. We clapped one another on the back, congratulating ourselves on our significant contribution. The apostles, too, praised our work. They appreciated the time and energy we had invested in Jesus's kingdom-building.

While I sought out the apostles' comments, I did not talk to Jesus.

In truth, I had not spoken to him in two weeks. *I am too busy,* I justified to myself. Yet in my heart I knew this was but an excuse for I could make time to say hello to my fellow disciples but not to our leader, opting to ignore Jesus and nurse my bruised feelings at not being properly noticed than deal with the problem. I knew it was silly but I did not feel like exerting the effort. It was simply easier to concentrate on my work. So, without even having supper with Jesus, Judas and I left for Bethany, the group's next destination.

Judas and I made a good team and were well-suited to work with one another. Judas often told me how gratifying he found promoting Jesus to the business and religious communities. With each new town we learned and applied more, refining our ideas while collaborating on new strategies to give purpose to what, despite being stuck in my mire of self-pity, I still believed to be a virtuous goal.

It also helped that I truly enjoyed Judas's company. It was obvious why Jesus had chosen him to be an apostle. Judas was self-made and knew well the costs associated with success. Extremely intelligent, his expertise shone most brightly in the areas of finance and politics. He was ambitious yet seemed to know the value of people, careful not to abuse them or the system in his quest for wealth. He had integrity. He told me that he believed our nation needed a king and sincerely felt that Jesus was that man. Consequently, he chose to make it his life's work to achieve Jesus's reign. His history of success proved that he pursued his beliefs with conviction and had the ability to make them a reality. I was glad that he was on our side.

We arrived in Bethany a full week before Jesus and immediately sought the home of Lazarus and his two sisters, Mary and Martha, where Jesus would stay.

Jesus had met this family of siblings almost a year earlier during a visit to Bethany. Lazarus and his sisters had made numerous trips to Capernaum over the past seven months and Judas and I had gotten to know them, too.

Lazarus's was a man of considerable wealth. For as long as his family history had been recorded, his family had grown grapes.

Lazarus, the oldest living male in the family, had inherited this legacy and now owned a large vineyard and wine press, employing a good many people between the two ventures. His family was known throughout the region for their superior wines.

Lazarus was a large burly man about my age. The gray tinge to his beard and hair, however, gave him more of a hearty grandfather quality than one of dignity. From the moment I met him I held him in high regard, not because he was wealthy, but because his personality did not reflect what I typically associated with prestige. Money had not made him contemptuous; his friendliness was as generous as his stature.

When we arrived and located Lazarus, it was like coming home. He grabbed both Judas and me in a monstrous embrace.

"Ah, finally you are here!" he exclaimed, his voice booming as he ushered us down the city streets towards his home. "Come and we will show you the hospitality of Bethany."

We chatted lightly about our journey and how Jesus's wandering group had fared in its meanderings. Jesus had discussed his intended road trip with Lazarus on Lazarus's last visit to Capernaum so he had been expecting us.

We were politely welcomed by a servant at the door of Lazarus's house. As I entered and surveyed my surroundings, I made a conscious effort not to appear too astounded; the home Lazarus shared with his sisters was beyond imagining.

The outer mud brick wall had been built in the shape of a gigantic rectangle. Inside this wall half of the home was open to the sky while the other half comprised a number of rooms. The outer courtyard was beautifully landscaped and boasted a stunning centrepiece: a circular limestone cistern of water intricately carved with a grapevine motif. Around the cistern had been placed potted olive trees, delicate flowers and stone benches. Truly, this inviting place rivaled many of the public gardens of Jerusalem.

Lazarus led us to the rear of the open courtyard where enclosed rooms constructed of hewn stone two levels high joined together on three sides to form the back half of the complex. The central two-story space created by these rooms was covered by a thatched roof supported by six pillars. Grapevines entwined these columns before branching across the latticed ceiling. Beneath this greenery, inlaid on the floor of the inner courtyard, was a stone mosaic depicting a cluster of dusky grapes. Polished limestone, smooth and cool, had been used for the remainder of the flooring throughout. The overall effect was one of gracious welcome and serenity—a perfect place of respite for Jesus.

A small movement from the doorway of one of the rooms caught my attention. Mary and Martha emerged to greet us and make us feel at ease.

Mary was the next oldest of the siblings yet was considerably younger than Lazarus. I guessed her age to be in the mid-twenties. Neither she nor her sister Martha, who was only a year younger than Mary, had ever married. Nor had Lazarus, for that matter. Their parents had died when Mary was only five and the girls had been raised by their older brother. Lazarus once told me that he knew beyond a doubt that his strengths did not lie in parenting! Nevertheless, as a teenaged boy he had done the best he could. By the time his sisters were old enough to marry they were both headstrong and picky. They balked at any man Lazarus proposed they wed and, surprisingly, there were blessed few of them despite the money involved. It would be a desperate man who might take on Mary or Martha. I, too, found their tenacity a little unnerving at times for they spoke their minds freely, a trait that I, along with most men, did not appreciate.

Although I could easily believe Mary and Martha to have been the young malcontents Lazarus had described, they had changed considerably. Despite their opinionated nature, I found them to be vivacious and determined. Lazarus attributed their change in demeanour to Jesus. He said that after embracing Jesus's teachings their edge and abrasiveness had become spark and passion.

Except for the enthusiasm of their spirits, the two sisters could not have been more opposite. I must admit, I appreciated Martha more than Mary—probably because Martha was more like me. She was organized, methodical and had an eye for detail; a diligent perfectionist who loved structure and was at her best when it surrounded her.

Mary, on the other hand, could not be bothered with everyday tasks. She was capricious, pursuing life with reckless abandon and rarely considering the full implications of her decisions. She gloried in disarray and clutter.

Their home was not often peaceful, as can well be imagined.

Yet all three wanted to make Jesus's visit a memorable one. After supper we strategized about how to accomplish this. Lazarus told Judas and I about key men with whom to talk. Although it was a busy time for Lazarus, he was determined to help us. He decided to leave his servant, Obed, the same man who had met us at the door upon our arrival, in charge of his business so Lazarus could accompany Judas and me. Lazarus, it seemed, treated Obed more as a personal assistant than a servant, saying that he always left the daily operation of his lucrative business in Obed's capable care whenever he visited Jesus in Capernaum.

Martha volunteered herself and the sisters' servant, Joanna, to help with the town clean-up. Mary, much to my disdain, politely excused herself from all of my suggested activities, claiming that she had her own ideas about how to welcome Jesus.

The following morning, despite Mary's contrary nature, I left the house refreshed and invigorated by my group of helpers, determined to win the town for Jesus.

Lazarus, Judas and I talked to the town elders and rabbis. We held meetings, lobbied and convinced the townsmen of the importance of Jesus's visit. Judas, whose abilities inclined towards the business community, was soon adding money needed for daily expenses to Jesus's purse.

Martha took her talent for organizing to the streets. She convinced women to sweep the road, wash down dusty old carts and weed flower beds. Martha was in her element. At one point I saw her stand on an overturned pot with her hands on her hips and her lips pursed to better survey the frenzy of activity. Then she quickly jumped down and ran to help an elderly woman struggling to dislodge a stubborn buried root.

It seemed obvious to me that Martha wanted to show Jesus through her work how much she cared for him, how much she loved him. I did not think it was the type of love that sparks a romance but rather the love you feel towards someone who makes you a truer person—like loving the bright soothing sun after the wind of a torrential rain has ripped at your soul.

Mary, however, was not once seen helping with the improvements to the town. In fact, throughout the day I caught but one rare glimpse of her as I passed the city gates on my way to a meeting with the head Pharisee. She was in a field just outside of Bethany, bending briefly to gather something from the grass, then she moved forward and bent down again. A group of children hovered around her like bees clustered together looking for a new place to build their hive.

That evening the seven of us worked on the house. Mary did help with this activity, but certainly not with the same diligence as the rest of us. I often had to keep myself from sighing too loudly as I readjusted a mat that Mary had just straightened or revisited an area she had weeded.

Finally, Martha declared our day a success, dismissed the servants and suggested Lazarus, Mary, Judas and I accompany her to the hearth. We readily collapsed on some cushions beneath the leafy green latticed ceiling.

The evening was cool and dark but the stoked oven robbed the chill from the night. The lanterns hanging from the surrounding pillars made our shadows dance on the mosaic floor with their flickering flames.

"Tomorrow I believe I will get some of the workers," Martha commented as soon as everyone was comfortably seated, "and start on the road leading into town. Joanna can look for a few extra buckets before she goes to bed and make some thick mud in the morning so we can start on the holes first thing."

"Thank you, Martha, that would be a great help," I beamed, happy to relax and rely on her high standards.

"What were you doing today, Mary?" Judas asked. "I seemed to see

Martha everywhere, but you were hard to find." His question sounded abrupt and harsh, yet I was glad he asked it for I wondered the same thing.

"I was gathering berries and flowers," Mary answered perfunctorily, seeming not to appreciate the undertone of Judas's inquiry.

There was an odd silence. Martha shifted in her seat as if she sensed the mounting tension that I knew I was feeling.

"If quantity was your intent then I would say you were a success," Lazarus said lightly with a chuckle and a generous smile, trying to soothe Mary. "When I saw you it looked to me as if you had the interest of almost every child from the north end of the city. What are you going to do with the products of your hard work?"

"I have talked to a number of men who have businesses along the main road and they have agreed to let me paint their outer walls," Mary said proudly. "The children and I are going to paint giant pictures to welcome Jesus."

The four of us stared at Mary blankly, the shock on our faces easier to read than words on a parchment under a bright light.

"Well," Martha finally offered, "that is a creative idea."

"Yes," Mary replied defiantly. "Yes, it is."

The conversation lulled, no one sure what to say next. Lazarus played with a fringe on the corner of his mantle. Then he asked, mostly, I presumed, to fill the awkward moment, when I had first met Jesus. Happy to steer the conversation in a different direction, I told them about James's exuberance and how he had convinced me to go to Nazareth to hear Jesus speak. Despite the lateness of the hour I reciprocated the question and asked about his first meeting with Jesus.

"Martha and I heard him speak at a synagogue, as well," Lazarus returned. "I was amazed by his teachings. It was not that his words were that different from other rabbis, it was the fact that he spoke with authority. While other teachers guess at the meaning of passages, as we all do, Jesus explained them with certainty. That day he spoke of sins and forgiveness. He said that all sins were equal, that lusting after a woman was the same as committing the act of adultery."

Leaning back slightly in his seat, he extended his large hands to place them on his knees and shrugged a bit as he continued, "That pretty much put us all at the same level now, doesn't it? Who has never sinned in his thoughts? I knew I must meet him. And," he added, with a glance at Mary, "I knew that if there was any hope for Mary to find redemption, I had to get Mary to hear what Jesus had to say."

Judas and I looked at Mary quizzically.

She was not shy. "I was a prostitute," she stated matter-of-factly.

I am sure that my eyes grew to be the size of the full moon in the dark sky above the courtyard. I knew Lazarus had had his challenges in raising his sisters but I was shocked at the full implication of his troubles.

"I was very unhappy back then, always dissatisfied," Mary explained, picking up the story. "I wanted more. More money. More notoriety. When I was sixteen I met an older man, John, with whom I fell in love. He was rich, suave and handsome. But the thing I loved most about him was that he listened to my rants and always let me speak my mind. Oh, he hosted the most elaborate parties and bought me incredible gifts. I felt like a queen."

She paused. I noticed her fingers quiver as she lightly touched her forehead to brush some wayward strands of hair back into place.

"However, he was also manipulative," she said softly, clearing her throat. "I found out too late how he had gained his wealth."

Mary jutted her jaw out determinedly, stared at the wall and cleared her throat again before speaking more forcefully.

"It started with him telling me how his money was drying up. He soon told me he was penniless. Then, playing on my emotions and my love for him, he said that desperate times demanded desperate measures and he arranged for me to spend a few evenings with some of his wealthy friends. At first he was apologetic, sorry that he had to arrange another meeting. I so desperately desired his love to be real that I resolved to believe him and lived in his lies."

She spoke dispassionately, like someone telling a third-person narrative. I supposed that was how she had lived, the only way that she could have done the unthinkable.

"One night a friend of his beat me up. I had black eyes, a broken nose and fat lips. I wondered if I would ever heal properly and look the same again. So did John. He left me that night. He went off to another town. Another girl, I suppose."

She paused again, shifting her eyes to gaze at the enclosed garden, then glancing at Lazarus to smile slightly before staring into the garden again. Lazarus returned her faint smile, rapidly blinking his glistening eyes.

"Lazarus begged me to come home," Mary sighed, shaking her head, "but I was too proud. Instead I went to a woman who had 'worked' at some of the parties I had attended. Her name was Suzanna. Her story was similar to mine so she felt sorry for me and agreed to let me stay with her as long as I promised to stay out of sight when she had customers. I healed eventually. Suzanna and I made an arrangement. We took turns working and shared our accommodations. Finally, I had money and I was known—but it was hardly the notoriety I had expected."

Mary inhaled deeply, trying to find the strength to tell what happened next. Her eyes looked like dull, dead orbs.

"I lived like that for three years. By then I was used up and tired. I felt like an old hag. Cynical and completely disillusioned with people, I knew no joy. I cared about nothing. I sold my body. I had no soul. I existed, that was all.

"One night, Lazarus came to see me, adamant that I go to hear a man called Jesus," she chuckled softly, a smile lingering on her lips as she continued. "To tell you the truth, I only went to prove Lazarus wrong. If Lazarus said Jesus was like no man he had ever met, I was going to prove that this man was exactly like every other man on earth." She gave her brother a wink and then for the first time looked at Judas and me. "I was sure that Jesus just told people what they wanted to hear, that he was a manipulator, another man spouting promises he wouldn't keep.

"The next day Jesus spoke to a group of about a hundred people outside of town. I went and stood at the back. As he spoke, he looked at each one of us. His eyes were like nothing I had ever seen before."

Two small wrinkles formed between her eyebrows as she pushed them together, looking as if she was trying hard to think of a way to describe what she had seen. After a few moments her face relaxed and she said, "It was as though his eyes were pure as if they had never been hardened by the harshness of the world. They were like the eyes of a child who doesn't realize the true ugliness of the place that he has been born into." She smiled, satisfied with her portrait. "He spoke about what I thought was impossible: forgiveness for my sins. For three years I had lived in hell's clutches, feeling like there was no escape, my sins too great to atone for even with daily sacrifices at the temple. Adonai seemed so far away. Yet when Jesus spoke, I thought perhaps the impossible could happen, that Adonai meant it to happen. All I had known was condemnation, but Jesus offered mercy. All I had heard were accusations, but Jesus granted grace. I believed him. I had to, he was my only hope."

Her eyes took on their familiar shine, glittering again like the sun dancing on ripples of water.

"I trusted him and a miracle happened. I felt fresh and clean. It was a feeling I thought I had been eternally denied. Right there I determined to talk to Jesus, to thank him. After some discreet eavesdropping I discovered that he was having supper with a Pharisee named Simon. At first I was a little intimidated but, never one to let a thing like decorum stand in my way, I decided to go to Simon's home," she laughed, recalling her audacity.

"I went to my hiding place, retrieved some of my savings and bought a jar of perfume. Then I went to his house. I walked right in. I had a little speech of thanks prepared and rehearsed in my head but when I saw Jesus I could not say a word. I was completely flooded with emotion. Three years of feeling not a thing, then I saw Jesus and the dam broke. I could do nothing but weep. Helpless to do anything else, I walked to where Jesus was sitting and knelt, bowing my head before him. As I sobbed, I noticed that my tears were falling on Jesus's feet. I gently wiped them with my hair. All I could think of was how grateful I was for what he had given me, salvation from my hell. I took out my perfume and poured it onto his feet. I kissed them."

Tears again flowed down her cheeks as they had that day.

"I heard Simon shuffling restlessly behind me. He knew exactly who and what I was. I could feel his disapproval. But then I heard Jesus say, 'Simon, I have a story for you. There once was a money lender who had two debtors: one owed five hundred denarii, and the other fifty. Neither debtor was able to repay him, so he graciously forgave them both. Which of the debtors do you think will love the money lender more?' 'I suppose the one who was forgiven more' Simon said. 'You have judged correctly' Jesus said."

Mary paused and drew in a deep breath, trying to compose herself.

"And then Jesus placed his hand on my head and said, 'Do you see this woman, Simon? I entered your house; you gave me no water for my feet, but she has wet my feet with her tears, and wiped them with her hair. You gave me no kiss, but she, since the time I came in, has not ceased to kiss my feet. You did not anoint my head with oil, but she anointed my feet with perfume. For this reason I say to you, her sins, which are many, have been forgiven for she loved much; but he who is forgiven little, shows little love.'[1] Then Jesus took my hand, looked me in the eyes and said, 'Your sins have been forgiven. Your faith has saved you, go in peace.'"

"And I have. I have lived in peace. I know what it means to be forgiven. I have lived in hell but now I live in mercy. I will follow Jesus to the ends of the earth and back."

Mary's eyes bore into each of us, daring any of us to challenge her. No one did.

For the next few days I watched Mary with keener interest. Although her priorities were not like mine, I gradually began to appreciate her contributions.

True to her word, Mary set to work creating elaborate scenes on the outer walls of local shops. Early each morning she drew a basic landscape then, as her young helpers finished breakfast and congregated around her, she organized them into groups. Some she taught to make palettes of colour using crushed berries, flowers and a bit of water while others she sent to collect new painting materials from nearby fields. By midday there were toddlers giggling at the juice oozing between their toes as they stomped in buckets of berries, youngsters painting grass on the bottom of the giant work-in-progress, older children making simple animals or hills and teens painting the sky or clouds. I sometimes saw Mary teaching children new techniques of painting, at others times acting as a magistrate of disputes. I marveled at her patience.

In all honesty, the creations were not the most beautiful I had ever seen but they were not bad either, especially with the extra work that Mary did. Each evening she would return to the mural, lantern in hand, to work through the night long after her helpers had gone to sleep. She made a dark purple paste to outline a smudge that a four-year-old intended to be a flower or deepened the blue under a cloud to add definition to an eleven-year-old boy's contribution; her detailing accentuated each child's efforts. The next morning, following her painters' ohhs and ahhs over their collective masterpiece, they moved to the blank canvas of the next building.

Many elders scoffed at the futility of her labour but by the end of the week I saw in her art a love for Jesus, a gratitude for how he had affected her life. I just prayed it would not rain before he arrived.

chapter eight

B y the end of the week we still were not as ready as I had hoped to be despite my many helpers; Bethany was a large city. Luckily Jesus did not arrive the day he was expected, so I used the extra time to continue preparing.

Jesus, however, did not arrive the next day either. By the third day into our watch, worry began to consume me.

"I hope nothing has happened to Jesus and the others," Judas said into the blackness of our room that night as we lay on our woven straw mats and waited to fall asleep.

"Yes, me too," I responded, glad to hear him voice my concerns. Hoping that saying it alone would make it true, I added lamely, "I'm sure they are fine. A group that large would intimidate any bandits."

"Even so," Judas countered, "I intend to walk back towards Jericho in the morning."

"I will join you. Although it is unlikely they are hurt, I would feel better knowing what has happened," I said, pleased by his proactive attitude.

After a few hours of sleep, and with the sun still waiting to greet the day, Judas and I began our quest for our missing companions.

We traveled for most of the morning chatting about the weather, the road and other topics of little consequence. After an uncomfortable lull in the conversation, Judas unexpectedly asked, "What did you think of Mary's story about when she first met Jesus?"

Taken aback by the sudden change in the direction of our talk, I thought for a moment then answered, "I was surprised, actually 'stunned' would be a better word, that she had lived such a life."

"But what about when she said that Jesus forgave her sins?" he queried further.

I was quiet, contemplating his question.

"I don't know," I finally answered. "I didn't think about it much, I suppose, because I was so shocked by the rest of her story."

"That is not the first time that Jesus has professed to forgive sins, you know," Judas spoke under his breath as if scared someone might overhear us even though we had not seen anyone on the road for at least an hour.

"It's not?" I asked incredulously. "When else have you heard this?"

"It was in Capernaum. I had come up from Jerusalem with a group of Pharisees and teachers of the law to find out about this teacher who was causing such a stir. Jesus was teaching in a house. The place was so packed I could barely turn around. Suddenly the tiles in the roof above Jesus's head started to wiggle and move. I looked up and saw an opening in the roof through which four heads peeked. Then they disappeared. The next thing I saw was a stretcher suspended by four ropes being dropped from the ceiling. I could see the men on the roof slowly lowering their friend right in front of Jesus."[1]

I listened, astounded by the tale.

"The man on the stretcher could not walk or use his hands," Judas continued. "I overheard someone behind me whispering that the invalid had fallen from a cart a few years ago and broken his neck. Jesus looked at the man on the mat and said, 'Friend, your sins are forgiven.' I glanced at the faces of the men I was with. At first they looked shocked, then angry. Imagine saying he has the authority to grant forgiveness! Although they did not say anything and Jesus had been focusing on the man on the mat, Jesus turned to them and said, 'Which is easier, to say your sins are forgiven or to say rise and walk? But so that you will know that I have authority on earth to forgive sins…' Then Jesus looked at the paralytic and said, 'Rise, take up your stretcher and go home.' And he did! Just like that the man sat up, rolled up his mat and left. That was when I knew that I had to find out more about Jesus."

I thought about what Judas had said. Only blood sacrifice made by the priests in the temple at Jerusalem had the ability to atone for sins. Why would Jesus claim to be able to forgive? Yet Jesus *was* doing amazing miracles. His authority was undeniable. But authority to nullify past sins? Was that possible?

"What do you think, Judas?" I asked, genuinely curious about his assessment of Jesus's claims. "Do you think Jesus can forgive sins?"

"I honestly don't know," he confided. "However, I am sure of one thing: there are things you simply do not say if you want to be a king and that is on the top of the list. I don't think it matters if he can forgive sins or not. It isn't relevant. But we can never hope to win over the leaders of the law if they feel Jesus threatens their authority. It just isn't prudent for him to claim such things."

Judas's arguments made sense. As the sun progressed across the sky we continued to discuss the image that Jesus should exude in order to make his reign a reality.

By noon we spotted a cluster of tents and shelters to the left of the road. Deciding to investigate, we approached the camp which, as we drew closer, looked more and more familiar. I sighed in relief and hurried my steps as we approached the dwellings. It was indeed the friends we were searching for.

The smell of quail roasting over open firepits tempted my nose and I remembered how hungry I was. Philip saw us first.

"Hello, Hello!" he yelled, coming out to welcome us. "Your timing is impeccable. We were just about to eat."

"Is everything all right?" I blurted out before Philip even reached us. "You are four days late."

"Oh yes, yes," Philip calmly explained. "Jesus was invited to visit the village of Rissa so we have been here about a week." He smiled generously.

As Philip's news slowly sank into my mind, any relief at finding my friends was pushed away by swelling anger.

"Do you not realize the welcome that is waiting for Jesus in Bethany?" I exploded. "And now you tell me that he simply decided to stay in this insignificant town for the past week? Did someone prepare this place for his arrival? Were the people prepped and informed how to greet Jesus properly? Was any preliminary work done?" My voice crescendoed with my litany of complaints.

Philip stared at me blankly.

"Where is Jesus now?" I demanded.

"He is over that hill," Philip said, motioning lamely to a nearby incline. "He has been teaching there since early this morning."

"Judas, why don't you stay and have lunch," I called over my shoulder, stomping off in the direction Philip had indicated. "I'll go and talk to Jesus."

I walked up the hill and tried to gain control of my emotions and calm myself down. *Obviously Jesus does not know the amount of work that has been done on his behalf,* I thought to myself in an attempt at soothing my rage. *How is he to know that an entire city waits for him, alight with anticipation?* Jesus was probably tired and wanted a break before entering another hotbed of activity.

Realizing that I was probably overreacting, I decided to take some time to gain a more balanced attitude before confronting Jesus. I sat down on the ascending grassy hill and forced myself to refocus my thoughts.

Surprisingly, achieving the perspective I sought was not as difficult as I anticipated, for it was a lovely day. I closed my eyes, breathing deeply of the grass-scented air as the sun's warmth graciously welcomed me into the day. Feeling a little better, I opened my eyes and squinted against the brightness. As my eyes adjusted to the glare, I watched the grass as it swayed under a slight breeze like the gentle roll of waves across water, splashes of colour from spring flowers spraying through the green now and then. The sky, brilliant blue, was dotted with small balls of fluff. It was a carefree day, the kind that is meant for nine-year-old boys to play and laugh with friends.

I stood, feeling more in control, ready to continue looking for Jesus. Cresting the hill, I heard laughter and shouting. A group of children had captured the day, refusing to let it go. Entranced by the picture before me, I sat again deciding to watch the frenzy of activity below me and enjoy the day a moment longer. The descending hill was not too large and at its base gurgled a small stream that I could walk across in four steps. Beyond the creek was a flat meadow where the group appeared to be playing a game of tag. Children ran in the open field, calling and chortling, forming a rough circle where they wove in and out amongst themselves, swerving to avoid one another. The organized chaos revolved around someone in the middle whom I presumed to be "it."

Now and again I caught a glimpse of the one in the middle of this mayhem. He appeared to be an older child on all fours with a two or three-year-old on his back riding him like a horse. Children of all ages played, older and younger ones running hand in hand. Their laughter was wild and freeing; it danced and sashayed with the grass and the wind.

The boy on all fours collapsed in laughter and rolled through the grass with the child who had been on his back, each giggling at the other's silliness. Then the boy stood and I realized that he was not a boy at all, but a man. I stared incredulously, shocked. Had a bird happened by I'm sure it could have built a nest in my gaping mouth.

What self-respecting man would play children's games in the middle of the day? What man would play with them at all?

Then I heard the man call, "I'll race you all to the river!"

Horrified, I recognized his voice. It was Jesus!

I gawked as the group of children squealed and tore towards me. Taking the rear, Jesus herded them towards the water and swooped up a little girl who was lagging behind to ride on his shoulders. When he reached the rest of the children, Jesus placed the girl on the bank and ran into the water with total abandon his bounding feet splashing those on shore. He turned, cupped his hands and scooped water on the heaving, panting, laughing group. Soon all the children joined in the fun. Although the water was only knee deep, everyone was so wet you would think they had just swum across an ocean.[2]

Jesus stood up straight and stopped to catch his breath. I stared at the water dripping from his drenched hair and beard and was haunted by the image of the suave, sophisticated visionary I had promoted to the dignitaries in Bethany. If the 'nay-saying' Pharisees from Capernaum ever witnessed such a spectacle, they would have all the ammunition they needed to destroy any hope of kingship for Jesus. While I had been trying to establish respect and a sense of decorum for our future king, Jesus frolicked with children. I turned and walked back to the encampment, renewed in the justification of my anger and disgust; Judas's warnings about the necessity of prudent behaviour ringing in my ears.

At camp the disciples were sharing their lunch with a group of men and women whom I assumed were the townspeople, many were probably the parents of the children with Jesus. Emboldened by my righteous fury I took the opportunity to voice my displeasure.

"I was just over the hill," I began, "and I saw Jesus playing with children."

"Yes," a woman interrupted, smiling and looking pleased that she could give me a helpful explanation, "Jesus offered to take them for the afternoon."

"Well, I hope you realize the damage your childless afternoon could cause." I spat, realizing too late that I sounded harsher than I had intended. Some men lowered the food they were about to eat, others stared at me with puzzled expressions. I remembered that many of these people did not even know who I was.

Andrew stood, extended his hand and introduced me, saying, "This is Judas, he is a fellow apostle of Jesus who has been traveling ahead of our group for some time to prepare each destination for Jesus's arrival."

He did not excuse my outburst but instead added his gaze to the rest of the assembly waiting for my explanation. The concentrated attention was nervewracking and I tried to vindicate myself by speaking less severely, "There are many men who would love to see Jesus in such a compromising position. Just a glimpse of what I saw over that hill could destroy all that we have worked for. Is your afternoon of freedom worth such a great cost?" My accusation hung in the air.

The parents around the fire were quiet, one woman sheepishly drew circles in the dust with her toe.

"We meant no harm," a father exclaimed. "Jesus is a great man. We simply wanted our children to know him too. The children were so curious, so excited when Jesus said he wanted to spend time with them. Anything we can do to make things right, please, just ask. We will gladly do it."

Softened by the sincerity of his apology yet not wanting to lose the opportunity to stress the importance of propriety, I gently instructed, "A great man cannot afford to act like a child."

"No damage has been done," Andrew interjected, attempting to console the distraught parents. "There is no one here who wants to compromise Jesus. We will just have to be more careful in the future with Jesus's reputation."

"What should we do?" a women asked.

"Well, we should probably get our children," suggested the man who had offered to do anything to help. With many nods, men and women began to stand and walk towards the hill. Relieved that I was no longer the centre of attention or was required to defend my opinions, I sat down on a knobbled log by the fire. An old woman with a toothless grin brought me a spit of meat that had been roasting over the coals. As I ate, I overheard Judas advising Peter, Andrew and John that it would be wise for them to discuss the incident with Jesus in order to avoid similar situations in the future.

Finished the meal and satisfied that Jesus's character would remain intact, Judas and I told our friends that we would head back to Bethany and expect to see them within a day or two.

Jesus arrived in Bethany two days later. The important men of the town were present to meet him as he passed through the city gates. The Pharisees acknowledged Jesus with a nod of their heads, Lazarus greeted him with a kiss. The women, showing great dignity, bowed their heads as he walked by and the children revered him in quiet awe.

Jesus made his way to Lazarus's home and, once inside, gave each of the three siblings a giant hug, happy to see his old friends again. I watched all the activity, pleased to see my handiwork accomplish its purpose. When Jesus learned of Mary and Martha's preparations, he raved about the murals, saying he had suspected her involvement when he saw the artwork. He also thanked Martha for her integral part in the beautified city.

Lazarus washed Jesus's feet beside the cistern of water to formally welcome him and received Jesus's companions in the same way.

With the formalities complete, Martha left the gathering to join Joanna in preparing supper. Jesus sat on a bench close to the cistern, chatting with Lazarus. Mary, at Jesus's feet, took in all that he was saying, peppering him with questions.

I found Mary's behaviour strange and wondered why she was not helping Martha with the food. *Supper must be ahead of schedule,* I reasoned to myself. Deciding to ask Martha how soon I should direct everyone to the lattice-roofed room to eat, I went to the kitchen.

It did not take long to realize that dinner was far from ready. Beans, cucumbers and onions lay mid-chop on a bench, a pile of cuttings beside them. Bread dough rose on the window sill, waiting to be baked, beside it cloth-covered *leben*, soured milk mixed with yeast, sat curdling in the sun. Cutting boards, knives, peelings, pots and half-prepared food littered the work area. So completely engrossed in her activities was Martha that she seemed oblivious to me standing in the doorway—even after she turned from stooping over a pot of boiling water and walked in my direction. With rigid shoulders, fixated eyes and pursed lips, her frustration seemed to be bubbling more than the churning pot of water on the hearth. Joanna was nowhere to be seen.

"I don't know why I should be expected to get all this food ready by myself." I heard her mutter as she picked up a knife and stared at the half-sliced heap of figs before her. She continued her rant as she chopped the fruit and the figs quickly deteriorated from diced to demolished. "A houseful of guests and Mary can't even lift a finger to help. How would she feel if I left her alone to prepare all this? I can't believe that no one even cares that she is sitting out there visiting while

I slave away in this heat-baked kitchen!"

She nicked her finger with the knife and let out an angry grunt. Turning away from me, she dunked her finger into a bowl of cool water at the end of the table.

"I agree with you, Martha," I offered.

She jumped, jerking her head in my direction, then quickly recovered—giving me an obviously forced smile.

"It is inappropriate for a woman to be visiting with the men," I continued, reassuring her that her feelings were justified. "Her place is here in the kitchen with you. Where is Joanna?"

"I sent her to the market for more cucumbers and onions," Martha explained, wiping a sweat soaked strand of hair from her crimson cheek. Scanning the mess around her she pursed her lips again, "Look at this place! This is all Mary's fault."

She slammed the knife down beside the water bowl, placed her hands firmly on her hips and declared, "You're right, Judas. It's about time that Mary learned her place." With that she stomped into the outer courtyard.

I followed close behind to give Martha my moral support, but when we reached the gathering, I stayed at the back uncomfortable about pushing my way to the front as Martha had done. She stood beside Jesus and waited for him to finish speaking.

Jesus, noticing Martha, paused in mid-sentence, smiled up at her and grabbed her hand, giving it a slight squeeze before letting go and returning to his story.

"...so by the end of it," Jesus continued, "this little grasshopper was surrounded by six grown men all watching him dance. Take a step, do a little jig, take another step, do a little jig."

As Jesus spoke I remembered his talent for storytelling. His eyes twinkled and the corners of his lips turned up playfully as he exaggerated the supposed dance moves of the locust in his story.

This brought a chorus of laughter. Even I smiled, despite my sour attitude, for it was hard not be drawn into his tale.

Once the chortling had subsided, Jesus raised his eyes and his hands toward the sky, grinned broadly and exclaimed, "And I thought what a beautiful world this is where a little bug can entertain the likes of us!"

"Of course he is leaving out the best part of the story," Matthew interrupted. Everyone cocked their heads towards Matthew. "Jesus was standing beside Philip at the time. With everyone completely entranced by the grasshopper, Jesus reached out and ever so lightly tickled Philip on the side of the neck. Oh! Did he jump!"

A new peal of laughter filled the air. Thomas, who stood beside Philip, gave him a good-natured jab in the ribs.

When the merriment had quieted, Jesus turned to Martha and said, "I'm glad you've decided to join us, Martha."

"Actually, Lord," Martha began tentatively, "there is still a lot of work to be done."

The jocularity seeped away as a cloud passing over the sun dampens the heat's intensity. Gaining the attention of the crowd around Jesus and confident in her position, Martha minced no words in her complaint. "Do you not care that my sister has left me to do all the dinner preparations alone?" she asked, her words sounding more of a plea than a whine, as if she sought relief more from her inner stress than from her work. "Please tell Mary to come into the kitchen and help me." Jesus reached out and took Martha's hand again.

"My dear woman," he said tenderly. "You have worked ceaselessly for a week to make me feel welcome. Now it is time to let the dinner fend for itself. I do not care if we eat now or hours from now. I promise not to get sick if the food is cold and mushy. I know the efforts that you have made for me. But tonight, Mary has chosen something better and I will not take it away from her. Please, Martha, join us. I want you to hear of our adventures too. There is room here beside your sister. Have a seat and rest. The time for work is finished. It is time to laugh and visit."[3]

As Martha looked around at the faces staring back at her, her cheeks darkened to a deep red hue. Mary scooted over closer to Andrew, leaving a space on the ground beside her, then smiled up at her sister and patted the spot. Slowly, Martha lowered herself to kneel beside her sister.

"Mary was telling us that she has never seen the city work together with such vigor. She said that you convinced mortal enemies to work side by side," Jesus offered, easing the awkward moment and making Martha feel welcome.

Martha stared at her sister. Mary reached her arm around Martha's back to gently squeeze her shoulder.

"Oh, yes. She was a marvel," Mary grinned.

As the chatting resumed, I watched and listened from the shadows. It did not take long for Martha to relax and become one of the group. Everyone took turns relating stories about the past week. The travelers told of the hospitality of Rissa, Mary of the antics of the children and Martha of cleaning mishaps and their hilarious results.

Conversation flowed naturally to Jesus. He spoke of time.

A time to work, and a time to tell stories.

A time to play, and a time to teach.

A time to tear down, and a time to build up.

A time to weep, and a time to dance.

A time to fast, and a time to feast.

An appointed time for every event under heaven.[4]

chapter nine

a s I stood on the fringe watching my assembled friends, I must admit I did not follow Jesus's logic or his nonchalant attitude towards life. I thought again of how little regard he seemed to have for the preparation it took to set events in motion. Time is the enemy, I reasoned, not a commodity to be embraced. We seek a noble cause and all else must be sacrificed to see its completion. The luxury of time is something that must wait until this work is completed.

It was dark when we finally ate our barely palatable meal. The cold, bland food stuck in my throat along with my assessment of the past few days. I ate half the food on my plate, made my apologies and rose to go to bed.

Jesus was quick to rise as well, saying, "Judas, I need to speak with you. Come, let's go for a walk."

I agreed, assuming Jesus needed to confirm some plans for the coming week.

Although the full moon shone brightly, I carried a lamp to help us see the path. The air was cool and refreshing, something I was grateful for after the stifling evening.

"Why do you think that I asked you to be my apostle, Judas?" Jesus's opening question took me by surprise.

Jerking my head to look into his eyes, I immediately felt uncomfortable. His intense gaze pierced the flickering glow of the lantern. Yet I did my best to answer.

"Well," I began, "as more people joined us, it became necessary to have someone look for places to stay and to coordinate food. I have many contacts and an ability to organize so you asked me to tend to this."

"That is what I asked you to do but it is not why I wanted you to be my apostle. I wanted you to follow me. I asked you to be my ambassador. Lately you have been running so far ahead of me that you have lost sight of what I seek to establish."

"I have been working very hard, Jesus," I responded defensively. "I am trying to make your kingdom a reality. I am doing my best to have people treat you with the respect you deserve."

"You are keeping people from me."

The frankness of his comment stopped me.

"I do not understand what you mean, Lord," I said, honestly confused.

"You plan who sees me and when. You have told parents to keep their children from me. You rank people in an order of importance dictated by your own judgment. You are separating me from my people. This must stop."

"You are my king. You deserve to have men of privilege pay you homage," I justified.

"I have come not only for men of privilege," Jesus firmly countered. "I have come to bring all people to me. Women and children need me too. Children need to be blessed now when they are young as well as when they are grown." Jesus's voice mellowed as he went on. "I want to bless the children. I want them to come to me. They will know that they are blessed when they are loved as they are. How else will they understand?"

Discouraged, I looked at Jesus and said, "Perhaps I am not the man you thought I was. I have been doing all I can think of but it never seems to be good enough. Maybe you need to find someone else to tend to your needs."

"I do not want someone to tend to my needs. I want you to know my kingdom," Jesus implored. "Oh, Judas, how different my kingdom is from that of the world's. It is imperative that you grasp it. In my kingdom the first shall be last and the last first. People will not be allowed to enter because of prestige or laurels but will have to humble themselves as children. In my kingdom past transgressions and present status will not preclude anyone. You will find sinners behind every door. Harlots, teachers of the law and businessmen will walk the streets together. Toddlers and the highly educated will dine at the same table. Murderers will be welcomed there, men of despicable background who have done heinous crimes. Mothers, fathers and families of respect will be as sought after as earnestly as adulterers. I want them all, Judas. I want every one of them."

He paused to let me absorb the awful magnitude of what he was saying, then continued.

"The common bond which will hold them together is forgiveness. People need to know Adonai's love and forgiveness. I want them to experience the joy of being called to a community, a kingdom, to know that they have a place to belong. I want them to see themselves the way I see them, as creations of Adonai, to realize that He desires them to live in His love. I want them so secure in that love that they love others with the same abandon."

His vision was so far beyond my comprehension it seemed surreal.

"At the very least," I offered with a weak smile, "you are more popular than ever because of the important people who greet you."

"No, never think such a thing," Jesus addressed me with renewed vigor. "My kingdom must never be reduced to a cause. I will not have people treated as pawns to accomplish an end no matter how virtuous that end may be. The process is as important as the goal. The construction as imperative as the completed structure. It is the individual I seek, not a cause."

Totally defeated, I slumped my shoulders in silence.

Jesus placed his hand on my shoulder and gave it a slight squeeze.

"Go to bed, my friend. We will talk again tomorrow. But before you sleep, think on what I have said and try to remember what brought you to wait by that rock outside Nazareth those nine months ago. Recall what kept you in Capernaum. Come back to my vision. Please, Judas, follow me again."

I went to bed, but I did not sleep.

I did as Jesus asked. I thought back to my first encounter with him at the synagogue in Nazareth. I thought about the way his eyes had bored into my soul. I recalled my terror at feeling that Jesus could see my inner being. It was impossible to hide my wretchedness. Then I remembered the peace and thinking, *I found it*. I had an intense desire to live in this forever. I felt complete as if something that had been missing was now discovered. But what treasure had I found? What inner need had been miraculously satisfied? These questions I mulled and churned through my head for most of the night. It was when the sun began to stretch its fingers across the horizon to begin a new day that dawn broke through my mind's dark night as well. I grasped it again. And this time I determined to hold on to it with all my strength.

I was loved.

I was loved by Adonai himself.

At that moment in the Nazareth synagogue, I had realized my desperate longing for Adonai's love; a love that embraced me as I was, a love that existed even when it was utterly aware of all my defects. I discovered that the love of Adonai is most fully revealed when I understood that in the midst of complete exposure to my sins, He still loves me.

I was loved as I was—not as I should be.

No charity, no matter how good, and no act of devotion to Adonai, no matter how sincere, would increase His love for me. No evil I could commit, no matter how depraved, could diminish it.[1]

As I thought through these feelings, I was not satisfied to realize that I had experienced Adonai's love. I wondered at my intense longing for a love that was not based on action. Indeed, it was a curious thing. I had never been taught that love needed to be deserved, that I needed to be worthy of it. On the contrary, my parents were adamant that I was loved no matter the circumstances. As a child, discipline was never about depriving me of love. It was however, administered by people who loved me most. Justice and love were therefore like two cords lying parallel on a path. The cords lay dangerously close to one another. So close, in fact, that they often become tangled and entwined.

Was humanity's curse, I pondered, that these two concepts should lie so closely together? Their proximity seemed to make it far too easy to apply the philosophy of justice to that of love.

Justice is natural and necessary, our society relies on it to function. Truly, mankind cries out in one voice for fairness. A fairness created by Adonai. A man who sits lazily by a cool stream day after day should not eat as heartily as someone who labours a full season in his field. A criminal should not live a life of freedom while his victim suffers.

Justice must prevail.

But this is not to apply to love for love is to be irrespective of action.

Yet love remains the motive, the push behind justice. It is as if love is like water pushing the dirt of justice down a path. Water and dirt are separate entities, each essential. At their interface is mud. I had been living in the mud, the confused state where justice and love intermix.

In this interface between love and justice, I recognized my desperate desire for love but felt I did not deserve to be loved: I had to hide my ugliness in order to warrant love.

The profound irony I discovered that first Sabbath with Jesus was that only when I fully came to grips with my total unworthiness, living and wallowing in it, could I fully embrace Adonai's transcending love.

It was as if all my life I knew in theory that love was not earned; it was an argument in my mind that I could communicate but found hard to believe. On that day in Nazareth Jesus made it a reality. Like straining to see a tree that I knew was planted a few yards away but was shrouded in fog, Jesus's gaze into my heart was the bright sun's heat dissipating the fog to undeniably confirm the tree's existence.

Adonai did not want my virtue. He wanted my heart. He did not need anything from me. He loved me.

I grasped the wonder of it.

I gloried in the beauty of it.

I understood what Jesus had told me on our walk.

Adonai's love was for every man, woman, and child. Jesus had come to show everyone the amazingness of this love. How could I deprive anyone the bone-deep knowledge of such a fact?

I crawled out of bed, dressed for the day and headed out of town for a walk so I could solidify all I had just perceived. After walking for most of the morning, I found a stream and sat down. I took off my sandals, dangled my feet in the cool flow and listened to the water gurgle to itself.

Suddenly, I felt a hand on my shoulder. Startled, I jumped and turned to see Jesus sit down beside me. He took off his sandals as well, lowering his feet into the stream.

I turned my face from him, ashamed of myself.

"I am sorry, my lord," I said. "I have presumed too much. I have hurt your kingdom in my attempt to prosper it. How stupid you must think I am. You must be so …"

"Judas," Jesus interrupted, "all is forgiven. Forgiveness is not meant to tear a person down but to build him up. I did not want you to be left behind while you ran so far ahead."

I looked at his face and he smiled back broadly. "I will not always be with you and I need you to know what my kingdom is like. My ambassadors must grasp why I have come. I want you to meet the people who have joined me. You will be amazed! We have quite a diverse spectrum of people traveling down the road with us."

We chatted for another hour, getting caught up on the things I had missed. It was wonderful to again laugh and enjoy each other's company.

When we returned to Bethany for lunch the frenzy returned, too. We were surrounded by ceaseless hordes of people clamouring to see Jesus, shoving and calling.

This time, however, I stayed and listened to Jesus's teachings. I determined also to get to know this growing contingency of disciples who had attached themselves to Jesus.

Jesus stayed in Bethany for a month. With renewed resolve I made up my mind to learn about Jesus's dreams for his kingdom rather than rely on my own perception of what I thought his convictions ought to be.

Bethany was within an hour's walk from Jerusalem so I took every opportunity to hear Jesus teach in the Holy City from the Torah, the Prophets or the Writings. I often thought of Lazarus's comments about the authority with which Jesus taught; it did seem as if he had true insight into the intent behind each phrase and law written in the Holy Scripture.

Besides reacquainting myself with Jesus's philosophy, I decided to take his advice to appreciate more members of his following. I therefore set a goal for myself of meeting at least two of Jesus's followers each day. This I did beginning on our return trip to Capernaum, whether we were in a village or on the road.

As we traveled from place to place, I realized that Jesus's gang of followers had an ebb and flow quality, people came and went as monetary and family demands allowed. Very few were with him continually. It made for a dynamic group. When we passed a town close to someone's family, that family would join us for the next few weeks until we moved to a place too far for the commute.

There were times that I wondered about the rag-tag group which often seemed to me to be full of misfits. There were people who had the most disturbing pasts. Then someone would surprise me and I would marvel at this follower's commitment and love for him. He was accomplishing the desires he had told me about that night in Bethany. His followers included children, whores, healed cripples, cleansed lepers, Pharisees and tax collectors. Yet Jesus did not seem to see any human categories, he just saw his people.

Our group's perceptions and ideas, the way we saw the world and each other, were constantly challenged. There was always something to discuss, some teaching to contemplate. My favourite way to begin a discussion with a newcomer was to ask about his or her first encounter with Jesus.

Oh, the stories I heard!

Many had first met Jesus through a healing, their own or another's. Others had been intrigued by Jesus's authority. One fourteen-year-old young man said Jesus's ideas were upside-down and backwards, bizarre yet invigorating. He said that when Jesus quoted the scripture, he breathed new life into ancient words and texts.

Many women now traveled with us. Some were prestigious. Joanna, for example, was the wife of King Herod's steward. It was many of these women, I learned, who were among our chief financial backers. Judas was quite distraught over this fact and insisted that it be kept quiet lest the 'nay-saying' Pharisees find out and discredit us. He begged Jesus to be discreet but Jesus, while never publicly announcing any of his financial benefactors, did nothing to hide the information.

One particular morning, following my usual routine, I fell into step beside someone I had not yet spoken to, a woman whom I had noticed often in our group. I judged her to be about ten years younger than me and knew she'd been traveling with Jesus since Bethany. She seemed quiet and unassuming. As we walked I introduced myself and asked her name. She told me it was Mary. We laughed about the number of Marys and Judases following Jesus then she said I should call her Magdalene to help differentiate her from all the others.

"So, how did you first find Jesus?" I asked, using my favourite opening question.

"He actually found me," she said with her eyes on the road.

I was surprised for in all my conversations so far each person's story had revolved around how they sought Jesus, their pursuit of him. I had never gotten a response like Magdalene's.

"What happened?" I asked, intensely curious.

"My story is very different," she began, her look assessing whether or not she could trust me with her secrets. I do not know what she saw in my face that convinced her to confide in me but I was honoured that she felt she could share her haunting tale.

"My life has not been spent with people," she stated softly. "At the age of twelve I ran into the woods close to my home and grew up there alone."

"Why? What happened that made you ran away? Were you sick?" I asked.

She focused her eyes on Thomas, who was walking ahead of us.

"No, I wasn't sick. Not in the way you thinking of illness," she explained. "I just had to run. I can always remember feeling like I had to run. It was like being chased by bees. An incessant buzzing in my ears, a sense of impending doom. It was my perpetual nightmare, to flee but never escape, my soul urging me to run away but my feet never able to break free from the mire.

"Voices screamed in my head and drowned out reason. I couldn't speak over them. I was a still, small voice whispering in the shadows of my own head. It is strange to feel so dissociated from your own reasoning, so disconnected from sanity. I think being oblivious to the knowledge that I was going insane would have been better but I knew I was a raving lunatic. I knew I was powerless to do a thing about it.

"Rage yelled at Guilt. Guilt screamed at Torment. Torment hollered at Accusation. I craved focus and yearned for singularity of thought. I needed something so pure it could overpower everything else. I wanted to live in a fire's blaze so that, even for the briefest of moments, I could know only heat. I was starved for purpose. Oh, to know where to be, what to do or why to do it. I did not care what 'it' was. 'It' could be anything. Oh, what utter bliss that would be.

"That was my life. My body screaming through the forest, running. My spirit rocking inside my head with hands cupped over my ears thirsting for quiet."

Magdalene stopped and stared at me as if trying to survey the impact her life had on me. I was completely enthralled. I had never known someone possessed by demons.[2]

"How did you survive such torture?" I asked.

Satisfied that she could confide in me further, she shook her head slightly and said, "Adonai alone knows." She again fixed her gaze on Thomas's back. Her voice quieted as she continued so that I had to lean towards her as I strained to listen.

"One morning when I was scavenging for food, I heard a shuffle of feet. A man stood in front of me. He was alone, tall and ominous. 'His head and His hair were white like white wool, like snow and His eyes were like a flame of fire and His feet were like burnished bronze, when it has been caused to glow in a furnace.'³ His face was like the sun shining in all its strength. I was terrified.

"I heard a hideous sound pierce the air," she said, her voice quivering and she twitched slightly as if to cast away a shiver that crawled up her back. I almost jumped as her tone returned to its normal volume again, so absorbed I hadn't realized how hushed her voice had become. "I shrieked and heard a guttural hiss escape my lips my mouth spoke these words: 'I know who you are! You are Jesus, Son of the Most High God! What are you doing here?' I heard myself whine. 'It is not yet time. You can't have her. She is ours.' I went into a screaming frenzy. I felt my eyes bulge and my mouth foam. I lunged at him. 'Enough' Jesus yelled. His voice was like a crack of thunder. The voices in me cowered under it. It was so horrible. 'Leave her,' he commanded and this time his voice sounded like many waters. Then all was quiet. The silence for which I had always yearned was mine."

She paused, drew in a deep breath and turned towards me again.

"This may sound strange, but the quiet terrified me. I had lived in chaos for so long that, when it was gone, I was horrified. I was a captive reliant on my tormentors and did not know what to do without them. I was empty. Totally alone.

"But Jesus was there. I was *not* alone. He was all I saw, my singular purpose, my one true thought. He took my hand."

Her face was stern, her jaw set, her eyes steely as she turned to survey the horizon. "I have lived with the enemy," she stated. "He is ruthless and cunning. Never underestimate him. His power is terrifying, his torment real."

She stopped, grabbed my arm and turned me to face her—white indentations appeared on my skin under her fingertips. Her stare sent chills down my spine. "He's preparing for battle, you know," she said in a haunted voice.

"Who is?" I asked, uncomfortable.

"Our struggle is not with world powers or rulers. The fight is with the principalities of evil.⁴ The power they wield is beyond you and me.

But I have seen a greater power. A power that sends them howling to Hades. They will attack but they will not prevail. Of that I am sure."

I could think of nothing to say so I stared back at her, waiting for her to release her grip and start walking again. Finally she did. Sobered by her prophesy we walked on in silence. Soon I saw Matthew and lamely excused myself, anxious in my desire to retreat to a more comfortable environment.

I thought for many days about what Magdalene had said. Her comments were disturbing and I could not easily dismiss them. I hoped she was wrong yet feared that she had much more insight than the rest of us.

chapter ten

or the next few weeks we traveled back towards my home region of Galilee. Just as we had done on the road to Jerusalem, we stopped at villages along the way so that Jesus could teach. Although the stops were of shorter duration and we made good time compared to the journey south, we were still far behind fellow pilgrims who had attended the feast in Jerusalem. While the bulk of Galileans, even though they had taken the long way home in order to avoid Samaria, were doubtless back to their work and studies, we were only at Jacob's Well— still in the heart of Samaria with half our journey ahead of us.

The slowness of our trek did not distress me. Because I was spending more time with Jesus I was again constantly aware of his passion for people, his delight and joy in them. I wanted to see people the way he seemed to, to see their lives as a canvas on which Adonai created an intricate painting or a parchment on which their Creator composed an insightful poem. Yet, despite my appreciation for Jesus's joy in the artwork of people, I was tired: we had been on the road for over two months. I yearned for a familiar home and marketplace.

Although it was only noon by the time we reached Jacob's Well, Jesus instructed us to make camp. Thomas and Philip said they knew of a gully west of the well that was sheltered from wind and had ample room for the tents. After supplying me with detailed directions to the area, the majority of our group turned off the road in search of the site to set up our goat skin tents. James, John and I, along with two men who had joined us a week earlier, headed for Shechem, the closest town to the north from which to buy supplies.

It did not take long to make our purchases at the market for I had good helpers and had become a proficient shopper for our group. With our packs full of dried lentils, sun-baked figs, cheese, two days worth of bread and a treat of milk and leben, we headed back to camp to make supper.

The smell of fresh bread tormented me as we walked back. The baker, who had been pulling the loaves from the oven as we approached his booth, had wrapped the bread in extra cloth because of its heat. Now, walking back to camp, I salivated from the aroma, my tastebuds anticipating the coming meal.

As we approached the crossroads to turn west towards camp I noticed two people, one sitting, one standing, beside Jacob's well. Fearful that they might be Samaritans I slowed my pace, hoping that by the time we reached the well they would have collected their water and gone on their way —and that any contact could be avoided. My friends, probably of a similar mind, reduced their brisk walk to a saunter and then a snail's pace. The two at the well, however, remained in place, more interested in chatting than drawing water.

I had never spoken to a Samaritan and had no desire to begin now; they were a hybrid, impure nation who believed only in the Torah and did not even acknowledge the prophetic teachings. The Pharisees I knew, refusing to disgrace themselves, would not even utter the word "Samaritan." Truly, the only time I did hear the term said out loud was when someone was so angry they had used up every other foul word they could think of, or during daily prayers at the synagogue when a rabbi would pray for God to deny the Samaritans the right to eternal life.[1]

I watched the two warily as we approached. The one who had been seated stood. My heart sank as I recognized Jesus's familiar robes. I thought, *Oh no Lord, not the Samaritans!*

As we drew closer I saw that the other person was a woman. From her clothes and the type of jug she carried I was sure that she was from the loathsome nation. *Jesus,* my inner voice agonized, *not just a Samaritan, but a woman?*

The woman turned to look at us as we approached and, forgetting to take her water jug, headed towards Sychar, a village to the east.

As we closed the distance between us and Jesus, I remembered again Jesus's admonition in Bethany regarding my exclusionary attitudes and readiness to prioritize people. I heard him again say that he wanted all people to follow him. At this moment, however, in the heat of the day with my stomach gurgling and the smell of warm bread in my pack, the last thing I wanted to do was have a talk about the merits of accepting Samaritans. I wanted to avoid the subject at all costs, take Jesus to our camp, have some food and leave Samaria in the morning. Perhaps if we left I would not even have to trouble myself by thinking through why Jesus would talk to a Samaritan woman in the first place.

Turning towards the newcomers in our group I suggested, "Why don't you two go on ahead and get these lentils to Thomas. I'm sure he is anxious to start the soup. James, John and I will bring Jesus."

The saucer-eyed men huddled together, nodded absently then immediately headed towards camp by cutting across a neighbouring field probably happy to avoid the juncture in the road where Jesus waited.

When James, John and I reached Jesus, we did not even acknowledge that we had seen him with anyone.

"We had great luck at the market," I began, grinning broadly and purposefully taking a few steps down the road towards the camp. "The bread was being pulled out of the oven and is still hot in my pack. Come, let's go and eat before it gets cold."

Jesus looked back at me and made no indication that he planned to move. "I have food to eat that you do not know about,"[2] Jesus answered, squinting into the sun's brightness at my back.

"Did someone from camp bring you some food?" I asked, willfully ignoring the possibility that he may have accepted food from a Samaritan.

"The food I am talking about is to do the will of the One who sent me."

I let out a sigh and smiled slightly in relief, thankful that he had at least not accepted their food.

Jesus was silent for a while then sat on the well's edge, leaning forward to rest his forearms on his legs and entwine his fingers. He turned his face eastward towards Sychar and gazed at a field full of grain. A breeze toyed with the pliable green stalks, pushing them gently to and fro. Nodding at the field, Jesus asked, "What do you think? Do those crops have about four more months until they are ready for harvest?"

Glad for the change of topic, I stepped off the eastward road to stand beside Jesus and assess the field more closely. Before I could say anything Jesus went on, "Take a good look at what is in front of your eyes. These Samaritan fields are actually ripe. It is time for a harvest!" His voice quickened and crescendoed, laced with excitement.

Confused, I leaned toward the grain and squinted, trying to determine why he would say such a thing. To me the stalks still looked short, the grain maturing. Extending my gaze further east to the edge of the field, I saw movement. Small figures in the distance advanced towards the well. I focused on the image and realized that about twenty people were walking towards us: Samaritans from Sychar.

Shocked at the sight, I shuffled backward and inadvertently bumped into James. I moved to stand beside him.

No one spoke.

Jesus rose and began to walk towards the advancing group. "Come, our harvester isn't waiting any longer," he said, looking back over his shoulder at us and grinning broadly. When he saw that the three of us did not move, he came back to stand in front of us.

"Adonai loves these people," he exclaimed, his eyes dancing with energy and excitement. "He's planted seeds in their lives, wooed them to come to Him. He has called to them through the splendour of His creation, demonstrated His power through nature's ferocity and confirmed His reality through the miracle of a newborn babe. He has sung to them through His holy scriptures, loved their souls through the words and goodness of their fellow man. And now Adonai is calling us to the harvest! The seeds He has planted are ripe for eternal life. How He longs to gather it in. How true it is that in

Adonai's pursuit of us, one person sows a seed yet someone else may harvest it."

He turned again towards the approaching villagers and hastened his step, obviously thrilled to be a part of Adonai's passion for these people. James and John slowly made to follow him, though they didn't look at all like they shared Jesus's excitement.

"Why don't you two go with Jesus," I said, taking the opportunity to excuse myself. "I really think I should get this food to the others. They are probably ravenous."

James and John acknowledged my comment with a wry smile then turned again to follow Jesus.

As I walked the other way towards camp, I mulled over Jesus's comments. They were consistent with what he taught and how he lived. He wanted all people to follow him. I did not disagree with Jesus and no longer wanted to correct his behaviour yet at times I wearied from the full implications of his teachings. *I'm just tired and hungry,* I reasoned to myself.

The savoury smell of bean soup greeted my nose when I reached the assembled tents. Peter and Andrew, who stood by the fire talking to Thomas, noticed me enter the inner circle of tents and waved me over to the hearth.

"Where is Jesus?" Peter asked when I was close enough for the four of us to talk quietly. "The two men who arrived about half an hour ago said they thought he was talking to a Samaritan at the well."

"Yes, he was," I confirmed, nodding my head and pursing my lips. "It was a Samaritan woman. She went back to Sychar when she saw James, John and me, but I think she must have told the whole town about Jesus because when I left a number of people were coming to the well and Jesus, of course, was anxious to talk with them."

Peter, Andrew and Thomas were quiet.

"James and John stayed with him," I added in the silence.

"Oh," was all Peter said in response, the three of them staring blankly into the orange and yellow flames.

"Do you think he will be long?" asked Thomas as blandly as if he was asking for a bit of salt to be passed to him at supper. "The soup is almost ready."

I sensed that these men, like me, sometimes tired of the challenge of living with what Jesus professed.

"We should probably eat when it is ready," I answered with resignation. "I think Jesus will be a while. The bread in my pack is still warm. I'll hand it out while we wait for the soup."

Thomas and Peter smiled weakly and nodded. Andrew continued to examine the fire. I passed a hunk of bread to those waiting for the meal then lowered myself onto the cool ground beneath a shady tree on the edge of the encampment. Leaning my back against the tree's gnarled bark, I willed my mind to focus on the activity around me and savoured the taste and feel of each morsel ripped from the round loaf in my lap.

Thomas stood over the steaming pot of soup, stirring it with his favourite well-worn flat stick which he always carried in his pack. Magdala and Peter spread out the *shul-khan*, a piece of tanned leather which formed our dining surface, on the ground. A smile lilted across Judas's face as he reclined against a large slanted boulder, crossed legs extended before him, arms folded over his chest and eyes closed as he soaked in the day's sunlight. To the left of the fire a clump of men visited, to the right five men played a game with the ankle bones of goat and sheep.

Soon, Thomas motioned people to the shul-khan. As Thomas placed the pot of soup in the centre of the leather and I passed out more bread, Peter explained that Jesus had some business to attend to and would not be eating with us. Most, satisfied with the explanation, were happy to go ahead without him and delved into the meal while others who knew Jesus better were probably aware that sometimes it was better not to know what Jesus was doing.

We ate quietly, dipping our bread scoops into the community soup and enjoying the fresh cheese chunks and leban. Occasionally I heard the soft hum of appreciation for a good meal or a compliment about Thomas's soup. The delicious flavour and texture of food not dried or otherwise preserved for travel rolled smoothly from my tongue to throat. I loved the meals proximity to a town allowed.

When the meal was finished and cleared up, everyone resumed their pre-supper activities. I again pushed my back into the trunk of the shady tree I had found and was soon dozing lightly.

The sun had set before Jesus, James and John returned to camp. Jesus called all his apostles together to form a circle beside the fire.

"Now that we are almost to Galilee," Jesus began, "I want to tell you of my plans." He paused, looked at each of us in turn, then continued, saying, "It is time for you to go out and share what I have taught you."

I was transfixed by his words and stared at him, hoping I had not heard correctly. He could not be serious. What did I know of speaking in public, of teaching? I pulled my eyes from Jesus to my fellow apostles. Some of them actually looked excited. Peter, Andrew, Philip, Judas and Bartholomew all smiled, glancing at one another beneath raised eyebrows. They leaned in closer to Jesus. Others seemed to be as intimidated by the daunting task as I was. Thomas and James stared at Jesus with their mouths slightly agape, my friend James's eyes were downcast, studying the ground. John focused his attention on Jesus, rubbing his hands nervously up and down his thighs. I felt as though someone had just placed an imposing featureless wall in front of me then declared that I had to climb it. The expectations seemed unattainable, the job insurmountable. I swallowed hard and stared at the folds in the worn fabric of my robe.

"Take nothing for our journey," Jesus was saying. "Stay at one home and use it as your base of operation. If any place does not accept you, do not force the issue but simply shake the dust from your feet as a testimony against them."[3]

"What will you do, Lord?" Peter asked.

"I will stay a while here in Samaria. The people of Sychar have invited me to teach in their town."

I heard a gasp escape from Thomas and Matthew. I imagined that this information about Jesus's plans gave them an added incentive to pursue the challenge of preaching in Galilee, as it did for me.

"After that," continued Jesus, "I will go to Bethsaida. We will meet there in one month."

"Lord," said James, almost so softly I wondered if Jesus would hear him, "I am not a teacher or a preacher. I don't know if I will be of much use to your kingdom building."

"Not everyone is a teacher or a preacher," Jesus returned, smiling reassuringly at him. "I am not asking you to be something that you are not. But I do want you to share the good news that I have taught you. Here is what I suggest." Turning to me he asked, "Judas, do you think your son will need help selling some of his supplies?"

"Most likely," I answered "Usually by this time of year I have all my merchandise collected and was preparing to sell it at market."

"Why not go and help him," Jesus suggested. "Take James along, too. Go to those towns and villages where people know you. When they ask where you have been, simply tell them your story. James, your enthusiasm brought Judas to the synagogue in Nazareth. That is all I am asking of you now."

Jesus's words comforted some of my anxious thoughts, his plans for the Samaritans silenced those that were left.

It was late when I turned to my tent, apprehension running hand in hand with excitement at the prospect of going home to Nain. I fell asleep listening to the drone of my fellow disciples discussing their plans for the next month.

In the morning, amidst many good-byes and plans for where and when to meet up again, James and I headed up the road towards Galilee. Peter and Andrew had agreed to meet us in Capernaum at the end of the month so we could sail across the Sea of Galilee together. Most of the others had arranged to travel to Bethsaida by boat and meet up at various locations. Levi and Thomas decided to spend the month walking the northern shore to arrive at the town on foot.

As James and I walked we saw more familiar sights daily, the crook in the road that took us to Nain instead of Capernaum, the neglected grape vineyard of Hezikiah's widow and, finally, the monstrous tree stark against the sky which signalled the dirt path that would bring us home.

Since speaking with Jonathon in Capernaum, I had seen my children and grandchildren only three times. Soon after Jonathon and Tabitha's daughter, Ruth, was born, their family (along with Mara and Josiah), had come to Nazareth when Jesus was speaking there. I had also spent two Passovers sharing the Seder supper with them in Jerusalem.

As we entered town my churning emotions and thoughts from the past few days intensified; I tingled with anticipation at seeing my children and grandchildren and wished the torrent of foreboding about their reaction to the reason for this homecoming would leave. I forced a smile and returned good-natured waves to the hellos and surprised looks on the familiar faces of old friends and colleagues.

Approaching the town centre, I saw our rabbi surrounded by children receiving their morning lesson. He sat on a well-worn rock and gave instruction to children my grandson Caleb's age, just as he had done for my son Jonathan as well as James and I when we were eight. Back then, however, the rabbi had been a young man of twenty. The brood surrounding him this afternoon seemed easily distracted, looking in as many different directions as there were children. One boy, noticing the commotion we caused as we walked into town, whispered to another until all the faces in the group turned towards us. Then one of them jumped up and began running towards me. It was my grandson, Caleb.

"Grandpa, Grandpa!" I heard him call as he made short the distance between us. I opened my arms to receive his hearty welcome, holding him with the same voracity he lavished on me.

"I have missed you!" he said.

"I missed you, too," I responded, blinking back tears, "especially your hugs."

Holding him at arms' length, I assessed him, "My, how you've grown!"

He beamed back at me. Behind him I could see the rabbi, flanked by his students, hobbling towards us down the street. I was glad to see him for secretly I had feared that he might have died while I was away. Nain would not have felt the same without the dearly loved man's caring presence. Realizing his teacher was near, Caleb turned to face him. The rabbi approached, extending his arms first to James, customarily placing his right hand on James's left shoulder, kissing James's right cheek, repeating the gestures with his other hand and James's left cheek, then turned to greet me likewise. He stepped back slightly, gave us a toothless grin and said with as much strength as his frail voice could muster, "Peace be on you!"

"And on you, peace." James and I responded in unison.

"So, our prodigals have returned," Rabbi said with a nod as he looked us over from sandal to turban, evaluating how we had fared over the past year.

"Only for a month," James clarified.

"Oh, how so?" Rabbi asked, his bushy eyebrows pushed together causing the crevasses across his brow to deepen.

"Jesus has asked us to return to our homes to tell people about what we have been doing," James responded matter-of-factly.

"Well, that is something I am indeed curious about," Rabbi smiled with another nod of his head. "But for now I am sure you are anxious to visit with your families. I will assemble everyone tomorrow morning at the well to hear of your adventures. Caleb," he said turning his face towards my grandson, "you may take the rest of the day to be with your grandfather. Come early tomorrow and I will talk to you about what you have missed."

James excused himself politely and headed towards his parents' home in the opposite direction to Caleb's persistent tugs on my arm. As we walked, Caleb eagerly told me about all I had missed. Upon reaching their dwelling, Tabitha, who had been grinding grain outside the door, looked up curiously, no doubt alerted to our arrival by Caleb's enthusiastic recounting of a recent frog hunting expedition that he and his friends had been on. She laid the pestle into the bowl and greeted me with a great hug and kiss. She then sent a reluctant Caleb to find his father and invite Mara and Josiah to supper.

I could have been fed baked sand that night and enjoyed the evening no less. The courtyard rang with the voices of my children and my children's children, laughing and telling stories of the past year. I, too, had amazing tales to tell about miracles and interesting people. My grandchildren in particular leaned in close, wide-eyed, chins nestled into the palms of their hands, fascinated by the healings that I had witnessed. Jonathan's four-year-old son, Abner, kept us amused with his questions about Jesus's power, like, "Is Jesus big enough to run across the desert in one day?" or "Is he strong enough to move a mountain?"

It was late when I finally left to find my sleeping mat, knowing that the morning would come far too soon. Before I went to bed I thought about what I would talk about the next day, how I would describe the past year. I grabbed some parchment, jotted down notes, then scribbled them out, rearranging my ideas. After a few hours of sleep, before anyone else in the house stirred, I got up to fidget with my writings again.

After a hurried breakfast, Jonathan's family accompanied me to the town centre. Word had traveled quickly, as it always did in Nain, so most of my friends and family were already assembled by the well, curious about what James and I had to say.

Everyone there had likely already formed some sort of opinion about Jesus, either based on listening to him or on what others had said; Jesus was quite a phenomenon. But all those assembled knew James and me, they had lived with us and we had lived with Jesus. Naturally they were interested in what we had to say.

When I arrived, James was already sitting on the edge of the well chatting with a few men close to him, every now and then scanning the growing number of townspeople. He looked anxious and uncomfortable, as though he was sitting on a spiny sea urchin. When he spotted me walking towards him a smile broke across his face and his shoulders and chest lowered slightly as he released a breath in relief.

"Quite a number of people here," he said when I was close enough to hear.

"Yes," I nodded back, feeling waves of nervousness crash over me. I had never had so many people assembled just to hear what I had to say.

Rabbi stood and motioned our friends and family to sit, then gave a quick welcome and surrendered the time to me and James.

I sat rigid on the cool stones, feeling too conspicuous and wishing I had better prepared myself. James sat straight as a slab of slate and fumbled with his hands as if trying to figure out what to do with them.

I cleared my throat and said as clearly and audibly as possibly, "Well, I first heard about Jesus from James after he had returned from a trip where he had heard Jesus speak."

Then I told them about my first meeting with Jesus and my impressions of him, why I had decided to follow him and the things I had seen and heard just as I had shared with my family the night before. James did the same, simply telling what he had witnessed, what Jesus had taught. We were careful not to censor our account, even speaking of Jesus's radical notions. When my old neighbour, Jacob, asked where Jesus was now I even told them that he had stayed with the Samaritans.

The news brought scowls, 'tsks' of disgust and murmurs—yet one thing I had learned from being with Jesus was that he bore his uniqueness unashamedly, purposefully.

When we described the miracles, some believed us, some explained them all away. In what seemed like minutes the sun was halfway across the sky and it was time to have lunch and disperse for an afternoon of work.

Each morning for the next week, James and I met at the well to visit with friends, talk about our time with Jesus and answer questions. In the afternoon, I returned to Jonathan's home to help him prepare for his upcoming business trip to the markets surrounding Nain.

Each day had new ventures and experiences. I woke with excitement, but also trepidation; would I be able to handle people's questions? Would they understand what I was trying to say?

One day a man named Jonah, whom I had known for at least fifteen years, came to me following a recounting of one of Jesus's healings.

"Do you think you could heal my eye?" he asked.

Jonah's eye had been lost in an accident when he was very young. I had only known him as a one-eyed man.

He looked at me hopefully with his one good eye. Terror pulsed in my veins as I glanced at James. Was this wise? Could I do it? Could I be an agent of Jesus, of Adonai? Was I that favoured?

Truthfully, my greatest fear was *what if it doesn't work?*

Do I risk being labeled a fraud? Do I chance jeopardizing Jesus if I fail? I swallowed hard.

Did I hinder Jesus by not trusting that he could heal Jonah? I had witnessed Jesus command diseases miles away to leave and they obeyed. These past few days I had given countless examples of Jesus's far-reaching authority. Any great king must have the ability to be obeyed with or without his immediate presence. Just today I had told Jonah that Jesus's kingship was one of power and authority, one that deserved respect and reverence.

Now, Jonah asked me to stand behind my claims. How foolish I was not to realize that someone would one day challenge me in this way.

With trembling hand I reached out and placed my fingers on his empty eyelid. In a clear, distinct voice I prayed, "Our Father, who art in heaven, hallowed be Your name. We ask, dear Father, for the sake of our King, Jesus, that You heal Jonah. We ask in the name of Jesus so that his power and authority may be seen."

I took my fingers off his eyelid.

It fluttered and then very gradually opened, blinking rapidly as it adjusted to the light. Then both eyes opened wide.

It was perfect! The white of his eye sparkled. The deep brown iris shone in the sun, the pupil adjusting to a perfect size to compensate for the day's brightness.

"Judas, I can see!" Jonah yelled.

He covered his other eye with his hand and looked with his new eye. He covered his new eye and looked with the old. His eyes were enormous with wonder as he took in the same terrain that he had looked at all day.

"It works even better than my old eye!" he said gleefully. "This Jesus you have been talking about is indeed powerful! He really does have the blessing of Adonai."

I stood astounded. Shocked that my hand had been an instrument of restoration, thrilled at the part that I had played in changing Jonah's life yet disturbed that I should be so astonished that Jesus's name could accomplish this miracle. Why was I surprised?

Jonah's healing seemed to be more of a validation to me and James than it was to Jonah. Even though we had lived with Jesus, we were the ones who seemed to finally comprehend how real Jesus's power was.

During the next week of preaching both James and I healed often. After a lengthy discussion however, we decided to heal privately, in people's homes and behind closed doors for we had seen the popularity that Jesus had gained through public healings and did not feel that we were ready for such notoriety.

In our second week we went to Cana, Magdala and Tiberias. Because I wanted to help with the business yet knew part of my day would be spent talking about Jesus, Jonathan gave James and me a small quantity of merchandise for the towns I was to visit. Jonathan took the bulk of product to other locations.

Jonathan agreed to let Caleb accompany James and me as we traveled. Not, I am sure, because Jonathan believed in Jesus and his kingdom, but rather as an opportunity for Caleb and me to spend some time together.

Caleb asked many questions about Jesus and his followers. After discovering all the tasks that Jesus had assigned to his apostles, Caleb decided that he would like to be a "heralder" and he took it upon himself to let the townspeople of each village we visited know that we would be speaking about Jesus.

In Tiberias we met the lepers whom we had seen Jesus cleanse. They now lived in the village with their fellow townsfolk. The residents of Tiberias flocked to hear us speak; the proof of Jesus's power lived with them daily.

I never thought of myself as a preacher yet talking about Jesus became natural. Our stories themselves taught about who Jesus was. We related the parables we had heard Jesus tell and discussed what they could mean. It was exciting.

Soon the month was spent. We took my grandson back to Nain; Caleb all the while planning arguments and bribes to convince Jonathon to take him to see Jesus. It was then time to go to Capernaum to meet Peter and Andrew. It was great to see the brothers again and we wasted no time in preparing to rejoin Jesus because we knew that our meeting was just a taste of the reunion that awaited us across the sea. The four of us loaded the boat and set sail.

After traveling the night we approached the opposite shore and saw someone cooking fish on an open fire. It was Jesus. He greeted us as our rabbi in Nain had. We spent the day eating, relaxing and talking. Over the next two days we waited with Jesus as more boats carrying our friends arrived. Jesus welcomed each arrival.

We spent a week resting. I had not realized how exhausted I was. The crowds had been invigorating, pulsing with energy, but their mental drain had been hidden from me until I sat in this solitary place to reflect.

Jesus instructed us to spend time by ourselves and recall the things we had done and seen. We thought about what people had said, questions they had posed and remembered miracles that had been achieved. Then we spent time with Jesus sorting through our thoughts, hashing out parables he had used, talking about healing we had seen or been a part of and clarifying what we had heard him say, what he had meant.

Our time of teaching others had forced us to solidify Jesus's teachings in our own minds. I had once taught Jonathan to balance the financial books of my business. I learned more than he did as I explained the procedure because I was forced to think about why I did things a certain way. Similarly, as we explained Jesus's teaching to others, we gained a new and deeper understanding of them ourselves.

Now that we were back with Jesus we had new questions. We were learning anew.

Over the past year-and-a-half I had thought that I was sure of Jesus's right to the throne. Now, as I was compelled to work through my opinions about Jesus, I was more certain than ever that we needed him as our king.

chapter eleven

t he people in Bethsaida soon realized who was staying close to their village. Again we were inundated with the sick and the curious who wanted to witness a miracle. While Jesus taught I tended to tents, boats and supplies. In three days we would set sail back across the Sea of Galilee to Tiberias. The break gave me time to ready our group for the intensive campaign ahead.

There were some local men who, when they found out where we were heading next, took to their boats that very afternoon, sailing to Tiberius to arrive there before us.

After three days Jesus said farewell to the villagers and we set sail for the west shore.

We sailed that day and all night, the gentle waves rocking us to sleep.

By mid morning we could see houses, fenced in by gentle foothills and mountains.

"Look at those hills," Thomas suddenly said, pointing starboard. "Aren't they an odd colour?"

Indeed, the foothills beyond the town were not green like the ones behind and south of Tiberius. Instead they were a bizarre mix of muted browns, blacks and tans. Their most peculiar aspect was that the surface of the hills appeared to be moving. The ground did not sway like grass. It was more as if the ground was alive; the hills jiggled and agitated like ants swarming a sweet piece of fruit.

"Let's go see what it is," said Peter, a man always up for an adventure.

We all agreed and turned our boats north.

The hills loomed larger and larger as we approached the shore.

"They're people!" shouted John, "Have you ever seen so many? There must be thousands!"

I gaped over the railing along with the other apostles. Never had I imagined that so many people could be gathered in one place. Their mass covered hill upon hill. It was like surveying the endless water at the edge of an ocean; the sea of people went on and on as far as my eyes could see, men and women replacing grass, children playing games to pass the time.

Judas, our master of numbers, gulped in awe. "There must be at least five thousand people there!"

"They look like lost sheep desperate for a shepherd," Jesus said, as he looked upon the expanse. "They need to know that their quest has not been in vain. Pull the boats close to shore. The water will help carry my voice."

This we did.

Jesus taught from his boat for the next two hours, the slow current pulling the boat down the shore as he spoke.

Then Jesus went on shore and healed many people. He moved through the crowd, making his way towards the mountains bordering the foothills. Where the mountain ascended he turned to address the multitude again and his voice ricocheted off the rocks to boom through the valley.

We apostles spent our time mingling in the crowd. At times Jesus was too far away to hear so we chatted with people close by.

I met many people James and I had talked with over the past month. As I walked with Andrew, he too saw and introduced me to men he had visited during his preaching stint.

"Grandpa, Grandpa!" Caleb's jubilant call rang out above the crowd.

I turned to see him running and winding his way through the myriad of people. Catching him up in my arms I tousled his hair and said, "Caleb, my boy, how have you been?" Caleb grinned a toothy smile back at me. "Andrew, I'd like you to meet my grandson. He has been my invaluable assistant over the past month."

"Pleased to meet you, Caleb," Andrew answered back.

"This is quite the gathering," I heard another familiar voice through the crowd as Jonathan appeared behind Caleb. "You are certainly reaping the fruit of your labours."

"Andrew, this is my son Jonathan; Jonathan, my friend, Andrew," I said continuing the introductions. "What do you mean 'the fruit of my labours'?" I asked.

"The twelve of you apostles have gotten everyone curious for the past month. Some men arrived a day or two ago and started running around the countryside saying that Jesus would be arriving any day. It's been crazy ever since. Everyone's been trying to get here before you docked."

I was astonished by the excitement Jesus was generating—like a spark had landed on dry grass and a wild fire was now spreading over the countryside.

"We arrived early this morning," Jonathan continued. "Caleb was determined not to miss the big welcome. I must admit I am glad that we came. I have never seen so many people in one place. It's amazing."

"I brought us a lunch to share, Grandpa," Caleb offered enthusiastically. "I have some bread and fish."

He showed me his basket of food. He had five barley loaves and two fish. It smelled delicious.

"Thank you, Caleb," I said. "Perhaps a little later we can sit down and have a picnic just like when did when we were traveling together."

"I'm hungry," Jonathan pouted, rubbing his stomach and feigning hunger. "How about sharing some of that with your dear dad?"

"No way!" countered Caleb, yanking his basket out of Jonathan's reach and jutting out his chin defiantly. "There is only enough for Grandpa and me."

"All right, then," laughed Jonathan, "I guess I'll have to find my own lunch."

"Can I go with Grandpa?" Caleb asked hopefully.

"If it is all right with him," answered Jonathan, motioning to me.

I agreed readily and we arranged a place to meet Jonathan later in the day.

Caleb accompanied Andrew and me for the rest of the afternoon. We spoke with many people. Having Caleb by my side reminded me of the fun times we had had together over the past month.

We worked our way through the crowd towards the base of the mountain where Jesus now stood teaching. Caleb hung onto my robes tightly as we walked, tugging now and then on my belt to say that he could see Jesus or hear him speaking. I noticed his knuckles growing whiter and his hands shaking with excitement as he neared his hero.

We met the other apostles a short distance from Jesus. They were huddled together having a discussion in hushed tones.

"Don't you think he knows what time it is?" James asked Thomas.

"If he does," returned Thomas, "why doesn't he send them home? Sooner or later these people will be hungry. What if they get unruly? I think we should talk to Jesus before a situation develops that could get out of hand."

"You know how Jesus can be," offered Nathaniel. "Sometimes his passion is so great the details of life escape his attention. If we convinced him to send the people away now they could get to the surrounding villages before supper."

"Ah, Judas and Andrew," acknowledged Thomas as he noticed us outside the huddled group. "Don't you agree that Jesus may need a small reminder about the lateness of the day? Judas, perhaps you could convince Jesus of the necessity of daily bread."

"I will try," I said.

When Jesus finished speaking, we quickly surrounded him. Caleb, my shadow, tagged along behind still clinging to the back of my robe.

"Lord, I think it would be wise to send the people home now," I began, voicing the group's concerns. "It is getting late and this place is rather remote. If they left now they could find food and lodging before it is too late in the day."

Jesus looked at his hedge of friends and smiled slyly.

"Hmm, yes, it is getting late," he said, "As you say, Judas, I'm sure they will soon be getting hungry." His eyes wandered over his apostles' faces, settling on Philip. "Philip, where are we going to buy enough bread to feed all these people?"

Philip looked dumbfounded.

"You…you can't be serious, Lord," he stammered. "It would take a year's worth of wages to give everyone here only a taste of bread."

"There is a lad here who has some bread and fish," joked Andrew. "But luckily it is not enough for all these people because we may have a hard time convincing him to deprive his Grandpa of his supper."

The apostles looked confused.

I was about to elaborate when I heard Caleb take a deep breath and push himself into the middle of the group to stand before Jesus.

"I'll share," he said staunchly, squaring his shoulders and looking directly at Andrew, "and Jesus is big enough to make enough for everybody."

Those around me began to snicker and smile.

Jesus crouched down to better look him in the eye.

"Well, hello!" said Jesus.

Caleb slowly turned his face to look at Jesus. Jesus smiled broadly at him, eyes sparkling.

"Hello. My name is Caleb," my grandson stated respectfully, "and he is my grandpa," he continued, jutting a thumb towards me. "I have been helping him tell people about you all over the place." I was surprised at how completely at ease Caleb looked, as if he was sure that Jesus would care about all he was saying.

"Yes, your grandpa has told me a lot about you, Caleb," Jesus returned. "Thank you for telling your friends about me. You have great enthusiasm. Thank you, too, for offering to share your supper. I intend to make good use of it." Then he gave Caleb a wink.

Jesus stood up and told us to have the people sit in groups of fifty and a hundred. He took the bread in Caleb's basket, prayed over it and broke it into pieces, returning the pieces into the basket.

Jesus tore piece after piece off the same cake of bread. He tore and tore until the basket was full. Half a loaf of bread remained in his hand. He continued to tear the same loaf into pieces, again filling another basket. Still half a loaf remained in his hand. This he did over and over again.

He asked us to take a basket to the group farthest away, the ones congregated by the sea. I wondered at the wisdom of this. Surely if everyone saw us carrying baskets of food to the groups of people, they too would expect something to eat. However, I did as I was told and walked to the furthest people to hand a basket of bread to a group of three families who were sitting together.

I walked back through the throng of people. Someone had started a fire where Jesus stood. Caleb's two fish were cooking on a spit. Four more baskets waited for me by the fire. Jesus continued to break the bread while the apostles and I took the bread to the people seated on the hillside. Caleb ran back and forth too, distributing two baskets for my one in his excitement.

It is strange but I did not wonder at what was happening. For some unexplained reason it just seemed natural to me that Jesus would feed the multitude. I was like a child coming to the table for meal after meal, never questioning the presence of food steaming in bowls, never wondering at the immense process required to make a meal available. What child contemplates this when he is hungry? The growth of a seed in sun, rain and soil, a farmer's harvest of grain, the grain ground to flour and a mother to form the flour into bread are not part of his thinking. No, the child just sees the food and eats it. Like me. I did not question why the bread did not disappear. The baskets were full and I handed them to the people around me. The fish was cooked and cut so I passed the steaming fillets to the community surrounding me. I cannot explain why I did not see the miracle of which I was a part.

Caleb saw it. That evening, as I boarded the boat to sail for another shore, he came up to me, glowing.

"I knew it, Grandpa! I just knew Jesus was strong enough," he bubbled, adopting the language of his younger brother, Abner. "He's big enough to do anything!"[1]

Vicki Clarke
124

chapter twelve

*t*he next year passed in a blur. We traveled north to visit countries I had not seen before: Syria, Ceasarea Philippi and even the city of Tyre on the Mediterranean Sea. Jesus healed and taught. When we came back to Galilee people thronged everywhere. Jesus again sent his apostles out to preach. This time, however, he also sent his disciples, seventy of us in all.[1] Jesus's popularity was mind-boggling.

As his notoriety grew, so did our challenges.

With swelling, unmanageable numbers came unruly crowds. Our security men, Simon, Bartholomew, James and Thomas, were kept busy deflecting obnoxious people who rudely pushed others aside to be cured. The biggest complaint these four men had were those wanting to be healed of a cold or an annoying headache that they had developed that morning.

"I would have Jesus fix my own aching head if a miracle was simply a matter of personal convenience!" James steamed one night.

The multitudes that now surrounded us were more volatile. Some were impressed by Jesus, others convinced that he was leading us all astray. Jesus did nothing to alleviate their concerns and continued to invite controversy as if he thought *If people want to be my disciples, then they are going to know who they will be following.* Once he even defended a prostitute who was dragged into the street, naked. He guarded her against her angry mob of accusers.[2] Such acts hardly brought cohesion to our growing numbers.

The money flowed through Judas's fingers like sand through a sieve. Often the temptation was too great for him and he would pilfer funds.[3] We all knew it. Jesus confronted him more than once but Judas always had some excuse for taking the money. He was never able to accept that he had done anything wrong. I believe that he felt justified in his mind because the only person he seemed to be fooling was himself, yet for Judas that was enough; he was completely convinced of his righteousness. What's more, I think Judas knew the slight regard that Jesus held for money— which provoked him all the more. I did not understand why Jesus did not send Judas away or at least give his job to someone else, but it was Jesus's decision and Jesus seemed loathe to give up on anyone, especially over a little thing like money.

My job was one of the few that actually became easier with time. With our growing popularity and a base of friends with whom to stay in each city, and because I was responsible for finding accommodations only for Jesus and the apostles, hospitality readily availed itself.

We adopted a much more rigorous itinerary than when I had first begun traveling with Jesus. We walked the majority of the time but also made use of boats to decrease travel time. I grew to love sailing. We often traveled in three boats, four or five of us to a craft. On each trip we shuffled men around so that each venture gave us different boat mates.

When we were on the water away from the crowds it was quiet, rejuvenating. We either chatted with one another or rested and slept. My favourite spot was in the front of the boat on top of our stored packs and bedding. It was perfect. I wriggled into this lumpy mattress until it conformed to my body. The sun was my blanket. The low drone of friends in the background and the sloshing waves rocked me to sleep.

Unfortunately, I was not the only one to appreciate the benefits of this location and I took my turn along with everyone else. Sometimes, on nights when I had to sleep ashore on a hard mat, I would imagine I was on a boat snoozing in the heat of the day.

Such a day was today. The sun was bright and promising, a light breeze cooled me, the sun cheered me and the lazy, undulating waves were soothing. For this trip, I was boat mates with Thomas, Philip,

John and Jesus. Jesus and Thomas took the first shift, rowing out into the water until we were far enough from shore to stretch out the sails. The wind immediately caught the white canvas and we all settled down for a relaxing afternoon. Philip took the rudder to keep us on course. I slept first, cozying myself into the front of the boat. When I awoke refreshed, Thomas replaced me on the makeshift bed.

I decided to try having a light conversation with John even though I had always found him difficult to engage. Despite his age (he was then in his late teens), he seemed to me to live in the clouds: focusing on the theoretical and constantly mulling over the deeper meanings of Jesus's teachings. Once when I asked him what he thought about after Jesus had healed a man near John's age, he said that he had not even realized that a miracle had occurred. He was instead engulfed in some minor philosophical dilemma implied by a statement Jesus had made earlier. He seemed to me to be oblivious to the obvious. Perhaps I was merely intimidated by the depth of perception in one so young.

Despite my lack of appreciation for John's company, I politely asked him a few questions. His answers were either short and abrupt or full of notions far too layered for such a beautiful day and I soon gave up. Not wanting to interrupt Philip and Jesus's discussion, I stared at the water and sky.

Thomas woke and Jesus took his turn to nestle into the coveted sleeping spot.

A short while after Jesus nodded off I noticed a few clouds forming in the distance, distinct puffs intruding on the blueness of the sky. Along the horizon a hedge of darker clouds began to gather, then crept into the sky. Casual stories Peter and Andrew had shared over supper the day before echoed in my mind, tales of the unpredictable sea and the speed with which storms sometimes descended upon sailors. As the sparkling sapphire expanse slowly began to turn an eerie murky green, seeds of fear took root in the pit of my stomach and grew. I shifted uneasily in my seat, my eyes transfixed by the sky which was now the colour of a translucent olive leaf. The clouds morphed into ominous, hideous monsters.

It will pass by. I'm sure it is not as bad as it looks, I tried to convince myself.

It did not take long, though, to realize that nature's building rage would not be easily appeased. Soon the sea churned, the wind's breath seethed. Thunder cracked its mighty whip and waves lashed. Lightning gripped the sky, inciting the frenzy.

I cowered under the storm's wrath.

Looking desperately to the sailors among us for assurance, I saw instead fear etched in their faces.

"Get those sails down!" Peter yelled to James and Philip, his fellow boat pilots.

"Where did this come from?" screamed James into the wind's fury.

Rain began to pelt down. My white knuckles gripped the hull of the boat as the bow rose to a forty-five degree angle then smashed onto the rock-hard water, waves leaping into the boat.

"Get that water out!" hollered Philip.

"Where's a bucket?" I yelled.

"How should I know?" Philip bellowed back.

I looked frantically for a container, anything that could hold water, then cupped my hands to shovel water over the edge. Lurching with the pummeling waves I lost my balance and fell hard against the boat's side, bashing my shoulder. Sharp pain shot down my arm and into my chest. Panic took hold of me. There was no escape!

I was a powerless, defenseless victim.

The waves were a ruthless wall of water about to collapse upon us. Death was coming, looming, waiting to drag me down. Its vulturous talons threatened my soul, its hideous face paralyzed my thoughts. I was terrified.

Help me! Help me! my mind screamed. Death hovered, leering at me, so close I could feel its hot breath.

No escape, it whispered hoarsely back.

Black terror surrounded me. So deep I was lost in it, so consuming I was enveloped in it, so devouring I was swallowed up by it. Never would I find my way home again.

Vicki Clarke
128

And then Jesus stood and planted his feet firmly against the boat's gunwales.

He stood in the midst of death's dread, at the pinnacle of nature's wrath and spoke.

"Be still!"

And it was so.

It fled, all of it. The wind, waves, and noise, the terror, panic and dread were all gone. I was safe.

I stared in disbelief at Jesus, this man who had calmed the sea, who quieted the force behind my terror and panic. Questions assaulted my mind, replacing the storm's turmoil.

What power *was* this? What authority was required to dictate to nature what it must do? Who was this man? Why was he here? How could a man tell nature how to act? How was this even possible? What did it mean?

What did he want?

Jesus spoke again.

"Why is your faith so small? Haven't you seen mighty works daily? Do you think Adonai cannot handle a little wind and rain? It is His creation! Can He not control His own handiwork? Why are you so afraid?"[4]

The other boats moored in close to us, the faces of the men in each craft mirroring my own. Amazement overshadowed the fear that moments before had lurked close. The boats' sides bumped periodically as we huddled them around Jesus. He taught about the immensity of Adonai and man's desire to keep Him in a confining box. As Jesus spoke no one said a word or asked a question. It was too much to fathom, to witness a man command nature.

That evening, camped on the shore, I began to grasp the possibility of Jesus being not just a king but our promised Messiah!

I remembered the teachings of the rabbi as I grew up. The Messiah would come from the root of Jesse with the spirit of the Lord resting upon him. He would have a spirit of wisdom, understanding, counsel and strength. With his words he could slay the earth, with the breath from his lips he could slay the wicked.[5]

For thousands of years our people had anticipated the Messiah. Through prophesy Adonai had said that the Messiah was His servant, the chosen one in whom His soul would delight and upon whom He would place His spirit.[6] The Messiah would bring justice, gather Israel to Adonai and bring restoration. My mind swelled with the implications. Kings would see and arise, princes would bow down.

It was more imperative than ever that Jesus be crowned as king of the Jews. I was sure that the Messiah's reign would secure prosperity for Israel; once Jesus was established, peace would flourish.

We must be at the precipice of freedom from Rome, I reasoned. Did not the scriptures promise liberty from our yolk of burden?[7] Rome had invaded our country, forced their rules and standards upon us. We worked to benefit them, paid taxes and tributes to prosper their nation instead of our own, were treated as inferiors in our own land and had our rights revoked.

The Messiah would right these injustices. Oh, how our people cried for justice. The Messiah would increase our joy.[8] How happy I would be if the Romans were defeated and cast from Israel's land; how happy all of Israel would be to have our oppressor broken!

Jesus must be more than a king, I thought, *for kings come and go.* Rulers can be great men who affect change and better their people's situation but the anticipated Messiah was different. He would christen a turning point for our nation, a decisive beginning. He would be a man as influential in the making of our nation as Abraham or Moses, ushering in a time of peace and gladness, a new era where Israel would rise up, other peoples would stream to us in search of Adonai.

How blessed am I! I rejoiced. Not only had the Messiah's time come but I was a part of his inner circle, creating a beautiful land for my grandchildren, a land once again flowing with milk and honey.

chapter thirteen

mazingly, my fuller understanding of Jesus as the promised Messiah did not change my life. My daily interactions with him and his disciples remained as they had always been, for with my decision to follow him and devote myself to his king-making already made, my new revelations simply reaffirmed my judgment and made me more confident of my ambitions.

Passover was nearing again. The forlorn tone of the ram's horn, the *shofar*, sounded from Judea to Galilee, transmitted from one man to the next and reverberating from hill to hill to beckon us to our Jerusalem pilgrimage. As usual we immediately prepared for the trip we were required to make twice a year. This time however, Jesus did not seem at all himself.

His jaw was set, his determination characteristic of the last year, the last six months in particular. An urgency in his voice, which had started just after the feeding of the five thousand, had become all too familiar during the past year's intensive campaign that had tripled the number of cities visited and quadrupled the distances traveled. It seemed as if he was living on borrowed time, driven to teach. He had a disturbing intensity.

I sensed the time when Jesus would stake his claim to the throne must be fast approaching; great power was at hand. Prestige whispered her promises in our ears. We who had been working so hard for the past few years felt we must be at the precipice of greatness.

Not surprisingly, with Jesus's disciples believing his kingdom so close at hand, aspirations rose unabashed. Now was the time to vie for positions in the soon-to-be-formed government. I thought Judas and I would be the most astute in capitalizing on this understanding but it was in fact James's and John's mother who first lobbied Jesus for a plumb appointment for her sons.[1] Such presumption, although anticipated, still caused dissension—especially since James and John were the youngest of the inner twelve. How ridiculous to assume that they were the most qualified to serve as Jesus's governors. The pursuit of their personal enterprises insulted the rest of us, their desires at the expense of everyone else. How selfish.

In truth I was probably angry mostly because their ambitions mimicked my own. My mother used to tell me to beware of those issues that bothered me the most in others for they are often the very ones that I needed to change in my own life. Jesus once said, "Do not worry about the splinter in someone else's eye while you have a board in your own."[2] James's and John's splinter reflected my fierce longings and aspirations—whether I wanted to admit them or not. It helped to soothe my hurt feelings, however, that Jesus did not give in to their petty pursuits for superiority.

The mounting tension was evident not just amongst Jesus's apostles but also in the nation around us. Many in the religious establishment were becoming direct and aggressive in their opposition. Some Pharisees tried to stone Jesus more than once but Jesus always escaped their death wishes. We knew it was only a matter of time before they tried again. The naysayers, that minority within the religious community that James and I had labeled what seemed a lifetime ago in Capernaum as more interested in retaining power than assessing if Jesus was our promised Messiah, continued to be a problem, scheming to use every opportunity to trap Jesus. Other chief priests and Pharisees however, whom I believed had hearts of noble intent, were also concerned about Jesus's popularity, for I think they realized that Jesus's ambitions would impact not only his supporters but affect our entire nation.

If Jesus became king, Rome would not stand idly by as the Jews put in their own government. If Jesus was established as our ruler war would be inevitable. Speculations about the fate of our people were rampant.

Jesus had been openly critical of the religious establishment, condemning religious activity devoid of devotion. If Jesus won a war with Rome, the leaders of the law would surely be expected to change, their future was thus uncertain. Should Rome win, our nation could be destroyed for Rome would undoubtedly retaliate and quash the very thing that defined us as a people: our religion. This concern went beyond our religious leaders' personal safety, it was a fear for our national identity.

Conflict was inevitable. Our world churned with emotion, apprehension mixed with expectation, excitement with fear, ambition with anger.

And Jesus, the man at the centre of it all, offered no help.

Jesus, usually so confident and assured, had never seemed so conflicted. He constantly gave mixed signals. The man who had no doubt that he could calm nature itself talked one moment of establishing his kingdom and the next of dying. He had confidence enough to tell a mountain to move and believe that it could sprout legs and walk into the sea yet now, at the apex of establishing his kingdom, he did nothing to assure us of its certainty. Never had I seen Jesus display such direness. He was fatalistic. It was completely unnerving. While we looked to Jesus to convince us of victory just as he had done through countless miracles in the past, we received only a sense of expectation clouded by doom.

It reminded me of the ominous feelings I had battled for weeks before my arranged marriage. I wrestled with two possibilities of this woman I had not met who would be responsible for shaping my entire world. Would she be lovely and full of joy and bring me children and happiness? Or would she be cantankerous, laced with disdain and bring only misery and hardship? For weeks I fought this double-edged sword of possibility.

That same sword was now sharper than ever. As Jesus's time of coronation neared, a battle to establish his kingdom seemed certain, yet the result was unknown. Would we succeed and be the instruments that set Israel on a new course? Or would we fail and be branded traitors and rebels? History, I knew, tended to be interpreted by the victors in the aftermath of its events, the judgment of actions taken dependent on who was christened the winner and who the loser.

Win or lose I had thrown in my lot with Jesus. My decision was made. The time of reckoning would soon be upon me. I often felt as Thomas did when he once said, "Well, let's go up with him so we can die with him, too."

When the shofar blew almost a month ago we had already begun our southward walk towards Jerusalem, stopping at villages along the way. Jericho was our latest delay, Jesus wanted to teach here for a week. I decided to continue to Bethany to visit Lazarus. Passover was still a month away and his home would be a good place to finalize arrangements since Jesus would soon be staying with him. Today my usual checklist was crowded out by my recent frustrations with Jesus.

The day of traveling did not help. The air was moist and muggy and the thick heavy clouds partially covering the sky sporadically let loose a fine drizzle. Throughout the day I pulled my leather wrap from my pack only to put it back about an hour later when the sun broke through the cloudy sky again.

The clouds never truly committed themselves to rain nor the sun to warmth. The next two days alternated between wet and dry, shade and light. At one point, after repacking my wrap in my bag for the third time in one afternoon, I glared at the sky, shook my fist at it and yelled at the uncooperative day, "Would it be so hard to make up your mind?"

The weather mirrored my frustration with Jesus. Why was he not capturing the moment, moving to make his kingdom a reality? Did he not see how important it was to grasp control of the events around him and bring assurance to his followers? We desperately needed it. The signs that it was time for Jesus to make his political move were evident from the masses of people who gathered to hear him and the worries of the religious authorities. We could all see it. What was Jesus waiting for? Why was he leery? Why did he dwell on the thought of leaving us?

He kept talking about going to his Father, that we would not always have him with us or that we would not see him for a while. I did not understand. We were so close. We had worked so hard. Why leave with victory at hand? It was not a time to retreat but to march!

If only Jesus would be decisive. Was this the right time for his reign to begin or would it be better to wait? I wanted direction, certainty.

At the end of two days of walking along mumbling to myself, I arrived in Bethany looking forward to a warm hearth and a chance to talk to Lazarus about my concerns; Lazarus always added an interesting perspective and I respected his opinion.

I walked down the street to his home and rapped on the door. Mary answered. Her face was pale, her forehead wrinkled and her hair unkempt. She looked as if she had had many sleepless nights.

"Mary, are you all right?" I asked, forgoing the normal formalities of greeting.

"Oh, Judas! Praise be. It is heaven itself to see you!" She quickly ushered me in.

"Lazarus is sick," she continued absently, wandering through the garden courtyard towards Lazarus's room. I presumed that I was to follow her.

"He's been sick for about a week but it just keeps getting worse. We don't know what to do. He is listless. What will we do if we lose him, Judas? He has to get better. He has always been there for Martha and me. He has to get better."

On and on she babbled, long after we entered Lazarus's room where Martha hovered over the bed, worry creasing her face. I inched closer to the bed to peer at Lazarus and was horrified at the sight of him.

He was as pale and gaunt as a ghost, pasty and torpid with fever. His gray eyelids had sunken into his head, his barely visible lips were the same colour as the rest of his ashen face. He must have lost at least thirty pounds. I felt I was looking at a man whom death had already claimed.

"What happened?" I rasped.

"It was so fast," explained Martha. "About ten days ago he began to complain of feeling unwell, he had a stomachache and felt weak. He went to bed and has not eaten or gone to work since. The fever doesn't break no matter what we do. He was shivering until yesterday but then he stopped. Now he just lays completely still."

She wrung her hands, looking desperately to me to see if I had any notion of how to help, then pulled a rag from a bowl of cool water beside the bed and placed it on Lazarus's forehead. Mary took the bowl and ran to change the water as if she longed to be useful.

"I'll go back and get Jesus," I said. It was all I could think to say, all I could think to do.

It was almost suppertime but, with the urgency of the situation evident, Mary packed me some food and I started back on the road that I had just traversed. Jesus was Lazarus's only hope.

I got back to Jericho as quickly as I could, walking only when I could run no farther. When I felt I could not go on without rest, I slept lightly then set out again. It took me two nights and a day but I finally arrived early in the morning. Although I was exhausted I went immediately to the place where Jesus had been staying when I left.

Before I reached the home, I met John who told me that Jesus was out walking and praying, his normal ritual for this time of the day. I told John about Lazarus's precarious illness and he quickly started packing, confident that Jesus would want to leave immediately.

I perched myself on the roof of the house closest to the direction John had last seen Jesus and scanned the horizon. I finally spotted Jesus strolling leisurely over the hill towards town.

I ran to meet him.

"Jesus," I called, still a good distance away, "Lazarus is sick!" When I reached him I added between gulps of air, "Hopefully if we leave right away you will be able to get there in time to help him."

Jesus, concerned, asked about Lazarus, yet as I told him all I had seen he continued his slow saunter towards Jericho.

"You left only three days ago," Jesus observed. "You must not have stayed in Bethany long."

"No, Lord, I left the same night I arrived."

"You must be exhausted, Judas."

"Yes, I'll have a quick rest while you pack but I'm sure I'll be ready to travel again," I said, impatient to get back and quickening my step. I glanced over my shoulder at Jesus, trying to entice him to hurry.

"Take your time and have a good sleep, we will not be leaving here for a few days," Jesus stated matter-of-factly.

I stopped, staring at him incredulously. Had I not communicated the severity of Lazarus's illness? Had Jesus not understood my earnestness?

"But…but, Lord!" I stammered. "You must go now. He is close to death!"

Jesus, having firmly made up his mind, took a deep breath, squared his shoulders back and looked directly into my eyes and said, "I will go. But not now."

Silence hung between us.

"I have my reasons," he added quietly yet just as resolutely.

I glared at him, dumbfounded, and did nothing to hide my welling anger. How could he be so callous? I could not believe my ears. Yet Jesus would not be swayed and I knew it was useless to waste any more words.

"Well, I, at least, will go back and be with Lazarus," I said, with as much determination as Jesus had just shown.

"All right, Judas. Please let Mary and Martha know I will be with them soon," his eyes seemed to soften, and he looked sad.

"And what shall I tell Lazarus?" I snapped.

"I will see him soon, too," Jesus answered softly then, hanging his head, he turned and walked away from me.

I stared at his departing figure and muttered under my breath, "This is unbelievable! Completely unbelievable!"

Kicking the dirt in front of my feet and sending a cloud of dust to circle my legs, I stomped and 'hmphed' back to Jericho, grabbing my pack once again.

Although my eyes stung from lack of sleep, I stuffed and jostled supplies into my bag, righteous indignation filling me faster than the food going into the canvas sack. The absolute gall! Jesus would make time for complete strangers but would not go to help a friend in need! I left without stopping to inform John—Jesus could explain his inaction himself.

I kicked and stomped most of the morning, replaying all of the events of the past three days. How desperately I wanted to make sense of it all. Jesus had seemed sad. Perhaps he really did want to go but something prevented him. Maybe I was just making excuses for him.

My return trip to Bethany took a day longer than my original trek, for with my fatigue catching up to me I napped often. What did it matter anyway? I had nothing to offer. I would have to tell my dear friends that I had failed to convince Lazarus's only hope to come with me. At mid-afternoon, for the second time in six days, I knocked on Lazarus's door.

The door creaked open and Martha stood in the doorway.

She looked tired and ragged. Her oily hair hung in strings framing her face, her eyes red and puffy. She pulled me into the house and hugged me. As soon as she was in my arms, she began to shake and sob as if she had been trying to be strong for too long and could no longer hold on to her strength.

I held her and patted her back.

"Jesus says he'll be here soon," I said lamely, attempting to say anything that might bring even a little comfort.

"It doesn't matter anymore," she wept into my shoulder. "Lazarus died this morning. He is already in the tomb."

I let her cry as the news sank in. Lazarus was dead. I was assaulted by memories of the past two years, his laughter and smile, his warmth and compassion, his chats and jokes.

I thought about Jesus and his time with Lazarus. If only he had come to Bethany as soon as I had told him about Lazarus's illness he would have arrived the night before Lazarus died. Jesus could have healed him! This pain and grief could have been avoided. Why had he chosen not to help?

"At least you are here in time for our shabbat," Martha offered, interrupting my thoughts.

I ate the Sabbath supper with the relatives who came to comfort Mary and Martha then went to bed to struggle through another restless night. The next day during the synagogue service, I stood with the rest of the community during the weekly ritual of offering prayers for those who had lost loved ones over the past year, grateful to Adonai for His provision of this symbol of community support.

For the next two days I helped the sisters set their house in order. We talked with Obed to sort through the money that Lazarus had saved, made decisions about how the sisters and their servants would live. We developed a budget and made plans for the future. I also helped with their houseful of family and friends, many of whom had come from Jerusalem to pay their respects.

By my third night in Bethany I could finally sleep normally. The rest helped with my perspective. Crisis moments always make priorities fall easily into place. Things that used to seem important are no longer. Life's distractions and stresses fall away, for as peripheral issues fade to the sidelines, what is truly important stands stark and alone. You don't have to think about priorities, they just are. They have no competition.

In this critical time, I realized that it did not matter when Jesus established his kingdom, only that it happen. I knew he was my true king. Despite the fray of the world around me, he was still worthy of my loyalty. As I thought about Jesus's decision to stay in Jericho, I decided that Jesus must be accepting the burden of leadership, setting aside his personal desires for the sake of public obligations.

Just before lunch, four days too late, Andrew came to the house to tell us that Jesus was just outside of Bethany. Martha hurried out the back door while Mary, out of politeness, stayed with their numerous guests. I stayed at the house to wait with Mary.

It was not long before Martha returned, out of breath from running.

"Mary," I heard her whisper to her sister, "Jesus is asking for you."

Both women, abandoning propriety, left the house to see Jesus. Their guests, not knowing where they were going yet wanting to be of support to the sisters, followed them. So did I.

When Mary came to Jesus, her grief was unleashed. She fell at his feet. I do not think even she realized how much emotion she harboured. She wept, sobs shaking her body.

"Lord, if you had been here," I heard her mumble as she tried to stifle her crying, "my brother would not have died."[3]

Her grief was overwhelming. Mary's sorrow quickened the sadness in us all, each person's pain aroused anew as her anguish radiated to touch us and revitalize our common loss. The wonder of how one person's grief can enliven and deepen the feelings of those around them is a treasured gift from Adonai; it is one of humanity's blessed connections. As the spirit of our communal sorrow stirred each soul, tears flowed and sobs echoed. Jesus wept.

"Where have you buried him?" Jesus asked.

Lazarus's tomb was not too far away and we soon arrived at the stone positioned in front of his gravesite. A few women near Mary and Martha laid their hands on the sisters' shoulders in comfort. The group was still but for the occasional shuffling of feet in the dirt or sniffing nose.

"Remove the stone," Jesus pronounced. I stared at Jesus, trying to process what I thought he had said. He stood next to the stone and glared at it as if it was an armed enemy blocking his path. The muscles in his face and jaw looked chiseled, his eyes narrowed as if he was determined to meet an adversary straight on.

"Remove the stone," he said again, more forcefully this time, his eyes still fixed on the rock. Astonishment rippled through the gathering. Shock followed by disgust. What was Jesus asking? The smell would be rancid; Lazarus's body was already decaying.

"Lord," Martha ventured timidly, "by this time there will be a stench for he has been dead four days."[4]

"Martha," he replied gently, not yet taking his eyes from the stone, "if you believe, you will see the glory of Adonai."

Why was Jesus asking us to do this? Surely, he did not plan to raise Lazarus from the dead! Jesus had raised people from the dead before.

Those deaths, however, had not been like this. Jesus had once met a funeral procession outside of a town and raised a widow's only son.[5] Another time he privately raised a girl who had just died then gave her back to her ecstatic parents.[6] Both times skeptics had readily explained the miracles away, saying that the people weren't really dead.

This time though, Lazarus had been entombed for four days. This time the body had begun to decay. I stared at Jesus's determined face. Peter, John and Thomas moved towards the stone, pushing back their sleeves. I gawked, dumbfounded, unable to move my feet.

The three men heaved, throwing their combined body weight behind the mass of stone. Gradually it began to shift, pushing settled ground away as it scraped against other rocks blocking its path. As the stone moved, a shriek of anger like a hideous beast furious at being disturbed rent the air, sending a chill through my body. Instinctively, I rubbed my arms against the shivering. Peter, John and Thomas stepped back from the cave's opening and huddled together, gulping in air from the exertion then quickly pulling the mantle of their tunics over their noses as the smell escaped the tomb. My eyes began to water and I covered my nose and mouth as well. As the odour spread, people's faces turned sour. Those around me pressed closer together. I wondered if they too felt the icy presence of an invisible monster.

Jesus looked up to heaven and prayed.

"Father, thank you for hearing me. I do this, Lord, so that the people standing around me will believe that You sent me."

Jesus stepped into the opening, planting his feet firmly in the hollow left by the stone. He again reminded me of a defiant soldier— one who prepared to claim back land stolen by a marauder.

With his rigid body facing into the blackness, he leaned forward and declared loudly, "Lazarus, come out!"

I had no time to wonder at the ludicracy of his call for I immediately heard a muffled, shuffling noise from deep within the cave. Slowly the figure of a man appeared, covered in strips of cloth. A unified gasp went up from our entourage. The being before us did not look the size of a man, death having begun its feast on his flesh.

Then, just like in the days of Ezekiel when he saw the valley of dry bones, the Lord restored Lazarus's body before my very eyes.

My Lord said, "Behold, I will cause breath to enter these bones that they may come to life. And I will put sinews on them, make flesh grow back on you, cover you with skin, and put breath in you so that you may come alive; and you will know that I am the Lord. Come from the four winds, O breath, and breathe on he who was slain, that he may come to life."[7]

I heard tree leaves rustle. A gust of wind moved towards Jesus, accelerating as it traveled, leaving the trees it had just passed still and quiet. When it reached Lazarus, it whipped the dust around him then, beginning at his feet, entered his white linen encasement, filling the strips of cloth with wind and stretching them as a flag unfurled in a storm. When the wind reached his torso, his chest bulged as though his lungs took in a great gulp of air. The wind continued to the wrappings around his head then escaped to the heavens. Lazarus was left squirming, frantically trying to untangle himself from constricting cords.

"Unbind him and let him go," Jesus shouted as he began to tear at the strips covering Lazarus's mouth and nose.[8]

Matthew and I quickly ran to Lazarus, helping Jesus pull the strips from his face and body. Lazarus gasped and coughed for air as we rushed to release the tight wrappings from around his chest. His eyes darted nervously, gaping at us and the people staring at him.

"What's happening? What's going on?" he asked, looking more panicked as he realized what we pulled off him and where he stood. As we stripped the cloth from his body, Jesus draped his own outer tunic over Lazarus and took him aside to talk to him as soon as he was unencumbered enough to walk.

The two of them sat on some rocks, their heads tilted towards one another. Jesus reached out and placed his hand on Lazarus's shoulder. Behind me I caught snatches of conversation between friends and disciples, people talking about our nation's desperate need for a leader with the power Jesus had just demonstrated. Jesus had again performed the undeniable. The excited chatter built around me.

I breathed in deeply and allowed a sigh to escape my lips as a smile lit upon them. For the first time in months I felt assured and confident that Jesus was on the precipice of establishing his kingdom. Having performed such a deliberate public spectacle, surely Jesus had finally decided that now was the time to stake his claim to the throne.

chapter fourteen

*t*he resurrection of Lazarus certainly caused quite a stir. His relatives from Jerusalem returned home to tell all that they had seen to the chief priest and Pharisees. Whenever Jesus performed a miracle close to Jerusalem, the Jewish leaders from the synagogue came to investigate so I was sure that these experts in the law would travel to Bethany as soon as they heard about this 'incident' in order to assess, interview, interrogate, and judge the merits of the event.

Early in the morning the day after Lazarus's resurrection, Jesus decided that we were to leave. Taking only the inner twelve and telling none of us where we were going, we snuck out of Bethany before the city stirred. At noon he told us that we were going to stay for a week at Ephraim, a more remote village about three-days' walk from Jerusalem, but said nothing as to the reason for his decision or the abruptness of our departure. This gave my imagination great leeway for speculation. I presumed Jesus's obvious avoidance of Jerusalem's dignitaries was some sort of strategic political move. The Passover brought pilgrims from all regions to Jerusalem. It was an excellent opportunity to address a large forum of people representing a diverse population.

Perhaps the next time he enters Jerusalem he wants stories of Lazarus's resurrection fresh in people's minds, I thought. *Maybe he thinks that by not answering the religious leaders' questions, attention will be focused on his right to the throne instead of the distraction of a public inquiry into the details of his life.*

While in Ephraim, Jesus gave no indication of a hidden political agenda. He laughed, taught and enjoyed the people of the town just as he had done for the past three years of his ministry. When he relaxed with his disciples, he often spoke of Lazarus, Mary and Martha, wondering aloud how they were faring under all the scrutiny. A week before the Passover feast Jesus declared that it was time to return to Bethany.

Oh what a homecoming we received when we knocked on Lazarus's door and Obed called out that Jesus had arrived!

Lazarus's welcoming bear hug greeted each of us as we stepped over the threshold of his home. He had never looked so healthy, robust and energetic. Jesus and Lazarus immediately sat down together at one end of the outer garden. Lazarus had been sick, dead, and interrogated by experts in the law—the two of them had much to talk about. They huddled in the corner for the better part of the day talking in hushed tones, a hearty laugh ringing out now and then. The rest of us respected their privacy.

By mid-afternoon, Martha and Joanna had begun supper preparations. The day was warm so they kindled a fire outside to enjoy the inviting weather. They seemed to be making a meal fit for a king, the preparation and ingredients they used boasted of the importance of their guest. Wheat bread instead of barley had been left to rise on heated stones; veal, served only on significant occasions, roasted on a spit instead of being boiled.

I sat on a nearby bench and chatted with Martha, savouring the smells and anticipating the meal.

"How have you been?" I asked.

"Oh, I feel like I haven't had a moment to think," she answered with a laugh and a sigh. She picked up a knife and began slicing a cucumber.

"First Lazarus was sick," she continued, "then we had all of the company from Jerusalem. Then the questions from the chief priests, and now there are Passover preparations. I have cooked enough food in the past month to last me a lifetime. I think we have single-handedly cleaned out the vegetable fields of four families."

"How did Lazarus handle all the attention?" I queried.

"Ah, Lazarus. What a rock, or maybe I should say boulder," she laughed and stretched her arms above her head then slowly brought them down to outline Lazarus's height, broad shoulders and husky body.

"He has taken it all in stride. He answers all he can remember and shrugs at the rest. Actually, he seems to remember nothing about the time when he was dead so he provides very little for the curious. But my is he healthy! And so much energy! Well, I suppose I would be energetic, too, if I had been awakened from the dead! He seems to always be famished. 'Must make up for that week of sickness,' he has said at every meal."

I snickered at the gruff voice she used to imitate Lazarus.

"And Mary, how has she been?" I asked.

Martha put down her knife, paused and looked blankly at her cutting board.

"Mary has been very curious," she said slowly. "She has not seemed herself since Lazarus got sick. When he was sick, she worried incessantly. Not just for him but for herself and for me. How would we live? How would we survive? Then, after he died, she was despondent. She was so quiet, I couldn't get a word out of her. She helped with all the company but was completely reserved. And now that Lazarus is back with us, she is still not herself. It's not that she mopes, it's more like she is ..." Martha paused, continuing only when she found the right words. "Distracted. Preoccupied."

As if on cue, Mary opened the outside door a few feet away from the roasting meat. She saw me and a smile lit her face.

"Judas," she cried, "how wonderful to see you!"

"And you, Mary," I answered.

"Does this mean that Jesus is here?" she asked.

"Yes," I answered, "he is just over there talking with Lazarus."

I motioned to the corner of the garden where the two were deep in conversation. I barely heard her quiet, "Oh."

She stared at the two men. Just stared. Then, swallowing hard, she softly added, "I see."

With that she turned on her heel and walked back out the door through which she had just come.

I looked questioningly at Martha. She walked to the outside door and closed it gently.

"You see," she said, "not at all herself."

While Martha finished the dinner preparations, I was joined by Judas, James and John. They had met with some men in the city and had learned that the chief priests and Pharisees had given orders that anyone who knew Jesus's whereabouts was to report it at once so that they might seize Jesus. This must have been one of the concerns which had motivated Jesus to go to Ephraim, I mused. We had an impromptu meeting to discuss secrecy and security. At various times in the past, certain situations had become particularly volatile; sometimes, we knew, discretion was essential. As Martha bustled with supper, we prepared some suggestions for Jesus. After our talk, James ran to meet with the other members of his 'policing' force to finalize their recommendations before speaking with Jesus.

With supper finally ready, Judas, John and I joined Jesus and Lazarus in the outer courtyard. I was fairly drooling after spending two hours anticipating Martha's cooking. Martha served supper. Mary was nowhere to be seen.

We ate at a table and in a manner reserved for special occasions. I felt like I was eating in a king's circle. A knee-high table had been set up in a 'U' shape beneath the garden lattice of the inner court. Around the sides of the table were padded benches for each of us to recline upon and a row of thicker cushions was positioned closest to the table. Resting on our elbows with our feet extended out away from the table, we reclined, relaxing comfortably while we ate.

Partway through our meal, Mary appeared at the edge of the mosaic-tiled floor of the courtyard.

She was breathtaking. She was adorned in expensive clothes yet she was modestly dressed. Her dress was a deep royal blue trimmed in crimson red with a magenta purple mantle draped over her shoulders. Upon her head she wore a sheer purple cloth with specks of shell scrapings sewn into it that shimmered in the light, cascading down the veil like falling, glistening water. A tiara of cut gems secured it in place. The detailed embroidery and stitching on her gown revealed days of painstaking work. Her dress and demeanour indicated that this a sacred moment and that Mary believed she entertained royalty, the dining room transformed to throne room.

She came toward Jesus, approaching him slowly, head bowed to show him homage before kneeling beside his feet in her desire to show him fealty.

When she had kneeled, Jesus sat up and moved to the end of the padded bench so that his feet touched the floor. Although his back was to me, I noticed him reach out and touch the top of her bowed head. From her mantle, she pulled a pound of pure *nard*, an expensive perfume, a gift befitting only a king. When she opened the jar, the air slowly became saturated with fragrance, filtering through the room and hinting at a garden of spring flowers in bloom. It was subtle yet intoxicating, years of meticulous labour had captured nature's scent in a jar. Surely Mary's pursuit of such extravagance had cost her dearly. Between her clothes and the perfume she must have spent her life's savings. Now she freely lavished her sacrifice at Jesus's feet. She perfumed his feet, wiping them with her hair.

It was obvious that her heart sang through her actions. Yea, it verily shouted! As she reverently showed her esteem for Jesus, her king, her heartstrings joyously resonated that he was entirely worthy. It was an exquisite picture of a true king honoured by his loyal subject.

"This is a disgrace!" spat Judas Iscariot. "Why was this perfume not sold for three hundred denarii and given to poor people?"

The question broke the reverie of the room like a harsh stone shattering fragile glass.

The moment was lost. Mary's divine sentiment, robbed. Judas's words were the only ones hanging in the room. Quietly, in the silence, the seeds of doubt planted by Judas's question took root, entwining tendrils crept through my mind. Was Mary's time and money a frivolous waste? Was such extravagance ill spent? Was it prudent to pursue this excess?

"Let her alone!" Jesus suddenly declared, his voice laced with fury, his judgment of Mary's actions decisive and sure.

"The poor you will always have with you but you will not always have me. This is as in the day of my burial."[1]

It was a strange thing to say. I took it to mean that he would one day be buried as a royal king. That at the time of his death he would be prepared for burial as royalty is. If the meaning was obscure, the intent was not. He had named Mary's actions as righteous and Judas's words as corrupt.

This was not lost on Judas.

His crimson face matched the trim on Mary's dress. He said not a word for the rest of the meal, only glowered at Jesus, wallowing in his reprimand and reproach.

Mary rose and helped Martha serve supper, waiting upon her king and her guests. There was an uneasy spirit in the room. Unbridled joy shared space with seething contempt.

I was relieved when the meal was finished and I could excuse myself to my sleeping mat for the night.

chapter fifteen

*t*he next morning, as James and I were talking, Jesus came and asked us to do an errand.

"Go into the next village. When you enter, you will find a tied donkey; a donkey upon which no one has ever sat. Untie it and bring it to me."

Anxious to comply with his request but also concerned, I asked, "Lord, won't people think we are stealing it?"

"If anyone asks, tell them that I have need of it." he calmly reassured me. "All will be well."

Satisfied with his answer (after all when had I known Jesus's words to be proven wrong?), we set off to the next town. When we arrived everything was as Jesus had described. Some men standing beside the tied donkey did indeed ask what we were doing. James looked confidently at them and stated, "The Lord has need of it." That was enough for the men, who simply nodded and smiled.

We led the donkey back to Bethany near the Mount of Olives where Jesus and the rest of the apostles were waiting. Jesus mounted the donkey and we began to walk towards the gates of Jerusalem, joining the throng of people on their way there for the Passover.

It was a warm day, the brightly shining sun had no competition from clouds or wind. The well- worn, four-man-wide path was packed with old men and widows, husbands and mothers, chatting teens, frolicking children and screaming infants. Here and there five or six people tried to squeeze into a line across the road with those on the ends of the queue walking lopsided with one foot on the road and the other in the ditch. No one seemed in a hurry, content instead to keep pace with the slowest moving man or beast.

A little girl of about six a few feet in front of me gaily swung her mother's tightly clasped hand as they walked. Their hands moved to and fro in time with the child's bouncy step, her eyes wandering everywhere as her head swiveled and bobbed to take in all the new people and sights. Her eyes grew enormous as she focused on the man beside me riding the donkey. I presumed she must have seen Jesus at some point in our travels and recognized him.

She let go of her mother's hand and began to tug incessantly on the woman's blue tunic, demanding attention. Finally the woman turned to the girl and I heard the girl loudly whisper, her voice filled with awe, "Mama, isn't that Jesus, king of the Jews?"

Her mother followed the direction of her daughter's outstretched finger. She, too, seemed to recognize Jesus immediately. She quickly turned to tell her husband. Some fellow travelers overheard the conversation and began whispering as well.

The knowledge that Jesus was among them quickly began to spread.

The girl who had first seen Jesus pulled her mother down to whisper in her ear. The mother smiled at her daughter, nodded her head then, taking the child's hand again, ran into a nearby field full of wild palms and cut some leafy branches. They ran back to lay the branches on the path ahead of the donkey's hooves. Mother and daughter beamed up at Jesus, willing him to accept their tribute. Jesus smiled broadly back at them, his joy in their impromptu gift obvious in his glowing face and bright eyes. The two hurried back to the field to gather more branches.

Other travelers, seeing what these two were doing, dashed to join them. An elderly man ahead of us turned his leathery face towards the commotion, then recognizing Jesus, struggled to pull his old, weathered coat from his shoulders. With great effort he slowly bent, gently placing his cloak on the road to add his contribution to the green carpet being woven before the coming king.

I walked beside the donkey astounded as support for Jesus surged and pulsed, building around me.

Someone ahead of us called out, "Hosanna!"

"Blessed is he who comes in the name of the Lord!" a voice called back.

Still another bellowed, "Hosanna in the highest!"

A shout, "Blessed is the coming kingdom of our father David."

It is happening! my heart rejoiced. *Jesus's time is finally here!* My emotions swelled, erupted. I could not have imagined a moment more blessed than this! It was utterly spontaneous, wild, unabashed and raw.

This must have been like in the time of David, I thought, *when David returned with the ark of Adonai dancing before the Lord.* All around me pilgrims to Jerusalem now began to dance before Jesus with all their might. They shouted to their king with ecstasy, leaping before him, their adoration unadulterated and pure, their joy beyond propriety. It was their time of jubilee.

They chanted and sang and waved palm branches.

I looked from the throngs of people raving for Jesus to Jesus himself. The sight of him sent a shudder down my spine. This, I thought, is the reason I follow him, the reason I will serve him all of my days.

His countenance was beautiful to behold. The fullness of his heart showed undeniably upon his face; he did not restrain the smallest aspect of his true feelings. I saw no hint of arrogance or pride, only passion for his people, fervour for them, vehemence and zeal to be with them; there was nothing pretentious about him. I knew he loved the individuals before him and that they had touched his spirit. He thrilled to their adoration.

I readily joined the surging jubilation.

"Blessed is he comes in the name of the Lord!" I yelled then ran into the field, cut an armful of leaves and hurried back to lay them on the path. I yanked off my tunic and added it to the ground covered with wool cloth, tanned leather and fringed leaves.[1]

Jesus is my king and Adonai's chosen one, my heart sang. Memories of the past years flooded my mind, the reasons why Jesus deserved my acclaim and homage. I knew Jesus to be a lover of the human heart, a good shepherd who did not want even one sheep to be lost. He was like revitalizing, living water or like a lamp which shined on us with all its brightness so that all people would come to him.

With each armful of new palms, came more recollections confirming Jesus as the one worthy to be our king. He was a man of miracles: he made the dumb speak, the crippled whole and the lame walk. He was like the good Samaritan of his parable, pouring oil and wine on our wounds and bandaging them. He cared for us.

Jesus was a man of authority and power. He commanded wind and stormy water yet, amazingly, he was also the giver of quiet and great calm.

Imagery from Jesus's allegories burst into my mind. Truly he was like a hidden treasure in the field, an unusual pearl of immeasurable wealth. He was like a mustard seed sown in a field that grows to become the biggest of all plants, so that the birds come and make their nests in its branches. He was the supplier of our rest. He was like the yeast mixed in with the flour, causing the whole batch of dough to rise, drawing us to Adonai.

He was my inspiration.

I raised my voice to call out again, "BLESSED IS HE WHO COMES IN THE NAME OF THE LORD!"

As our parade made its way to Jerusalem's gates, the masses cheered. Those already in Jerusalem rushed to see what the disturbance was about.

"Tell them to stop!" I heard a man roar above the din.

A priest, his robes flowing behind him, strode in front of Jesus, his pomp and pageantry stark against the unbridled frenzy of excitement surrounding Jesus. The priest looked utterly indignant.

"Make your disciples stop this disrespectful display immediately! Who do you think you are?"

The people quieted, intimidated by the looming priest and his ostentatious grandeur.

Jesus's smile did not fade. In fact it widened, his eyes gleamed and sparkled, the very windows of his soul.

"If they keep quiet," Jesus answered back, "I tell you that the stones on this path would begin to shout."[2] The sheer joy in Jesus's voice was inescapable. He was undaunted.

A great cheer resounded from all the people and our procession continued down the street.

It was a transforming time of surging hope and belief in a magnificent future. Jesus had arrived.

Our king had finally arrived!

chapter sixteen

During the next five days Jesus did not perform a single miracle. Instead he taught in the temple and aggressively condemned those religious leaders and practices which lacked true meaning. Through parables and observations that belittled those rituals robbed of original purpose (and the people who represented them), Jesus forthrightly denounced many in the religious establishment.

Jesus also spoke about the future.

One morning as we walked towards Jerusalem from Bethany where we had spent the night, we overheard some men talking about how beautiful the temple looked with its fine stones and the impressiveness of the gifts offered to Adonai. Jesus stopped walking, turned to the small gathering of disciples following him, pointed towards the distant temple and asked, "Do you see all this? The time will come when not a single stone here will be left in its place, every one will be thrown down."[1]

I was horrified. The temple was a magnificent building but infinitely more important it was our access to our holy God. The twice-a-year pilgrimage to Jerusalem and the temple was our hope for atonement from sins, our way to become right with Adonai who was so holy that no man could approach Him.

"When will this be?" James gasped.

Jesus's response told of kingdoms attacking one another, war, revolution, terrible earthquakes, famine, and plague.

With each awful sign foretold by Jesus, the ball of fear in the pit of my stomach grew. While I never believed that Jesus's rise to power would come without cost, I had not expected such destruction. As the information assaulted me, I desperately tried to sort it into categories that made sense. Were nature and disease coming to Jesus's defense and declaring war on mortal man? Would the temple fall as a result of nature's revolt? Was Jesus foretelling a future that he had seen or one that he planned to orchestrate?

"Before all these things take place," Jesus continued, "you will be arrested and persecuted, handed over to trial in meeting houses and put in prison, brought before kings and rulers for my sake."

Jesus spoke as assuredly as if he was reporting on events that had already occurred instead of an unknown future. It was unnerving to hear such ominous forecasts spoken with complete confidence. Jesus looked intently at each of us, the tone in his voice reminded me of a reluctant parent intently giving last minute instructions to a child about to be left alone. "Make up your minds ahead of time not to worry about how you will defend yourselves; for I will give you such words and wisdom that none of your enemies will be able to resist or deny what you say."

Smiling weakly and looking as though he was communicating the distressing details of a decision no longer open to negotiation, he continued—never taking his eyes from us, the recipients of his foreboding prophesy.

"You will be handed over by your parents, your brothers, your relatives and your friends." Pausing, he added softly, "Some of you will die. Everyone will hate you because of me. But not a single hair from your head will be lost. Never give up, for this is how you will save your lives."[2]

We stared at him, silent. Jesus turned and we quietly followed him towards the city. Thoughts of my mortality had crossed my mind since becoming an apostle for I did, after all, seek to upset the accepted government. Yet hearing Jesus predict my impending doom took the concept out of the theoretical realm and into reality. Was this a call to arms? Should we prepare and harbour weapons for an upcoming battle? Just how much time did we have?

Throughout the day, whenever there was a free moment, I saw the rest of the apostles huddled in small groups or overheard them debating possible meanings for Jesus's prophesies and their horrible implications. We mingled amongst ourselves, sharing insights that we had gleaned from other groups of friends, gossiping and elaborating on our speculations. Finally, at the end of the day, Peter, James, John and Andrew decided it was time to end our questioning. They led our group to the Mount of Olives where Jesus had been resting, refreshing himself in the coolness of the night, exhausted from his day of teaching.

Jesus turned towards us as we shuffled up the hill. He did look tired! He reclined between two boulders, his back propped against the larger one and his feet resting on top of the other. A slight smile reached his eyes as we gathered around him.

"Ah, my friends," Jesus greeted us, fatigue in his voice. "Please sit with me and enjoy this beautiful night."

We quickly accepted his offer, surrounding him on the grass.

"Lord," Peter ventured, "today when you were talking about Jerusalem's destruction … when will this happen?"

Jesus sat up to look deeply into the eyes of the men around him. I was sure that he sensed the turmoil his earlier words had caused.

"No one knows when the day or hour will come," he began. "Not the angels in heaven; not me. Only the Father knows." The crevices between his eyebrows deepened slightly in thought then he leaned forward to say more earnestly, "You must be on your guard and not be deceived. Be alert. It will be like a man who goes away from his home on a trip and leaves his servants in charge. He tells his doorkeeper to keep watch. I tell you, that man had better do his job! His master may come back in the evening, or at midnight, or before dawn, or at sunrise. If he comes suddenly, the master must not find his watchman asleep!"[3]

Ah, I thought, *Jesus is calling us to prepare for battle.* I inwardly determined to be ready for the upcoming conflict. Jesus leaned back and gazed beyond us into the twilight sky, a far-away look lingering in his eyes.

"But, before your Master returns," he continued, "you will see 'The Awful Horror' standing in the place where he should not be." A shiver raced up my spine and I held my breath. I felt like a blade was about to drop, an axe head about to make contact with its target.

"Then those who are in Judea must run away to the hills. The man who is on the roof of his house must not lose time by going for his cloak. How terrible it will be in those days for women who are pregnant, and for mothers who have little babies. Pray to God that these things will not happen in wintertime. For the trouble of those days will be far worse than any the world has ever known, from the very beginning when God created the world to the present time. Nor will there ever again be anything like it."

What was Jesus talking about? One moment it seemed he was compelling us to arms, telling us that the time to capture his throne and rally his supporters was at hand, yet the next moment he talked of horrors, terrors and fleeing.

"But Adonai has reduced the number of those days," Jesus added, more to himself than to us. "If He had not no one would have survived. Yes, for the sake of His chosen people, He has reduced those days."

I felt like an intruder listening to Jesus's private musings as he convinced himself of a necessary course of action; the inner debate of pros and cons that a battle chief wrestles before the physical fighting commences.

"In the days after that time of trouble," he continued, "the sun will grow dark, the moon will no longer shine, the stars will fall from heaven, and the powers in space will be driven from their course. Then, the Son of Man will appear, coming in the clouds with great power and glory." Jesus paused, at last content with his deliberations. Then, noticing again that he was surrounded by friends, he smiled at us and finished by adding, "He will send out the angels to the four corners of the earth and gather God's chosen people from one end of the world to the other. Let the fig tree teach you a lesson. When its branches become green and tender and it starts putting out leaves, you know that summer is near. In the same way, when you see these things happening, you will know that the time is near, ready to begin."[4]

Obviously this talk with Jesus only added to my list of questions and accentuated my concerns. As we walked back towards Bethany for the night, I struggled with my fears and tried to bolster my courage. Was my home in order if I should die? Would I be able to do what was necessary when I was required to take up my sword to force Jesus's kingship? I had not been trained as a soldier yet I was sure of my course, sure of my direction.

There is an immense peace when the questions of 'why' are gone; a freedom to do what must be done when the reasons for the action are no longer harnessed to the judgment. Because I had contemplated my decision to follow Jesus many times, I was sure my intentions were noble and my cause pure.

When we reached Lazarus's house, Jesus went directly to sleep while the twelve apostles met together in the outer garden. We worried with one another about Jesus's grim forecasts and mulled over our lack of military preparedness. Little was confirmed but all agreed that Jesus's kingdom must be established no matter the consequence for he was our righteous king. I was commissioned to find and purchase some swords. If we had any hope of making Jesus our ruler, we needed to ready ourselves for inevitable conflict.

chapter seventeen

O ver the next few days I alternated between fretting over the daunting, coming clash Jesus had predicted and persuading myself of the victory at hand. Having previously only purchased items for domestic use, I nervously researched and made inquiries about weapons. I always carried a short sword, it was actually more like an oversized knife, under my tunic in case of animal attack or to threaten a roadside marauder, but in all my years the blade had not been needed for such noble causes and had been reduced to a tool for prying apart the over-tightened lashes on my pack or peeling the rind from fruit. Nevertheless, I managed to procure a handful of swords from a fellow merchant who I knew by reputation could acquire restricted blades and arranged to retrieve them on the day of the Passover feast.

On Thursday, in preparation for the Passover, Jesus sent Andrew and me into Jerusalem with specific instructions to get the meal ready. We were to enter the city, look for a man carrying a jar of water, follow him and at the home he entered say to the owner, "The teacher asks, 'Where is the room where my disciples and I may eat our Passover supper?'"

We followed our instructions exactly and, as usual, all happened as Jesus had said.

At the home, the owner showed us a large, beautifully furnished room. It was perfect.[1] Andrew and I spent the remainder of the day at the marketplace buying the food we needed for the Feast of Unleavened Bread. We also picked up the swords and hid them in a corner of the room so that, as Jesus had instructed, our master would find us ready and alert no matter if he came at evening, midnight or sunrise. His watchmen would not be asleep!

The Passover Seder supper was my favourite feast of the year, an event richly steeped in symbolism and poignant with significance; each taste and smell invoked memories of our forefathers and our deliverance from Egypt by Adonai's hand. The meal had a specific order that was followed faithfully each year and deliberately included children within its progression. I fondly remembered Jonathan, Mara, and later their own children, during the *Haggadah* or the telling, asking the four questions especially intended for them. 'Why is this night different from every other night?' 'Why do we eat only matzo tonight when usually we eat any kind of bread?' 'Why do we eat food spiced with bitter herbs on this night?' and 'Why tonight do we dip our food into salt water?' Parental instruction would follow as the story of Moses leading the Israelites out of Egypt was told. The bread reminded us that our ancestors' flight was quick—no time to wait for yeast bread to rise, the herbs spoke of the bitterness of their slavery and the salt water of their tears.

The meal also incorporated the joy of freedom, the anticipation of the promised land and the hope of the Messiah. At one point a piece of matzo was broken by the parents who then hid half of it in the house for the children to find after the *afikomen* or dessert. When the table was prepared for the feast, Elijah's cup was placed in the centre of the table as a symbol of hope for a saviour, for the holy scriptures said that Elijah would herald the coming of the Messiah. Four cups of wine were served throughout the meal, each symbolizing the four stages of the ancient exodus from Egypt: freedom, deliverance, redemption and release. Recitations, candles, smells, tastes and songs enriched each part of the meal. A final cup of wine ended the supper and words of hope were prayed in anticipation that perhaps next year, in Jerusalem, Israel would find its Messiah.

Since I had met Jesus, I had celebrated two other Seder suppers in Jerusalem. Yet those had been with my family who, of course, had also made the pilgrimage to the city for this sacred event. This feast, however, Jesus had requested be a private evening reserved and shared only with his closest friends, his apostles.

We arrived and chatted good-naturedly, relaxing around a short 'U' shaped table similar to the one we had eaten at the night Mary had anointed Jesus's feet with perfume. Our supper began by lighting the candles and reciting the *brachen*, the blessing to Adonai. Jesus poured the first cup of wine which symbolized freedom. We drank it together then performed the first of two ceremonial hand washings. Dipping parsley in salt water, we remembered the bitter tears of the Israelites before Moses led them in pursuit of the promised land. Next we ate *haroses*, a sweet mixture of apple, cinnamon, nuts and wine that was the colour of the brick mortar the slaves were forced to make yet boasted the wonderful flavour of anticipated hope. Jesus took the middle of three stacked matzo, split it in half and retold the story of Adonai's deliverance of His people through Moses. We drank the second cup of wine, the cup of deliverance.

Suddenly, a hush reached out to clasp a hand over my mouth, quieting me and my friends as we realized that Jesus had taken a towel and a basin of water and was washing Judas Iscariot's feet. Although the supper's progression dictated another ceremonial hand washing, I, along with the other apostles, gaped as our leader, knelt on the floor to quietly bathe Judas's feet and dry them with his towel. Then he moved to Thomas, Matthew, Philip and then to me.

Jesus knelt before me with his head lowered and gently lifted my feet into the cool water. It was disquieting, unnerving to have my esteemed Lord, the man I sought to place upon Israel's throne, the one whom I believed to be our Messiah, kneeling before me. He seemed to wear humility easily, like an old comfortable robe donned on a relaxing day. Though I had seen him serve people daily, Jesus's familiarity with servanthood did not sit well with me. I felt the rough cloth towel dry my feet.

Jesus moved on to Andrew. When he reached Peter, Peter tucked his feet beneath the hem of his tunic and, expressing what I was sure we had all been thinking, said with concern, "Lord, you will never, at any time, wash my feet."

"If I do not wash your feet you will no longer be my disciple," Jesus stated calmly.

After a moment of silence, Peter, ever loyal and quick thinking, replied passionately, "Then do not only wash my feet but my head and hands as well."

Jesus smiled at him, appreciative of the sentiment behind Peter's comment.

"I don't want to give you a bath, Peter!" Jesus chuckled.

We all laughed, grateful for the release from the tension created by Jesus's unusual behaviour. Continuing, Jesus said, "No, Peter, I am sure you are quite clean. You just need your feet washed. All of you are clean, all except one."[2]

His curious statement played in my mind as Jesus finished washing Peter's feet and moved on to James. Why would Jesus doubt any of his apostles? We had proven our commitment to him for years. I wondered if he was referring to the fears that had taunted me over the past few days. I swallowed hard, dreading that Jesus could be suspicious of my devotion to his kingdom.

After Jesus had knelt before each of his apostles, he stood at the opening of the 'U' shaped tables, focusing our attention on him.

"I am your Lord and teacher," he instructed, "and I have just washed your feet. I have set an example for you. I want you to do just as I have done for you. No slave is greater than his master, no messenger greater than the one who sent him. Put into practice what I have taught you."

Next in the order of the Seder was the eating of the matzo. Jesus walked to the plate of two whole and one broken matzo. He picked up the previously halved, flat, lumpy piece of bread, looked towards heaven and prayed, praising Adonai for His bread of freedom. Then he broke the piece into a quarter, looked at Judas who was at the furthest end of the table, handed him the quartered section and said, "Take it, this is my body."

Again, as he had done when he washed our feet, Jesus began to move about the table, giving the other quarter of matzo to Thomas while repeating the strange words. Three matzo are traditionally placed on the Seder table, Jesus quartered these and gave an equal portion to each of his twelve apostles.

As he picked up each piece of brittle bread, placing his thumb in the centre and splintering the square wafer, Jesus appeared more shaken as if inner strength was required to perform the simple act of breaking bread. I did not understand Jesus's variation of tradition or the torrent of emotion behind his actions but I guessed that it had to do with the closeness of his claim to the throne. When he handed me the matzo, telling me it was his body, I took it from him, unclear as to his meaning in the gesture but wanting to show that I meant to accept him as my king. It was my expression of loyalty.

Next we ate the main meal after which Jesus said another barach thanking Adonai for His provision, promise and the Seder supper.

It was time for the third cup of wine, the cup of redemption. Jesus picked up the wine skin but instead of filling our individual cups as he had done for the first two cups of wine, he walked to Elijah's cup at the centre of the table. A breath caught in my throat at the implication of what Jesus did next. This cup was traditionally left empty, waiting to be filled when the time for the Messiah had arrived. Jesus carefully poured the deep red wine into the cup, picked it up, faced us and said, "Drink from this cup, all of you, for this is My blood of the covenant, which is poured out for many for the forgiveness of sins."[3]

Just as with the matzo, he came to each of us and offered us the cup. My hand trembled as I reached out to accept it for I had never drunk from Elijah's cup. It symbolized a history of hope for our deliverer. Now Jesus offered me the cup to drink! Again he seemed to grow upset, his eyes about to spill tears, his tightened lips quivering now and then. By the time he took back the cup after the last apostle had drunk from it, his hand was shaking.

At last, mustering great fortitude, Jesus squared his shoulders decisively and said, "I will never again drink wine until it is given its true meaning in the Kingdom of God."

Now is the time! my mind whispered excitedly. Jesus was not even going to finish the Seder supper! After singing a hymn, the final order of the Seder was to drink the fourth cup of wine, the cup symbolizing our release, and express our hope that the Messiah would come the next year by saying, "Maybe next year in Jerusalem." Now Jesus had filled and offered Elijah's cup to us, declaring that no such sentiment was needed. Our Messiah had arrived. He would not drink the fourth and final cup at our Seder supper, not until Adonai's kingdom had come.

Jesus did, however, have something further to say.

"One of you is a betrayer!"

This accusation slapped me sharply. Fears from the past week flashed through my mind once again, muting the staunch allegiance I had just now felt when accepting the bread and wine from Jesus. *My apprehensions of the past few days are understandable, aren't they?* I inwardly defended myself, *Not tantamount to betrayal?*

"Not me, Lord!" Thomas's declaration rang through the room. "I would never betray you."

I joined my voice to the chorus of denials that immediately resounded around the table, desperate to silence any of my remaining inner doubts with a verbal affirmation. Jesus was about to become king. This room was full of friends who had lived, laughed and endured together for two-and-a-half years. We were brothers who had seen the glory of heaven. We had just pledged our fealty to Jesus by accepting the broken matzo and Elijah's cup. The immediate, insistent response of my friends eased the shock of Jesus's comment. How could one of us be a traitor working against comrades and our Lord? Surely Jesus was misinformed or overreacting because of all-too-human apprehensions.

"I am ready to die for you!" Peter blurted out in the midst of these proclamations. I smiled. Trust Peter to rise up and express what was in my heart.

"Oh, Peter," Jesus said with a sigh, placing his hand on Peter's shoulder and looking about the room of apostles, "Satan has received permission to test all of you as the farmer separates the wheat from the chaff."

His eyes settled on Peter as he continued.

"But I have prayed for you, Peter, that your faith will not fail. And when you turn back to me, you must strengthen your brothers."

Peter stared back at Jesus, wide-eyed with horror.

"Lord," Peter was adamant, "I am ready to go to prison with you. I would die for you!"

"I tell you, Peter," Jesus said, and his voice ached with sadness, "before the rooster crows, you will say three times that you do not know me." Peter hung his head, dejected and hurt that Jesus had not accepted his declaration of allegiance.[4]

Now I was sure that Jesus was misinformed, for Peter would never deny him.

"The one who takes this dipped bread will betray me," Jesus said. Then he took some bread that was left on the table and dipped it in Elijah's cup. As he pulled it from the cup, the wine dripped like blood. He offered it to Judas Iscariot.[5]

Their eyes met. I felt a terror, an awful horror invading the room. Evil itself crept among us. It was a terrifying bleakness, an absorbing blackness, a writhing hatred. A dark shadow moved across Judas's face, an expression so fleeting that I wondered if I had imagined it. Judas took the bread and stuffed it hungrily into his mouth, savouring the taste. Then he rose and left the room.

I did not understand anything that I had just seen or felt. Nothing made sense. The more I tried to sort through the significance of all that had just happened around me, the more muddled my thoughts became. In an evening I had traversed the peaks of devotion as well as the valley of doubt and disbelief. I felt exhausted, confused and longed not to think. Judas must be going to pay for the room, I reasoned, knowing this explanation made no sense for it was too late in the evening. How desperately I wanted some easy answers to my many unanswerable questions.

"When I sent you out last year," Jesus asked, ignoring Judas's abrupt departure and his apostles' obvious confusion, "without purse or bag or shoes, did you lack anything?"

"Not a thing," Matthew replied quickly.

"Well, this time," said Jesus, "whoever has a purse or a bag must take it. And whoever does not have a sword must sell his coat and buy one. I tell you, the scripture that says, 'He was included with the criminals,' will be true for me. For that which was written about me is coming true."

Completely baffled, my thoughts turned, folded and twisted on themselves, the only thing I felt certain of was that I wanted to please Jesus, to show him that he had my support. Running to the corner of the room where I had hidden the swords earlier in the day, I seized them in my hands and brandished them above my head, calling out triumphantly, "Look, here are two swords, Lord!"

"That is enough!" Jesus snapped, exasperated.[6]

I lowered the swords with a clang, slumped my shoulders and stared at my feet, discouraged. I felt deflated, completely at a loss as to what to think or do.

Jesus was still, as if gathering his patience, like a parent frustrated with his child's lack of understanding. I, in turn, felt like a child confused by his parent's irritation. Jesus's meaning sometimes seemed so far beyond my comprehension.

Inhaling deeply and closing his eyes for a moment, Jesus spoke, "Come, let's go for a walk."

We walked silently to the base of the Mount of Olives. Thomas and James, closest to me, looked as despondent as I felt. I could hear the shuffle of dragging feet from the apostles in front of me. The high hopes I had had for the Passover Feast had been replaced by confusion and disappointment.

Once in the public garden, Jesus gathered us around him in a tight circle, kneeling on the grass. We did the same. Then he began to pray for us, a beautiful prayer that I believe was his way of assuring and comforting us in our confusion and frustration.

"Father, the hour has come. Give glory to Your Son, that the Son may give glory to You. I have made You known to the men You gave me. They belonged to You, and You gave them to me. They have obeyed Your word, and now they know that everything You gave me comes from You. For I gave them the message that You gave me and they received it. They know that it is true, that I came from You, and they believe that You sent me."

Jesus's confidence comforted me.

"I pray for them. My glory is shown through them. And now I am coming to You. I am no longer in the world, but, they are in the world. O Holy Father! Keep them safe by the power of Your name, so that they may be one, just as You and I are one. While I was with them, I kept them safe by the power of Your name. I protected them and not one of them was lost, except the one man who was bound to be lost. I pray that they might have my joy in their hearts, in all its fullness."

A sense of peace descended upon our gathering, a feeling that One higher than us was in charge, fully capable of dealing with the turmoil both real and perceived in my mind. I need not worry, all was well.

"I gave them Your message," Jesus continued, turning his face to the dark sky, "and the world hated them, because they do not belong to the world, just as I do not belong to the world. I do not ask You to take them out of the world, but I do ask You to keep them safe from the Evil One. Make them Your own, by means of the truth, Your word is truth. I sent them into the world just as You sent me into the world. And for their sake I give myself to You, in order that they, too, may truly belong to You."

I felt a presence surround and enclose my circle of friends. So real was the feeling that I looked behind me into the blackness of the garden but saw nothing. It was not a feeling of foreboding or evil but rather an apprehensive fear that we were watched and guarded by invisible beings.

"I do not pray only for them, but also for those who believe in me because of their message. I pray that they may all be one. O Father! May they be one in us, just as You are in me and I am in You. May they be one, so that the world will believe that You sent me. May they be completely one, in order that the world may know that You sent me and that You love them as You love me."

The churning, twisted emotions that had tormented me earlier in the evening flowed from my mind, Jesus's prayer blessed me with a calmness impossible to grant through simple recitation of the right words. I felt touched by Adonai.

"O Father! I want the ones You have given me to be with me where I am, so that they may see my glory. You loved me before the world was made, O righteous Father! The world does not know You, but I know You, and these know that You sent me. I made You known to them and I will continue to do so, in order that the love You have for me may be in them, and I may be in them."[7]

Jesus's prayer stripped me of the fretting and rationalizing of the past week and refocused me again on Adonai, His love and intervention in all our plans. At the completion of Jesus's prayer of protection and blessing, he asked us to stay and pray in the garden while he, Peter, James and John went on to a more secluded area to pray.

It was late. With the quiet of the night, the coolness of the grass and Jesus's gift of peace, it was not long before I heard the measured deep breathing of my friends. Soon I was dozing as well.

Pounding footsteps awakened me. Disoriented, I looked around trying to remember where I was. Why I was on the ground? Before I realized what was happening, men with torches and lanterns were upon us. There were so many! One grabbed me roughly and yanked me to my feet by my hair. They appeared to be a hastily assembled, disorganized group wielding clubs and swords yet, with the element of surprise and the dark of night on their side, they used their advantages well. These men were rabble rousers, a number of temple guards, Jewish soldiers used by the priests and Pharisees for minor skirmishes, and a few angry civilians.

Each of us apostles, who only hours before had pledged our loyalty to stand and fight for Jesus, was now easily captured. I was both scared and ashamed as the mob dragged us over to where Jesus had gone to pray.

Jesus emerged from the trees to meet the ragtag group of men.

Judas Iscariot stepped out of the group and approached Jesus. In the erratic shadows of the flickering torches I saw Judas clutching a little pouch. Coins clinked with each footstep.

"Teacher," he said, sarcasm dripping from the words, a sneer playing on his lips. He stood inches from Jesus then leaned towards him to kiss his cheek.

"Is it with a kiss, Judas, that you betray the Son of Man?" asked Jesus.[8] He looked deep into Judas's eyes and it again seemed as if a shadow passed over Judas's face. Horror replaced Judas's dark, forbidding expression.

Jesus stood before the crowd, valiant and resolute.

"Who are you looking for?" he asked, back straight with strength and courage.

"Jesus of Nazareth," the chief soldier said gruffly, advancing with a menacing grimace.

"I am he," Jesus said.

A force like a strong wind swept out of nowhere into the group. They released their grip on us and fell back. Then the wind was gone, leaving the soldiers confused, wondering what to do next.

Jesus asked them again, a little louder this time, "Who are you looking for?"

"Jesus of Nazareth."

"I have told you, I am he."

I looked at my friends for a clue as to our next action. Peter was edgy and alert, looking for a chance to help Jesus escape. As soon as Jesus asked a second time 'Who are you looking for,' I saw Peter dig in his feet, planting them to steady himself. Then, when Jesus said 'I am he,' steel flashed from Peter's robe. It was so fast. So decisive. The adrenaline surged in my veins. *Yes, Peter!* I thought, and I prepared to fight, too. The guard beside Peter howled in pain and groped at the side of his head where his ear hung by a thread of flesh. Blood dripped from Peter's sword. Jesus's apostles turned to attack.

"Put your sword away!" Jesus yelled.

His command halted us. We waited, ready for his orders, for our leader's next directive.

But Jesus walked to Peter and admonished him softly, "Do you not think that I will drink the cup of suffering that my Father has given me?"

Jesus reached out to the man writhing and whimpering on the ground. He took the man's limp ear in his hand, held it to the bloody wound and ran a gentle finger from the top of the cut to the bottom, reattaching and mending the ear with his touch. When Jesus removed his hand it was wet with blood. The man's ear was perfect again.[9]

The head soldier stepped forward and tied Jesus's hands behind his back. Just like that, calmly and serenely, our Lord was arrested.

"Now, you have me. Let these other men go," demanded Jesus.

A holy terror filled my soul. I had to run and I did. We all did. I ran as if I was chased by evil itself and fled, screaming, into the night.

chapter eighteen

ran and ran, going nowhere in particular, just away. I was a leaf caught in the surge of water rapids, racing, bumping, slapping and careening past rocks in a mad panic to reach the bottom. I ran from a vile wickedness that seemed to be everywhere, powerful and controlling. It felt as if a trumpet had blown and a large star, burning like a torch, had dropped from the sky to seek destruction burning. It turned purity bitter. It poured hail and fire mixed with blood and burned all it touched. It burned the trees and every blade of green grass. It blotted out the moon and the stars, stealing their brightness.

I covered my head with my arms, thinking I heard an eagle flying high in the air and screeching in a loud voice, "Oh horror! Horror! How horrible it is for all those who live on the earth!"[1]

The abyss had been opened, its doors flung wide. Smoke poured from it as if from a large furnace, smoke so thick it could make the sunlight dark.

Unable to go any further, I collapsed, lying on my back and sucked great gulps of air into my burning lungs. My side ached and my throbbing head felt like it was about to explode. After several minutes I caught my breath, my sanity slowly returned and I began to think clearly again.

I had to find safety, some place to figure out what to do next. The safest place I could think of was Lazarus's home. Bethany was close and I could confer with Lazarus, he would help me, of that I was sure.

Getting my bearings, I realized I was not that far from Bethany. Without thinking I had run in the right direction. It was the middle of the night when I rapped on the familiar door of my friends.

Lazarus came to the door, disheveled from sleep. Quickly assessing my distraught state, he ushered me in, sat me on the closest bench and got me some cool water.

"What has happened?" he asked urgently as he sat down next to me.

I gave him a quick synopsis of the evening's terror.

There was a sharp knock at the door. Lazarus told me to hide behind the cistern while he went to see who else had arrived this late at night. It was Andrew.

Lazarus pulled him into the courtyard. I ran from my hiding place to throw my arms around Andrew, ecstatic to see him safe. Over the next hour, three more apostles arrived: James, Matthew and Thomas. Mary and Martha woke and prepared some food for us, all the while peppering us with questions.

Lazarus was a blessing sent by Adonai. He listened to our accounts, sympathized with our fears and asked questions about Jesus's abductors, nodding patiently and making sense of our garbled story.

"This is what I propose," Lazarus counseled at last. "From all you have told me, these soldier were all Jewish, the Roman legions were not involved. So there may still be something we can do. We all know that our religious leaders have wanted to kill Jesus for some time. But they can't get rid of anyone without proper authority and they will have to take him to Pilate. Pilate sets one Jewish prisoner free at each Passover feast so we will go to the assembly and call to Pilate for Jesus's freedom."

It sounded like it could work.

Lazarus continued, "Rest for an hour while I get some things ready and gather some people who I know are loyal to Jesus. Then we will head back to Jerusalem."

I sat on a bench in the garden for a few moments before deciding that a walk would do me more good. The night was almost over yet the full moon provided enough light to find the stream I was looking for— the stream where Jesus had confronted me over a year ago after my sleepless night of contemplation as to why I had followed him in the first place. I dangled my feet in the cool water, recalling my anger with Jesus and my rediscovered first love. I remembered his hand on my shoulder, his ready forgiveness.

"Judas!"

Startled to hear my name, I had a momentary thought that Jesus had done the miraculous again. That he was here to forgive me once more.

"Yes?" I turned expectantly.

"Judas, help me," the voice pleaded.

It was the other Judas. The traitor.

His face was red and puffy, the internal torment obvious. I almost felt sorry for him. Almost.

I shoved him, hard. He fell backwards into the grass to cower in a heap.

"You! You betrayer!" I accused.

"I know, I know," he moaned. He looked pathetic.

"How different my kingdom is from that of the world's," I heard a voice softly speak in my mind, Jesus's words whispered from the past. *"In my kingdom, past transgressions and present status will not preclude anyone. You will find sinners behind every door. The common bond that will hold them together is that they embrace forgiveness. I want each of these people to feel love and to know Godly forgiveness. I have set an example for you. I want you to do just as I have done for you."*

With great effort, I forced myself to look at Judas and squeeze the smallest drop of sympathy from my soul for Jesus's sake, his sake alone.

Judas sobbed.

"I tried," he babbled. "I took the silver back to the chief priest and the elders but they wouldn't take it. I told them that I had sinned by betraying an innocent man to death but they said they didn't care, that it was my business, not theirs."[2]

Sickened by his confession, I asked in disgust, "How much did you sell our king for?"

"Thirty pieces of silver," he answered, unable to look at me. Then, as if to vindicate himself, he raised his head to add, "But I threw the money at them. I don't have it anymore."

"Why?" I spat at him. "Why would you betray a man like Jesus?"

"I don't know!" he cried. "I first went to them after Mary anointed Jesus a few days ago. I was so angry that Jesus had sided with her against me. He has never appreciated me, never acknowledged my contribution. Jesus was out of control, off course. It was embarrassing …the people he was associating with…I had to do something."

His words sounded too familiar and mirrored my reprimand of Jesus the year before. I softened slightly, sadly realizing how similar Judas and I were beyond the name we shared.

"Help us find a way to rescue Jesus so you can ask him to forgive you," I counseled, surprising even myself with this suggestion.

Judas's face went white, his mouth fell open.

"No, I can't!" he said in shame and horror. "Jesus would never forgive me. I can't face him!"

"He will. I'm sure he will, if you want him to," I said more confidently, remembering the compassion Jesus had demonstrated for people living in sin.

"No, no. It is impossible. I can't do it. What I've done is too evil, too bad. He would never forgive me."

Judas turned away from me and left. He had refused to seek Jesus's mercy. I never saw him again.

chapter nineteen

my mind was a torrent of thoughts as I walked back to Bethany. How could all our plans change so suddenly? How could life be so out of control? When I arrived back at Lazarus's door and saw the group of about twenty people assembled, a spark of joy lit within me; at least there are some willing to try to salvage the situation and right this disaster. Perhaps all hope was not yet gone. With the sky lightening behind us we set off for Jerusalem.

The crowd in Pilate's courtyard was small, probably only about a hundred and fifty or so, for many of Jerusalem's visitors and residents were not even moving about the city yet. Our group of supporters was meagre due to the betrayal by one of our own group, so Lazarus had suggested we be cautious about sharing our plans for Jesus's release. I agreed with his reasoning.

We had decided that our best option was to disperse among the crowd to seek fellow supporters. Mingling with the throng, I soon saw some of the apostles as well as a few disciples who had often traveled with Jesus. Each one I approached greeted me with a broad grin and a look of relief. As I quickly shared Lazarus's plan in hushed tones they nodded enthusiastically and scanned the field of faces for more allies. Moving on I noticed Bartholomew standing in the corner of the courtyard. I wove my way through the crowd towards him. He looked like he was trying to remain inconspicuous, pushing his body against the stone wall behind him. When he saw me, the weariness in his eyes lessened though he sighed heavily and his shoulders dropped slightly as if the taut rope holding his muscles had slackened.

"Where have you been?" he blurted.

"I went back to Bethany, I've been with Lazarus," I explained, a bit defensively. "Where have you been?"

"I have been following Jesus. I watched them bring him here," he said, less abruptly than before. Then, after looking to the left and right, he leaned closer to me to whisper, " You see those priests over there?" He motioned to some austere-looking men waiting outside the gates of Pilate's palace. I nodded.

"They refused to go into the palace with Jesus because they wanted to keep themselves ritually clean for the Passover.[1] I heard them arguing with Pilate myself. Can you believe their gall? Getting Pilate to do their dirty work," he shook his head.

"Getting Pilate to do their work may be our saving grace," I answered, then told him of Lazarus's scheme. Bartholomew, grateful for something to do, followed me to where our friends where waiting.

There was movement on a balcony about ten feet above me. Four guards marched stiffly onto the parapet followed by Pilate, who was ornately decorated for this stately address.

"Greetings, good citizens of Jerusalem. On behalf of Rome, I welcome you." His voice boomed easily across the throng of people, expressing his comfort in his position as the representative of the ruling government.

"As is my custom, I offer you a gift," he continued, his over-exaggerated motions trained and polished for dramatic effect. "I shall release one of your prisoners to you as a symbol of good will during your Passover celebration. Just this morning, your chief priests brought to me Jesus of Nazareth." With a sweeping arc of his arm, Pilate directed our attention to the door leading to his balcony. I held my breath.

Jesus stepped out of the palace onto the parapet. My stomach lurched and a lump stuck in my throat. *My precious Lord. What have they done to you?*

He wore a torn and faded purple robe, a blatant mockery of his claim to the throne. His hands, barely visible beneath the fringed sleeves, were chained together. One side of his lip was fat; blood leaked from the corner of his mouth. As he slowly turned his distended face to look directly at the crowd, I saw that one of his eyes was swollen shut. He scanned the crowd. I wondered if he hoped to see at least one friend.

"Shall I release your King of the Jews?" Pilate called out magnanimously to the crowd.

This was what we had hoped for, yet the sight of Jesus was so shocking that I just stared up at the balcony completely missing the cue I had been anticipating. Jesus's accusers, however, knowing this was their chance also, attacked vigorously in the lull we afforded them.

"Barabbas! We want Barabbas released!" a few yelled and others quickly took up the cry. Better organized than we were, the courtyard was full of the chant within seconds. I, along with those standing close to me, began to yell frantically for Jesus to be released but our efforts were drowned by Barabbas's name.

For the first time since his speech began, Pilate looked nervous. He stepped forward to place his hands on the balcony railing and leaned towards the crowd. "B-but I can find no reason to condemn this man," he said, giving what sounded like an impromptu plea. "I have sent him to Herod and he also can find nothing wrong in what he has done. He does not deserve death!"

"Kill him!" the mob yelled back.

As more calls for death resounded and the crowd's rant built in intensity, Pilate's eyes jumped from man to man below him, his hands making tiny circles as they nervously rubbed his outer cloak.

"I will have him whipped," Pilate bellowed over the frenzy— probably hoping a little blood would placate those calling for this innocent man's death. "Guards!" he barked, motioning the soldiers to come and take Jesus.

The soldiers pulled Jesus from the balcony to reemerge a few minutes later in the courtyard amidst the jeering throng. Armed men cleared a path to the centre of the yard while four soldiers escorted Jesus to a pole protruding about seven feet out of the ground. One soldier yanked the chain binding Jesus's hands upward and hooked it into a ring near the top of the pole. Everyone backed up. A guard carrying a whip entered the arena to stand behind Jesus. Long black leather strips studded with sharp pieces of broken glass lay on the ground like huge talons ready to claw and tear at the flesh of Jesus's now bare back.

The whip cut the air and cut my Lord's skin. Jesus grimaced silently as the pain raked down his body. It cracked again, again and again. Jesus's wounds lay open, blood poured freely. The strips of skin were torn and ripped, lacerated and shred, until the leather dripped in blood. Nine, ten, eleven. His bone was exposed white. Still the guard snapped the lash.

Thirteen. Fourteen. Fifteen. Sixteen. The crowd began to count with the soldier, jeering and sneering at Jesus. "Twenty-two, twenty-three." Men's voices undulated with glee at the rhythm of the lashes, savouring Jesus's pain, reveling in his torture.

"Twenty-nine, thirty, thirty-one."

Jesus sagged against the pole, his legs buckling under the pain as he hung by the chains, limp and lifeless. The ground beneath him was stained brown with blood. His body now flung out with each blow for there was no resistance left; a dead leaf clinging to a tree limb wracked by the wind.

"Thirty-seven, thirty-eight, thirty-nine, forty!" the crowd yelled the fortieth count the loudest.

The lashes seemed to last an eternity. Tears ran unhindered down my face as I watched the methodical torture of a man who had only ever loved his fellow men. Jesus did not say a word during the entire beating.

When the crack of the whip stopped so did the jubilance of the crowd. It was suddenly quiet. Jesus moaned and coughed, blood flowed from his mouth, his teeth were crimson.

The bile stuck in my throat. I swallowed it down and nearly choked.

My Lord. My King.

Oh, my dear, dear friend.

As the guards came jerking the chains which held Jesus to the pole in order to release him, a whimper escaped his lips. The tension of the chain was released and Jesus fell to the ground. With great determination, he forced himself to his hands and knees and then to a standing position. Surrounded by soldiers, Jesus looked straight ahead and turned to walk back towards the entrance of the palace pushing his feet forward as though willing composure back into his body. After ten paces, Jesus's legs buckled again and he fell to the ground, hard.

"Get up!" a soldier beside him yelled and booted Jesus mercilessly in the stomach. The sickening 'thunk' of the guard's foot into Jesus's belly echoed awkwardly in the silence.

Slowly, painstakingly, Jesus brought himself upright, straightened his shoulders and continued his hobbled walk until he and his armed guard disappeared into the palace. I looked around for a friend, anyone with whom to share my horror.

A few feet away I saw Lazarus holding his sisters, the women's bodies shaking with sobs and Lazarus's head buried in their hair. Bartholomew had returned to the wall where I had found him earlier. He looked as if he wished the stones would surround and swallow him. Nearby, Matthew, was white-faced, encapsulated by fear. Magdala appeared, unmoving, as the crowd shifted around her. I immediately remembered her prophetic words: that our struggle was not with world powers or rulers but with evil itself. I wondered if she questioned the power that Jesus had over this unseen dominion. Philip joined me, looking angry, his eyes narrowed, his brows furrowed. Within the faces of my comrades I did not see a longing to establish a kingdom or crown a king—only friends who desired above all to have their friend free from pain.

Pilate again took centre stage on the balcony, having regained his confidence and composure, and triumphantly proclaimed, "Behold, Your king!"

Jesus staggered out to join Pilate. A crown of thorns, a wiry branch of two-inch spikes protruding in every direction, had been placed upon his head. It sat off centre, many of the thorns had embedded themselves into his forehead. Someone had hit him in the head as he wore it. The mock royal purple robe was now drenched in blood, scarcely a thread of cloth not stuck to his body with it. His disfigured, distorted face was barely recognizable. Jesus's anguish and agony were laid bare, as exposed as the bones and blood on his back had been during his whipping.

My very heart and soul wept.

"Kill him! Kill him! Nail him to the cross!" The chants from the crowd began again almost instantly. Those who had never been touched by Jesus's compassion were now incited; the dark side of human nature, that ugly part of each of us that we struggle to keep hidden, had awakened, smelled blood and craved more.

"Do you want me to nail your king to the cross?" Pilate asked, deflated. I think he had hoped that Jesus's mangled body would have drawn more compassion and appeased the bloodthirsty mob.

A chief priest, having found a small niche in the palace wall to stand in, called the attention of the rabble. He spoke in a clear voice for all to hear.

"We have no king but the Emperor!"

A look of surprise and then anger registered on Pilate's face. The priest had essentially declared that he was more loyal to Rome than Pilate. It was Pilate who had referred to Jesus as the King of the Jews, who had asked the crowd to vindicate Jesus and now a Jew, not a Roman, stated that Rome was the true authority.

"Fine!" Pilate spat. "Bring me a basin of water."

A large, intricately engraved clay bowl was brought and placed on the railing of the balcony. With great ceremony and exaggerated movements, Pilate washed and dried his hands then declared, "I am not responsible for the death of this man. This is your doing."

The priest, still standing smugly on his elevated platform, nodded his agreement. "Let the punishment for his death fall on us and our children."[2]

chapter twenty

oman guards escorted Jesus off the balcony, out of the courtyard and into a nearby barracks while the crowd that had witnessed the morning's events waited. Moments later Jesus emerged carrying the horizontal beam of his cross. I stared, stunned.

How could this be happening? It was nine in the morning. Yesterday at this time I had been bustling about preparing for our Passover supper. How could one day alter my world so completely? How could just one day transform years of planning and wonder into nothing but smoke and ash? It seemed impossible, a nightmare from which I desperately needed to wake.

I followed the mass of people and listened to the jeers of the throng ahead of me, feeling helpless and alone. I followed because I had to; Jesus was my friend.

Soldiers flanked Jesus as they climbed the hill of Golgotha, the Place of the Skull. I stood at the bottom of the hill and shivered despite the heat of the morning sun. I needed to be a witness, to attest to this atrocity, yet I could not bear to go any closer.

The plank was laid on the ground. Jesus was shoved onto the wood, his arms stretched across it.

CLANG!

The sickening, reverberating sound of metal striking metal, echoed through the early morning.

CLANG! CLANG!

Jesus cried out in pain with each thrust and jolt of the stake into his wrist.

The soldier moved to Jesus's other hand.

CLANG!

The metallic sound rang out again.

A rope, looped around the crossbeam that held Jesus's tattered hands, was strung through a pulley system on the top of a plank stuck vertically in the ground. With jerks and yanks, Jesus was hoisted up the vertical board until the horizontal beam was dropped into a bracket to hold it in place. The two pieces of wood met to form a cross. I heard Jesus groan with each wrench as the beam lurched into place. My heart fell deeper.

CLANG! CLANG! CLANG!

The guard pounded a stake into Jesus's feet.

Then began Jesus's grind for life. He pushed on his feet to raise his chest above the level of his arms, rasping deeply as he sucked air into his lungs. Then he fell awkwardly on the stakes which pinned him, excruciating pain etched into his now hideous face. Up and down he pulsed at the demand of his lungs as life itself refused to surrender. All his focus, all his concentration, was devoted to controlling the pain as his body, becoming his curse and tormentor, fell victim to its own convulsive instinct for survival.

On and on it went. When would this hell end?

I sat at the bottom of the hill, out of sight, with my head in my hands rocking, weeping.

Faintly, I heard Jesus's voice. Although I could not make out what he said, I saw that he was speaking to John. Jesus's mother was there, too. It was nauseating to watch Jesus take the three or four excruciating gasps of air necessary for speech. Jesus's mother moaned and begged Jesus to stop wasting his valuable air but Jesus was determined to be heard.

The soldiers crucified two criminals on either side of Jesus. The men on the other crosses screamed and writhed at the pain. One criminal called down curses upon the soldiers, damning them to the abyss. I hung my head, clapping my hands over my ears to stop their shrieks.

The soldiers placed a ladder against Jesus's cross. One of them ascended it and hammered a paper into place above Jesus's head. I squinted to read it.

It said: KING OF THE JEWS.

It was written in Hebrew, Greek and Latin, in every common language so that all men could see the fate of our king.[1]

I thought of the countless times I had rehearsed how we would usher Jesus into his kingdom. Now he struggled to live upon our world's most despicable symbol of death. Was it only six days ago that we danced in the street, blessing our Lord?

Two men with their families walked along the road at the bottom of the hill. They stopped to gaze up at the men who hung on the crosses above them.

"Look, Gabriel," one man motioned to the other, pointing to the paper above Jesus's head, "that sign says, 'King of the Jews'! Isn't that Jesus of Nazareth? You know, the one that all of the commotion was about this week?"

Gabriel looked intently at the man hanging on the middle cross.

"Yes, that's him all right," confirmed the man called Gabriel, sounding shocked then scowling.

"I thought he was supposed to be a powerful man," said a woman who stood beside the first man.

"I saw him perform that miracle in Cana," said another woman, taking a step closer to Jesus and studying him. "Remember, I told you about it."

"Oh, Mary," said Gabriel condescendingly, "I told you then that he was a fraud and now look at him. Everyone can see him for what he truly is, a deceiver and a liar."

"Come children," he continued, pulling his offspring forward to stand beside him and their mother, "see how Adonai punishes conniving impostors." The three boys obeyed reluctantly, regarded Jesus briefly then, shaken, turned into their mother's mantle.

Their mother, as though wanting to salvage something from the heinous lesson said, "That shows you how holy Adonai is, children. That," she said, suddenly angry and irritated as she pointed at Jesus, "is

Adonai's judgment for such a sinner. Now you know why we must go each year to the temple to make our sacrifices." This woman who had witnessed Jesus heal glared up at the cross then spat on the ground.

"A curse on you, you liar," she yelled up the hill, shaking her fist. "I thought you were real. What a fool I was. But now you are getting what you deserve. Go to Hades where you belong!"

Turning their backs, the families continued on to Jerusalem.

I did not hate that woman for her outburst. It frightened me but I understood her anger; her contempt for Jesus far outweighed that of her traveling companions for she had dared to hope in him, dared to believe.

As the group shrank into the distance, I thought about the woman's reference to the temple sacrifices. Oh, how Jesus's bloodied body looked like an atonement lamb. Each year at Passover, I chose a lamb for my offering. He had to be perfect—without blemish or flaw—for that was Adonai's demand. I would lead him silently to the altar and place my hand on his head as a symbol of the transference of my sins to him, an acknowledgment that he died for me. The lamb was then slain, blood flowing from the sacrifice's fatal wound. Blood was everywhere, sprinkled on the four corners of the altar and pouring down the front of the structure.

This ritual was our blatant confirmation of Adonai's abhorrence of sin. A vivid portrait of His purity and perfection painted on the waiting backdrop of our need for reconciliation. Were justice genuine, it would be me dying on the altar for so holy is Adonai and so sinful His creation.

The sacrifice was also Adonai's provision, the way He could again commune freely with us. This means by which sinful man could coexist with perfection was an astounding sentiment, a testimony to Adonai's desire to be near to us.[2]

I looked at Jesus's gaping wounds, his flayed body and the flowing blood, the symbol of Adonai's crimson pathway of connection between corrupt man and his flawless Creator.

A Pharisee walked by laughing and taunting Jesus. "You were so quick to save everyone else," he yelled. "Let Adonai rescue and deliver you if He delights in you so much. Come down off that cross if you are so powerful!"[3]

The Pharisee waited, his chin jutted towards Jesus, daring him to accept the challenge.

"Ha! I thought not. You're nothing but a swindler."

Jesus said nothing in his own defense. A silent lamb led to slaughter.[4]

I prayed to Adonai, imploring Him for the sake of my Lord.

My God, my God, why are you so far from saving your dear servant, Jesus? Why are you so far from his groaning? Can you not hear him crying out? Why are you silent? Jesus is scorned by men, despised. All who see him, mock him, hurl insults and shake their heads. Oh, God, take notice of your servant, your chosen one. Oh, God, have mercy. He is poured out like water. His heart has turned to wax and is melting away. His strength is dried up like a potsherd and his tongue sticks to the roof of his mouth. He is laid in the dust of death. A band of evil men have encircled him, they have pierced his hands and feet. People stare and gloat over him. They are dividing up his garments and casting lots for his clothes. He is despised and forsaken, a man of sorrows, acquainted with grief. God, why is he stricken? Why have you crushed him? Why do you punish him? Why is he afflicted? Smitten? Wounded?

My God, do not let his enemies rejoice over him. Heal him. Have pity, oh God. Bring his soul up from Sheol. Make him alive, please. Do not let him go down to the pit. Hear, O Lord, and be gracious to him. O Lord, be his helper. Turn his mourning to dancing. Be his rescuer, his deliverer. Amen.[5]

How many miracles had I seen during the past few years? Was this too hard for God to accomplish? Had I not learned that I just needed faith enough?

I hoped. I believed. I prayed.

But Adonai was silent. Jesus bore his pain alone for Adonai had hidden His face and forsaken him. I was asea in an endlessly pulsing tide as the minutes turned to hours and Jesus rose and fell, nailed to his cross, bearing his burden.

It seemed as though he carried more than physical pain, as if his very soul despaired as he became ever more alone in the knowledge that Adonai had taken His hand from him. How can a man who has known Adonai's favour bear such a thing? Darkness seemed to overwhelm him, the light became night around him for Jesus was deserted. Adonai, who had enclosed His servant behind and before, who had laid His hand upon him, was gone. It was as if Jesus shouldered hopelessness itself, a life without Adonai where he knew only God's reproach and rejection.[6]

For three excruciating hours I sat at the bottom of the hill unseen by passersby, unseen by my Lord and friend. I prayed without courage or faith, was vigilant but did nothing to show my support or align myself to him.

At noon, after a morning of harsh, unforgiving, hot sun, everything changed. The sky began to darken ominously, as though someone pulled a black curtain over the world's bright window.[7] Intimidating fear of the judgment Adonai must be about to dispense through nature began to encroach upon my sadness. Despite my pleas to Adonai, He was turning His back on His chosen king. I remembered the story of Moses asking to see Adonai's glory then hiding in a cleft of a rock when the unbearable brilliance passed by.[8] That same shining favour which had been bestowed on Jesus's ministry was now denied as Adonai's shining countenance went black.

I could stand it no longer. Ashamed, not man enough to stay and endure Jesus's torment, I, too, turned away.

A few steps away from me I saw Magdala straight and tall as she faced the three crosses, the wind whipping her hair about her face, unbidden tears streaking her face. I looked down and walked aimlessly away. Never had I felt such despair, such utter hopelessness. All was pointless. Nothing mattered. A shiver shook my body as I thought I heard a gruesome laugh, a malicious taunting behind me.

Depravity has conquered, the voice rasped. *Blasphemy is victorious. Lies prevail.*

I knew it was true. Evil's dominion held triumphant control, drunk with power. Love hung crucified, dying. Goodness and purity were bloodied and wretched. Truth groaned in anguish.

I walked in the unnatural darkness back towards Bethany, then decided instead to wait at my favourite stream for my companions to return to Lazarus's home. My thoughts wandered unfettered over the past eighteen hours processing nothing, just flashing images of grieving friends, incensed accusers and impossible events. Reaching the water, I sat and listened to the gurgling stream, wishing to be washed away, not wanting to think ever again.

I lay on my back, closed my eyes and eventually fell into a fitful sleep. Sometime during my rest the sun must have returned for when I awoke the sky was bright again. Judging by its position I had a few hours before evening, time enough to prepare for the Passover Sabbath, our most holy of Sabbaths in the calendar year.

At Lazarus's home every bench and cushion was filled with deflated, downcast friends. Reassured by our mutual sorrow and grief, knowing that at least I wasn't alone, I found a spot beside the wall where I sank to the floor to just listen and rest in our mutual melancholy.

"Did you hear the criminals on the crosses beside him?" asked James of Martha.

"Yes," she replied. "The one mocked Jesus but the other defended him. Then the one who defended Jesus asked him to remember him when Jesus came as King. Jesus said that today he would be with him in paradise. It was such a strange thing to say. What do you think he meant?"[9]

James shrugged, rubbing his forehead tiredly. "They were probably just delusional from blood loss. I just hated to see him say anything. It was horrible to watch."

"At least they didn't break his legs," Lazarus was saying in another corner to Thomas. "How could I have borne to watch that?" He added, "But then, how can we bear any of this? When the soldier pierced

Jesus's side he was already dead. The soldier went to the two criminals and struck their legs.[10] Their bones broke right through the skin. Oh, the ugliness we have seen today," he shook his head.

"Where was Jesus buried?" asked Thomas.

"Joseph from Aramathea went to Pilate asking if Jesus could be buried in Joseph's own tomb.[11] Pilate agreed," Lazarus informed him. Thomas nodded absently in acknowledgment.

I shut my eyes and let the drone of voices carry me, trying hard not to focus on what they were saying. After a few hours I excused myself, hoping a walk in the cool evening would better distract me. Eventually, I found myself at the Mount of Olives, the last place I had spoken with Jesus. Had it only been twenty-four hours earlier that Jesus had prayed for us and asked us to pray with him?

I heard weeping. Creeping closer I saw a man kneeling in the grass where Jesus had prayed the night before. As I approached I realized it was Peter.

"Peter," I said, quietly.

He jumped, startled.

"Judas?" he asked in a whisper, his eyes widening in recognition.

I nodded dropping down on the cool grass to face him. Peter stared at the ground and said nothing.

"How long have you been here?" I asked into the uncomfortable silence between us.

"Hours, I suppose. Does it really matter?" he paused. "Does anything matter?"

"I haven't seen you all day, were you at the sentencing?"

"I was everywhere…but I was a coward. Jesus knew it all along. He knew that I would have no courage, that I would deny him."

"What are you talking about?" I asked, disturbed by this self-deprecation.

"Jesus said that I would deny him three times. And I did."

I waited for him to elaborate.

"I was in the courtyard and a servant girl recognized me," he stopped, glaring at me before continuing in exasperation. "She was a wisp of a girl and a servant, no less! Not even anyone of authority! And I denied my Lord to her. Then a little later, I did it again. And before dawn someone else recognized me and I cursed Jesus a third time and swore that I did not know the man they were talking about. Just then the gates of the courtyard opened and the guards led Jesus out of the palace. I think someone said that they were taking him to see Herod. It doesn't matter because when he walked out he looked right at me." Shakily he sucked in some air in an attempt to control his emotions. "Oh, Judas! How can I live the rest of my life with that image burned into my mind? He looked sad and yet resolute. I remembered what he had said to me at the Seder supper. I knew that he was remembering the same thing. Then a cock crowed."[12] Peter looked past me blankly.

I couldn't believe it. Peter, our staunchest apostle, had betrayed Jesus as well. My kinship with Peter never felt stronger. It had been a day of betrayals. Judas Iscariot had turned his back on Jesus, Jesus had turned his back on his claim to the throne and Adonai had turned His face from Jesus. What was one more denial?

I pulled my knees to my chest and wrapped my arms around them to hug my body.

"It was all so fast," I mumbled, ignoring his confession. "I suppose it was the only way that his adversaries knew that they could ever accomplish it. Twenty-four hours ago we were praying in this garden, yet Jesus was tried before the sun rose on this day. At dawn Pilate offered to free him but by nine in the morning, before the Passover travelers had even risen for the day, Jesus was hung from a cross." I shook my head in wonderment. "How could we be so blind? So disorganized? They won so easily and now Jesus is dead."

Peter and I sat in silence.

"We all failed him, Peter," I said. "We knew this day would come. How many times did Jesus talk about it and predict conflict? And now in one day Jesus's kingship has been stolen away. In one day they have taken the greatest hope this world has ever known. In one day we have lost our dearest friend. And we let it happen. None of us did a thing to stop it. Not one of us lifted a finger or said a word in his defense. We are all guilty."

Finally, Peter took a deep breath. "You are right, Judas, we are all hurting. I have been thinking too much of myself. Tomorrow after synagogue we should all meet together here. We can remember our dear Lord and console one another. Spread the word. Tell everyone you see at the service tomorrow. But," he added, "be discreet. We do not want our enemies to know."

The time with Jesus's disciples and friends that Sabbath afternoon began as a Godsend. We laughed and cried together, relating stories and sharing what Jesus had meant to us. Jesus's mother was there. She talked about Jesus's birth and childhood, told about him getting lost in Jerusalem one Passover only to find him in the temple days later.[13] We recounted miracles that had astounded us, caring acts that had moved us and revolutionary words that had changed us.

As evening descended, however, I realized that my grief was beyond that of losing a friend. I had lost my hope as well for I had been convinced that Jesus was the Messiah, my bright future and promise in whom I had invested all my faith.

But I was wrong!

Now there was nowhere to turn for even my judgments were unreliable. Jesus's death had destroyed my beliefs, taken my confidence and made my own discernment treacherous. How could I ever trust myself again? What a fool. How could I be so easily duped? I had given up money, my livelihood and sacrificed time with my family. I had been sure, absolutely positive that my decisions were right.

Now all was lost, I had nowhere to go and I was certain of nothing. What was the point of eating and living when purpose was dead? Worst of all it was hopeless to look for direction again because I could not trust myself to know the truth.

chapter twenty-one

I spent the night with the other apostles and disciples camped outside of Jerusalem. As the sun pinked the sky and people began to stir around camp, I noticed Magdala beside the furthest tent in an animated discussion with Peter and John, her arms moving in large arcs as they conversed. The two men seemed agitated as she spoke and soon ran off in the direction of Jesus's tomb, Magdala following behind.

The day before, Magdala, Joanna, Mary, and James's mother had anxiously waited for the Sabbath to end so that they could prepare the burial spices to anoint Jesus's body. They had wanted to perform this final act of love for him early this morning. There must have been some problem with the stone at Jesus's tomb or perhaps with the guards, I thought. Confident that Peter and John were capable of dealing with any problem and that I would find out about the commotion soon enough, I began stoking fires and gathering food for breakfast.

Peter and John soon returned. Scanning the camp, Peter ran towards me—probably because he thought I seemed the most alert of the groggy campers.

"Quickly! Assemble everyone. Something has happened!" he said excitedly, before darting away without further elaboration to help wake people. Within minutes men, women and children were gathered around Peter, yawning and rubbing sleepy eyes, waiting for his news.

"This morning Magdala and her friends went to anoint Jesus's body," he began. "When they got to the tomb, it was empty."

A confused murmur rippled across the group.

"Is it not enough that they killed him? Do they have to steal his body too?" asked Philip incredulously.

"Are they sure?" asked James. "That stone was pretty big, how did the women roll it out of the way?"

Peter raised his hand to signal for silence before continuing.

"The stone was pushed aside when they arrived. Magdala came back here immediately when she found the tomb empty. We have just returned from there. It was empty!"

"What did you see?" I asked.

"The linen cloths were laying there," Peter said, shrugging his shoulders. "The one that had been around Jesus's head was rolled up at the top of where he was laid, bloody as ever. I am sure they were his linen cloths."

"This is a disgrace!" stormed Andrew. "To steal his body and leave the cloths. What are we going to do?"

"Look, here comes Magdala," James pointed to the base of the hill. Our group met her near the top of the slope. She was panting, perspiration dripped from her forehead.

"Has something else happened, Magdala?" Peter asked.

"Yes, yes!" she said gulping at air, swallowing as she tried to steady her voice.

"After you left I stayed at the tomb. Suddenly the inside of the cave seemed to be glowing. It almost seemed like someone had lit a fire so I looked inside and saw two men! They were dressed in white, gleaming white, like the sun reflecting on water. One was at the head of where Jesus had been lying the other at the foot. The one at the head said, 'Woman, why are you crying?' I was terrified but said, 'Because they have taken my Lord away and I don't know where they have put him.' Then the man said, 'Why are you looking among the dead for someone who is alive?'"

We looked at one another, confused, yet kept silent—interested in hearing more of what Magdala had to say.

"What does that mean?" asked Peter.

Magdala held up her hand in a halting motion, gulping more air as she continued. "He said, 'Jesus is not here. He has risen.'"

Whispers erupted as people exchanged questions and speculations.

"Did he say anything else?" Peter inquired loudly over the din, bringing quiet again.

"Yes," she answered. "He said to give you a message: 'Tell Jesus's disciples that he is going up to Galilee ahead of you and that there you will see him.'"

Talking amongst the group renewed in earnest, people wondered aloud what it could all mean, what we should do.

"Come," Peter finally announced, taking control of the turmoil, "let's eat before deciding what the day will hold."

"There is something else," I heard Magdala say quietly, almost sheepishly, to Peter—as if she wondered if she should say anything at all.

"There's something more," Peter refocused everyone's attention.

"After the men left, on my way here," Magdala paused to gather her courage, "I met another man in the garden. Shocked by what the two men in white had said, I was deep in thought trying to figure it all out and I almost bumped into this other man. I did not even look at him, simply excused myself and went to walk by but he said to me, 'You have been crying, are you all right?' I thought that he must be the gardener and that perhaps he knew something about what had happened so I said, 'If you have taken Jesus's body away, sir, please tell me where you have put him and I will go and get him.' Then he said my name. He said 'Mary.' Just as I had heard him many times before. I knew that voice! I looked at the man's face and it was Jesus!"

"What?!" asked Peter, astonished.

"Yes! It was Jesus," she said staring into Peter's eyes and nodding assuredly. "He looked just as I had seen him countless times. He was not bruised or bloody, he was healed. His hands were still pierced but it was as if time had healed the wound leaving only scars of what had been."

Her expression softened as she recalled this beautiful, treasured memory.

"I bowed to the ground and worshipped him, grabbing his feet, never wanting to let go. He laughed and said, 'Not so tight, Mary.' You know, just the way he used to talk. Then he said more seriously, 'I still must go to my Father. Let my brothers know that I must return to my Father and your Father, my God and your God.' Then he was gone." A smile played on her lips, a faint lingering echo of her joy.[1]

We were all silent.

"I am not questioning your story, Magdala," Peter began delicately, "but do you not think it is possible that you just wished that you saw Jesus?"

She glared at him defiantly.

"No, I know what I saw. I did not expect you to believe me. Why do you think I was reluctant to say anything?"

"Maybe it was a ghost, Jesus's spirit," offered John.

"No!" exclaimed Magdala. "I grabbed his feet. I felt his flesh. I have had experience with spirits, remember? He was no ghost, I can assure you!"

Staunch in her story, everyone soon realized that it was hopeless to convince her that she had seen anything other than what she believed to be true.

"Well," Peter said finally, deciding it was too early in the day to contemplate such theoretical matters, "let's eat and then discuss what our next move should be."

We walked towards the campfires knowing we had much more to chew on than food.

"We need more information," Peter stated, calling us together after a quick breakfast. "The only thing we know for a fact is that the tomb is empty. We need to find out more. Is this some elaborate hoax by the chief priests? How widespread is this news? What are people saying? I propose that we go in small groups to Jerusalem to gather information. Say nothing to anyone, just listen. John and I will talk to Nicodemus. As a Pharisee he can tell us what the religious leaders know. Judas, why don't you and James talk to Joseph of Arimathea? Find out what happened when he took Jesus's body down to bury it. Speak to only those whom you are sure were sympathetic to Jesus. We will meet back here at supper to share our findings. Then the eleven apostles will meet and give our recommendations."

The plan sounded good. As James and I got ready to leave, Peter motioned for the two of us to meet with him.

"Joseph was the last man to see Jesus," Peter began. "I need you to make sure that Jesus was dead and placed in that tomb."

"What are you saying, Peter?" I asked.

"Maybe Jesus was not dead when he was removed from the cross," Peter spoke in a hushed voice. "What if Joseph has hidden him somewhere?"

"We all saw him die," James whispered back. "The Roman guards are trained to recognize death."

"It's not likely, I know," Peter explained, "but we have to explore all the possibilities."

Agreeing, James and I set off to Jerusalem.

"What do you make of it all?" James asked as we walked.

"I don't know," I said. "I really don't. Magdala has always been a little strange, a loner, but she is no liar. I think that she believes that she saw Jesus. Whether someone tricked her or not, I cannot say. But why would someone want to do that? The religious leaders would never want to say that he is alive. I can think of no one who would want to think up such an elaborate deception."

"Besides us," added James.

"Yes, I suppose we could benefit from it," I mused. "But we have been together since yesterday afternoon. As far as this idea of Joseph taking Jesus's body, it seems virtually impossible. The guard pierced his side and blood and water flowed out, you can hardly fake that. But even if he kept the body out of the tomb and Jesus is alive, that cannot be who Magdala saw—Jesus's body was a mess."

James chuckled a bit. "Wouldn't it be just like Jesus though, if he did rise from the dead? I mean to appear to a woman instead of some man of high repute."

"Yes," I laughed. "Jesus was never one to do the expected."

We arrived in Jerusalem and went immediately to Joseph's home. As soon as he saw us at the door, he grabbed our tunics, one in each hand to pull us in.

"What are you doing out there?" He was brusque. "Don't you know that the chief priests are looking everywhere for Jesus's apostles?"

James and I exchanged bewildered looks and waited for Joseph to explain.

"The news is spreading like wildfire. Jesus's tomb is empty and you are the prime suspects."

"Us?!" I was incredulous.

"Who else?" he answered. "No one else stands to benefit from such a thing except Jesus's disciples. Why else would the tomb have been so heavily guarded? The Council has already met this morning. They were appalled to learn that I, one of their members, had prepared Jesus's body. I endured quite an inquisition! When they found out that Nicodemus had helped too, they questioned the two of us separately then together to determine if we were lying. At last they sent us to wait in the hall while they decided what to do. When they brought us back in, they told us we were to tell Pilate that it was our fault that Jesus's body was not in the tomb, that we had never even placed it there. If we refused they said they would immediately strip us of our titles and our jobs."

James and I listened, dumbfounded. The religious leaders seemed to be reacting more to Jesus's disappearance than we were.

"What did you tell them?" asked James.

Joseph was livid.

"What do you think?" he spat, throwing his arms in the air. "I lie for no one. I am an honourable man. I will not sacrifice my honour. I told them the truth. The day of the crucifixion I asked Pilate if I could take Jesus's body. It was Pilate's guards who pronounced Jesus dead and removed him from the cross, not me. Nicodemus and I prepared his dead body, wrapped it in linens as is our custom and laid him in the tomb. Pilate's soldiers were there—as were the chief priest's own guards—to make sure Jesus was dead and buried. The soldiers rolled the stone in front of the opening."[2]

"But, why?" I asked, surprised by the security measures taken to bury a dead man, criminal or not. "Why were they so thorough when it came to placing Jesus's body in the tomb?"

Joseph stared at me in disbelief.

"Are you so naive?" he exclaimed. "Were you not there when Jesus said that he would rise from the dead? The religious leaders' greatest fear was that Jesus would be inexplicably stolen away. The last thing they wanted was an unexplained disappearance that would shroud his death in mystery! They desperately needed a gravesite, a place to point to and confirm that Jesus was not who he claimed to be."

"I-I guess I never thought," I stammered, ashamed. "I was so caught off guard when Jesus died that I have thought about only that. We were devastated, the furthest thing from our minds was concocting an elaborate plan to steal Jesus's body. What would be the point? If Jesus is dead why seek to establish him as king? What cause would we be perpetuating? Beyond that, we were too cowardly to even help him when he was beaten and killed."

"So, you didn't take his body," concluded Joseph, then paused. "Are you saying that he actually *did* rise from the dead?"

"We are saying nothing," James interrupted, "except that we must go. If it is as you say and the religious leaders are looking for us we should not stay here."

He got up quickly and headed for the door. I followed.

"Thank you for your time," I said politely over my shoulder as we left.

James immediately motioned for me to duck down behind a stone wall as soon as we had left Joseph's home. Hidden in the shadows I asked him, "Why did we leave so fast?"

"You remember what Peter said, we are here to gather information. I have no reason to doubt what Joseph says but we must still be cautious. I don't want to be brought in for questioning. The religious leaders are sure to be watching the homes of Jesus's known supporters."

"Let's go back to camp," I said after thinking a moment. "I have an idea about how we can gather information without raising suspicion."

We needed to avoid attention and become unrecognizable to old friends or acquaintances yet still mingle with the public. We needed a disguise. At the camp we dug out and changed into our old travel-worn clothes. I then smeared some mud on our faces and lightly wiped it off, leaving streaks of the muck stuck in the wrinkles of our faces and causing the cracks to appear deeper. I hoped the effect might add at least ten years to our appearance. Next we took some flour and worked it into our hair and beards. A crooked branch supporting James's hunched back helped us appear to be two poor, elderly travelers getting ready to head home after the Passover. We refined our disguises as best we could then headed to the marketplace to see what else could be discovered.

For the past forty-eight hours I had felt completely hopeless; it was good to be doing something again. Although the tension was nervewracking, the rush of adrenaline also felt exhilarating.

We stayed together and circulated among the marketers—many of whom were gathering supplies for their trip home. Almost all of the gossip revolved around the death of Jesus and the disappearance of his body. Most thought that his apostles had stolen it while others thought that Jesus had not really been dead and had escaped. Speculation was rampant but reliable facts were scarce.

A group of Roman soldiers deep in conversation appeared at the edge of the market. Thankfully they did not look at us and I turned to walk in the opposite direction, anxious to increase the distance between us and them. James however, grabbed the sleeve of my cloak and stopped me with a hoarse whisper, "Let's get closer and listen to them!"

"Are you insane?" I gasped. "They're no doubt looking for us and you want to go closer?"

"They will at least have information beyond guesswork. These disguises are pretty good. I have already met a few acquaintances without being recognized."

I hesitated.

"Are you coming?" he said over his shoulder, setting off for the group of armed men without me.

I sighed and hobbled after him, more desperate than ever to play the image of an old man to the fullest. As we approached, it was obvious that the soldiers were indeed talking about Jesus's disappearance. Nudging James then snuggling my back into the wall of the nearest building, I lowered myself to the ground, brought my knees up and dropped my head onto them, feigning what I hoped looked like weary poverty. James followed my lead and sank to the ground, too. We listened intently.

"...been in a lot of battles but when that man died, well nothing can prepare you for that. It was terrifying, as if the whole earth protested what we were doing. How do you fight that? I mean, even the sun stopped shining! Rome can make men and nations do almost anything with a little force but can it turn the sun back on after it's gone out? For three hours darkness covered the countryside. Three hours! Until he loudly cried out, 'Father, into your hands, I place my spirit.' and died. Then the whole place shook—I thought the ground would split open and swallow us up. When it finally stopped, the shadow passed from the sun and it was light again."

There was a pause then the same man continued. "That whole crucifixion was eerie. It was as if spirits were swooping around us and things which we have no hope of understanding—let alone controlling—were running the show. We were just pawns."

"I agree, Troas," a second soldier broke in. "I have never felt anything like it. I never want to again. I have put in a request to be transferred back to Rome. It's like this place is haunted. When Markus saw how Jesus died, even he said, 'This man was really the Son of God.' And you know Markus, he believes Rome is God Himself."

"What are you going to do with the robe, Aquilla?" asked Troas.

"What are you talking about?" asked a third voice.

"We divided up Jesus's clothes while he was dying," explained Troas. "His robe was seamless and we didn't want to tear it so we played a game for it. Aquilla, here, won."

"I don't know," said Aquilla. "I feel like I'm cursed. But how do you get rid of a curse? Maybe I'll burn it. I could stop at Ephesis when I return to Rome to make sacrifices to some of the idols there but, to tell you the truth, that seems pointless. How do they measure up to a god who controls nature? I just want to get away from here and back to Rome. I don't care if I get sent out to a battlefield—at least then I will be fighting flesh and blood, things I can touch and see."

"Well, I was stationed at the tomb, and…" the third soldier spoke up, then hesitated.

"And?" asked Troas.

"I know what you're saying about the whole earth protesting. We had been at the tomb all night and didn't see anyone. There were a lot of us there because Pilate was frustrated with the chief priest's complaints. He wanted to be done with it so when the priests came asking him for a guard so that Jesus's disciples could not steal the body away, he gave them full disposal to as many guards as would satisfy the religious leaders. They took everyone they could find. I was there when the grave was sealed and stood watch throughout the night.

"Then, early in the morning before dawn, the earth began to shake. It started as a rumble but quickly became worse. Soon the whole area was moving as if the earth itself was angry. The rocks began to break and shatter. We didn't know what to do. There was nothing to hold onto. We were tossed to the ground by the vibration and I was glad to stay there sprawled on the grass. Like you said, how can you stop nature's revolution? We lay there just hoping to survive.

"Then I saw this being. I don't know what it was but it was twice as tall as us, dressed in white. Well, not really white, it was like nothing I can describe. Almost like the brilliance of bolts of lightning woven together to make cloth. It illuminated everything as if it was noon. Then the being touched the stone in front of the tomb and the stone fairly jumped out of the way! Whatever it was then sat on the stone. We were terrified! We became like dead men. When I regained consciousness it was almost dawn. The stone was still rolled away but the being was gone. My captain commanded me to look inside the tomb to make sure the body was still there. Staying as far away as possible yet still be able to see in, I peered inside. It was empty. When

I called out that there was no one inside, the captain's face went white then he ran away. We all did."

"Where did you go?" asked Aquilla.

"I went back to Pilate's palace. That's where most of us went. But they're still looking for our captain."

"This is the first we've heard of this," commented Troas.

"Yes," said the soldier. "I'm not surprised. I've been interrogated all morning, first by Pilate then by the chief priests and finally the Pharisees." After a pause he added, "I, too, have asked to go back to Rome. The powers here are beyond anything I know. The supernatural reigns here."[3]

"At least we can go back to Rome," said Aquilla. "The man who betrayed Jesus must've felt like he had *no*where to go. I heard he killed himself. Hung himself out in a field."

At the mention of Judas Iscariot's fate, James accidentally dropped his walking stick. It clattered to the ground, the noise reverberated along the road. Hurriedly I retrieved, it hearing footsteps headed in our direction.

"Hey, old man," snarled one of the soldiers, "have you been eavesdropping on a private conversation?"

I jerked my head up, slowly stood and nervously cleared my throat.

"Ah,…ah," I stammered, "we meant no harm."

"Well, you best be leaving or you may find some coming your way," snapped his companion, coming so close I could smell onion on his breath. His eyes narrowed as he stared at me, closely examining my face and hair.

"I wonder if these two are not who they appear to be," he said and grabbed my wrist tightly.

Without thinking I yanked my arm from his grip and yelled for James to run.

I dropped the walking stick and we hiked up our robes, running for the marketplace. The soldiers called for reinforcements and ran after us as we wove in and out of travelers buying their supplies. Thankfully I knew Jerusalem well. Ahead on the right was a narrow alley which led to a sewage canal. I checked over my shoulder for James and saw him run the opposite direction with three soldiers in pursuit. The soldiers chasing me yelled, "Someone stop that man. Stop him!"

I kept running. The alley. I had made it! Turning sharply, I slipped on the cobbled street and quickly scrambled to my feet again. My leg smarted, badly scraped from the fall. I kept running.

The soldiers must have lost sight of me for a moment because I didn't hear their pounding feet as I fled down the alley. Spotting the canal, I ran full stride into the stench.

"Look there he is!" one yelled.

They started down the alley but by now I had quite a distance on them. Where the canal began I heard one bellow, "Whoa! What a stink!"

I ran on, spraying filth all over me.

I heard one call, "You may have gotten away this time but you can't run forever! We'll catch you, you can be sure of that!"

At that moment I didn't worry whether he was right or not. All I knew was that I had escaped. I was safe…for now.

I took the long way back to camp through many bushes and rough terrain, all the while checking over my shoulder and listening intently for sounds of pursuit. After convincing myself that I was not being followed, I went back to camp.

James had beaten me there. I waved to him and called out that I was happy to see him then hurried to collect some clean clothes and bathe. Although I was curious about his escape, I was sure he would not have been able to stand being in my presence long enough to tell me. It took the better part of an hour and countless dunks in the river before the odour abated. By the time I was finished it was time to meet with the rest of the disciples to share what we had learned.

People milled about the camp, chatting excitedly. Peter called us all to order. As I looked around the group I soon realized that there were considerably fewer there than there had been this morning. Even one of the apostles, Thomas, was missing. We later learned that he had been detained.

"We have had a change of plans," announced Peter. "We must break camp immediately. This place is no longer safe. As you can see many of our number are missing. We know some have been captured and are now being questioned. The rest I assume are enduring the same fate. I have secured a room for the apostles to meet in which should be safe. If you have any information that you think will aid us in our decisions please let one of us know. Before you go, talk to one of the apostles to let him know how we can reach you tomorrow."

The apostles spread out and two or three people gathered around each of us. After spending the next few minutes being told tidbits of information about the day and recording meeting locations for the following morning, we hurriedly broke camp.

While a few men took down the last of the tents, Peter gathered the apostles together to plan the best way to sneak to the hideout.

As Peter spoke two men, Clepas and Simon, disciples who had left early that morning for Emmaus, ran into camp whooping and calling excitedly between gasps for air.

"The Lord is risen!"

"He has risen indeed!"

"We have spent the day with Jesus!"

Those left in the camp rushed to gather around the two men. Their faces seemed barely able to contain their smiles, their glee cut away the worries of our day.

"What are you talking about?" Peter asked.

"It was on our way to Emmaus," began Simon. "Soon after we started on the road we saw this man. We thought he was a traveler heading home from Jerusalem." He paused briefly to bend over slightly and placed his hands on his knees to take in another gulp of air before straightening up to resume his story.

"Clepas and I had been talking about all that has happened the past few days."

"What else would we be talking about?" Clepas interjected jovially.

"And this traveler," Simon went on, "interrupts us and says, 'You two seem deep in conversation. What has gotten you so focused on a beautiful morning like this?' We stopped walking, stood stark still and stared at him as if he was crazy. Surely he had heard about all that had happened during the Passover. Had he just dropped out of the sky? Clepas here," Simon said, nudging his buddy, "says to the man, 'Are you the only man living in Jerusalem who does not know what has been happening there these last few days?' And the man says, 'What things?'"

Clepas and Simon exchanged bemused smiles.

"I thought Clepas was going to shake apart with shock. Clepas almost knocked the man over in exasperation and told him, 'The things that happened to Jesus of Nazareth!!' The man stared back at us blankly like he didn't know what we were talking about so I decided to enlighten him. 'This man was a prophet,' I said, 'considered by Adonai and by all the people to be mighty in word and deed. Our very own chief priests and rulers handed him over to be sentenced to death and nailed him to a cross. We had hoped that he would be the one who was going to redeem Israel! It happened only three days ago.' Well, this traveler just looked at us and asked if he could walk with us along the road. It was as if he was unaffected by anything we had said. I was shocked. The traveler turned, started down the road and asked over his shoulder if we were going to join him."

"We ran after him trying to figure out who he was," Clepas said, picking up the story from Simon, unable to stay quiet any longer. "Why would such news just glance off him like a smooth rock skipped across the water? When we caught up to him, I said, 'Besides all that, this morning some of the women of our group went to the grave at dawn and did not find his body. One came back saying she had seen a vision of angels who told her that Jesus was alive! Some of our group went to the tomb and found it exactly as the women had said but they did not see Jesus.'"

Clepas looked sheepishly at Peter and apologized, "I'm sorry, Peter. I know you asked us not to say anything but he was so nonchalant about all we had told him about Jesus. I guess I was just trying to get *some* kind of a reaction from him."

Peter gave him a disgruntled look but said only, "I thought you said you spent the day with Jesus."

"Yes, yes," said Clepas, "I'm getting to that. Anyway, after I told him about what the women had seen, he said, 'How foolish you are and how slow you are to believe everything that the prophets have said. It was necessary for the Messiah to suffer these things and enter his glory.' Then he started reciting the books of Moses and went on to the writings of the prophets, explaining what they said about the Messiah. All morning he did this. It was amazing," his voice rose with excitement. "Did you know, that the prophet Jeremiah foretold about the deaths of children that happened when Jesus was born[4], that it was foretold that Jesus would use parables[5] or that Isaiah wrote that the Messiah would die by being nailed to a cross?"[6]

"This is all very interesting," interrupted Peter impatiently. "But you said you spent the day with Jesus."

"Yes, we're getting to that!" Simon exclaimed. "After a number of hours, we reached Emmaus and asked the traveler to stay to eat with us. He said he needed to continue on his journey but agreed to share a meal. We were about to eat when the man stood, looked to heaven, said a blessing, broke the bread and handed it to us. As soon as we took the bread from his hand it was as if our minds were touched by Adonai. I don't know how else to explain it. It was like we had been walking with a dark, heavy veil over our faces and someone reached down to lift it. The shroud was gone, we could see clearly, no longer looking through a barrier but directly, fully and unhindered. We recognized the traveler. It was Jesus! We understood what he had been teaching us. It was supernatural! Adonai-sent! Oh, his eyes were full of joy and splendour, peaceful yet vibrant. He pulsed with life. Then he was gone, disappeared. We ran back as fast as we could to tell you. Jesus has risen!"

We stared at them, dumbfounded once again.

"I don't understand," said Matthew. "How could you spend an

entire morning with Jesus yet not know it was him until the end?"

Clepas shrugged, trying to explain. "We don't fully understand ourselves. Like Simon said it was as if we had been walking with a veil over our faces, seeing but not clearly. Even when we had that veil over our eyes though, I tell you, when he spoke about the scriptures and their fulfillment, my heart burned as though I was being consumed by fire!"[7]

"This is amazing!" Andrew exploded, "What did Jesus… ?"

He had not finished his question before Peter jumped in, "I agree. This is a wondrous thing but unfortunately now is not the time or the place to discuss it. Although we want to hear more about your day, Simon and Clepas, Jerusalem has become rather dangerous right now. I fear that we have lingered too long in one place already. Thank you for coming and telling us. Let us know where you are staying so we can be in touch with you tomorrow with our plans."

I pulled the parchment from my pack to add Clepas and Simon's accommodations to my list of names then hurried to hear how to get to our safe haven.

chapter twenty-two

We arrived at the room that Peter had found in groups of two and three. The room was large and unfurnished—we had to sit on the floor—yet it had what was needed: a sturdy lock and a window through which we could easily crawl if escape to the back alley was required. Once we were all assembled the stories began.

James started the discussion. "We can be absolutely sure that every one has heard about Jesus's grave being empty. It is the buzz of the marketplace."

"His is not the only grave now empty," added Bartholomew.

"One man I spoke to said that he had seen his uncle who died two months ago walking outside of the city."

"Yes," echoed Matthew. "I met several people who had also seen dead relatives."[1]

"Let's stick to the matter about Jesus for now," directed Peter. "John and I spoke to Nicodemus. He was adamant that Jesus was dead and that the stone had been securely sealed. Judas and James, what did you learn from Joseph?"

"He, too, was sure that Jesus was dead and buried," nodded James.

"We have no reason to question his story," I offered. "It cost him his job. The religious leaders offered to pay him to say that he and Nicodemus had never placed Jesus in the tomb but he refused and his refusal cost him his position on the council."

"Yes, Nicodemus told us about the attempted bribe, too," confirmed John.

"Others were not as noble," said Simon in disgust. "We overheard some soldiers saying that they got paid quite handsomely to say they had fallen asleep at the grave and that we, Jesus's apostles, had stolen the body away."[2]

"What!" gasped Bartholomew.

"We will be marked men for the rest of our lives," huffed Matthew.

"I guess they thought 'Better them than us,'" Simon elaborated. "Apparently it was the only way that the chief priests could vouch for the soldiers and keep their superiors from punishing them. I suppose the soldiers didn't feel that they had any other choice."

"Well," snarled Bartholomew. "I am so happy that we could help them out. I suppose it is the least we could do."

The tensions of the day, along with the information that we would probably be hunted down, brought a wealth of discussion, to put it politely—or arguing, to put it accurately.

Suddenly, amidst the noise and clamour a strong, clear voice rang out.

"Peace, my brothers!"

The voice made my heart stop mid-beat. The air caught in my throat, every muscle in my body quickened, sharpening and tensing. It was Jesus! He stood in the middle of the room looking just as he had the day we praised and blessed him down the streets of Jerusalem. He was full of life yet seemed tranquil and content. His eyes were warm and accepting, his smile broad and rich, his complexion completely void of the ugly bruises and blood that had covered it only days before. He looked resplendent, earthy, glorious…alive! My head swam, soaked in a mixture of delirium, ecstasy and fear.

"He is a ghost," whispered James, then shuddered at the loudness of his words in the quiet.

"Why are you troubled?" Jesus asked in a soothing tone. "Look at my hands and my feet and see that it is me. Feel me. A ghost doesn't have flesh and bones as I have."

He stretched out his hands to invite our touch, asking us to confirm his reality. A knot tightened in my stomach as I saw the holes in his hands. They were scars now but they were still ugly, a jolt of reality that he had indeed been crucified.

Peter was the first to reach out to touch Jesus's skin. His eyes brimmed with tears as his trembling fingers brushed over Jesus's hand. He fell to the ground weeping, shaking at Jesus's scarred feet.

I could not resist. I, along with the other apostles, groped at Jesus's hands, desperate to enlighten every shadow of doubt that lurked in my mind. Over and over I touched him, resolving to never let my mind question his existence again.

The truth that Jesus had risen from the dead took hold of my being. It was like basking in a brilliant sunbeam. Oh, to be captured and held tight by Jesus's authenticity. How blessed am I among men! What delight to indulge in the assurance of his reality. I felt as if my heart would burst from my body singing in rapt bliss. My Lord was alive! I know that Jesus lives!

"Do you have anything here to eat?" Jesus asked.

"Yes, Lord," I said, running for my pack. "I have some fish that was left from supper. Hopefully it will hit the spot." I would have never supposed Jesus to be hungry. A ghost would certainly never ask for food!

I brought him back a piece of cold, cooked fish which he ate heartily, savouring the taste. We all watched him, silent.

"These things that have happened to me," began Jesus, "are the very things that I told you about while I was still with you, things that are written about me in the Law of Moses, in the writings of the prophets and in the Psalms. All of these prophesies had to come true."

We leaned in close to our Lord, soaking up his radiance, like men who had walked through an arid, parched desert alone and were now refreshed in sweet rain.

"Do you remember when the Pharisees asked for a miraculous sign and I said that the only one that they would receive was that of the prophet Jonah? That just as Jonah was in the belly of a huge fish for three days and three nights so the Son of Man would be three days and three nights in the heart of the earth.[3] Those three days and nights are now complete!

"It was all foretold. It all had to happen. The very night on the Mount of Olives when you all ran away was foretold by Zechariah when he said, 'I will strike the shepherd and the sheep of the flock will be scattered.'⁴ Judas's betrayal and death was also predicted by Zechariah over four hundred years ago, 'They took the thirty silver coins, the price set on him by the people of Israel, and they used them to buy the potter's field, as the Lord commanded me.'⁵ The soldiers dividing my clothes by casting lots was foretold by King David when he said, 'They divided my garments among them and cast lots for my clothing.'⁶ It all had to be fulfilled. The new covenant had to be fulfilled from the old one. *I am not an earthly King but your Messiah.*

I was the child born to you.
I was the son given to you.
A government rests upon my shoulders.
My name is Wonderful Counselor, God-Hero, Eternal Father.
Prince of Peace.
There will be no end to the increase of my government or of peace.
I reign on David's throne and over his kingdom.
I establish it and uphold it with justice and righteousness.
From this time on and forever.
The zeal of the Lord Almighty has accomplished this!"⁷

Jesus's proclamation was indisputable and victorious. My heart trumpeted his words. I knew them to be true.

I bowed my head in reverence. I truly believed Jesus was the Messiah. Yet this simple act did not seem to remotely convey the awe within my soul. With my head still bowed, I knelt before my saviour, redeemer and the world's only hope. Never before had I worshipped any one but Adonai, yet this felt right.

"Receive the Holy Spirit," I heard Jesus declare.⁸

Human language does not possess the vocabulary to describe the touch of heaven given to me. So beyond my understanding was this gift that I can only say that I must have glimpsed the freedom my soul will someday feel when it will be released from the confines of this temporal body and I will soar, worshipping Adonai, my Creator. The blessing Jesus gave was a reflection of the purest, truest joy of heaven. I glowed like molten metal burned free of imperfections and impurities, flowed like purest melted gold, sparkled like a precious cut diamond. I knew this immense beauty only because Adonai had touched me. I saw the radiance of Adonai's prevailing goodness in my life.

When I opened my eyes, Jesus was gone.

The angels at the empty tomb had told Magdala that we were to go to Galilee and said that we would see Jesus there. Having encountered Jesus once, we were determined to go to the next place he said he would be. In the morning, after contacting the disciples on our lists and informing them of the previous night's happenings, we departed. Most decided to come along hoping to witness the miracle of our risen Lord. Thankfully, after being questioned by the authorities, Thomas was released before we left and so was able to accompany us to Galilee.

It felt like we would never reach our northern destination; so anxious was I to see Jesus again that no amount of idle chitchat made the time go faster.

It took a week to reach the area of Galilee. When we finally arrived, I took a deep breath and looked around expectantly, hoping to see Jesus appear before me. But it did not happen. Our entire group slowed down, then stopped walking, wondering what to do next. After much discussion regarding our lack of direction, we decided to set up camp outside Dyadd.

For four days I rose each morning in anticipation that this might be the day that I would see Jesus—only to return to bed each night disappointed. Sensing the growing frustration of the disciples, Peter asked me to secure a room in Dyadd where the apostles could eat together and make some decisions.

That night at supper as I began distributing bowls of steaming lentils and round bread, I heard a familiar discussion between Thomas and John, the same discussion I had heard endlessly since leaving Jerusalem. During our journey to Galilee, and despite our repeated insistence, Thomas had staunchly stated that he did not believe that Jesus had appeared in the flesh. We had all been shocked and taken turns to convince him of our account, but after three days of arguing, I gave up. John, however, refused to drop the topic and kept bringing up some new indisputable proof that Jesus's appearance had been real. Personally, I was disgusted with Thomas. After glorying in the assurance of Jesus's resurrection I did not appreciate hearing denials of it by one whom I considered a friend.

"Ten men told you the same account," John pointed out tonight. "A figment of the imagination would not be the same for ten different people."

I rolled my eyes and placed two bowls of food between them.

"I'm not saying that you did not see *something*," Thomas returned. "I'm just saying that I don't believe it was Jesus in the flesh. Unless I see him with my own eyes, put my finger in the nail scars and my hand in his side, I will not believe."[9] He was adamant, far too sure of himself for my liking.

"Peace be with you."

The voice of Jesus reverberated through the room just as it had eleven days earlier when we had been locked in the room in Bethany. Joy and excitement leapt within me.

Jesus stood between the three tables of steaming food. Smiles broke across the faces of each apostle—except Thomas, who sat bolt upright, his eyes large saucers, his mouth agape. Jesus went over to where Thomas sat and knelt beside him to look into his face. Thomas shrank under the scrutiny.

Jesus put out his hands in front of Thomas and invited his touch.

"Touch them, Thomas. Touch them and believe."

The colour rose in Thomas's face but his hands remained tightly clasped in his lap.

"I'm sorry, Lord," Thomas said sheepishly. "Forgive me."

The Other Judas
213

"Yes, I forgive you, Thomas," Jesus said, "but I want you to touch me. I need you to believe and to stop your doubting."

Gingerly, Thomas reached out to touch Jesus's outstretched hands.

"You have believed because you have seen me with your own eyes and touched me with your own hands but the truly happy people will be those who believe without seeing."[9]

"Lord, what is happening?" Matthew asked. "We were preparing to establish you as our king. Is that still our goal? What are we to be doing?"

The questions had a number of purposes. As we had made our way to Galilee we had discussed what would happen the next time we met Jesus. First, we wanted to keep Jesus with us for as long as possible and determined that the best way to accomplish this was to keep him talking by asking him questions. Secondly, we sincerely wanted to know what the future held. Our Messiah had been killed and had risen. This was, for us, completely unexpected. Where did we go from here? What was our next step?

"Many years ago the prophets saw visions that foretold my coming," Jesus began. "They prophesied about the Messiah. Isaiah said that the Messiah would make things right again, that he would be a light to the nations and that Adonai's salvation would reach to the ends of the earth.[10] But what is the Messiah making right? Jeremiah prophesied about a new covenant. What new covenant was he speaking about?"[11]

I, and everyone else in the room, stared blankly back at Jesus. I didn't dare to even attempt an answer to his questions, keenly aware that my pathetic understanding of the scriptures had proven rather lacking over the past two weeks.

"When the first covenant was handed down to Moses," Jesus continued, "it was a picture of the true covenant, a representation of Adonai's perfect choice." Jesus looked around the room then walked over to a picture of a bowl of fruit hanging on the wall.

"Here, look at this picture of grapes. It is a good representation, isn't it? The painter was talented."

Jesus returned to the table and grabbed a handful of grapes lying in a basket in front of me.

"Now have a real grape," Jesus said, passing out some fruit to each of us. "Take a bite. Feel the juice on your tongue. Taste the sweetness. Smell it. The picture is an image of the fruit but it can not compare to the sensation of the real thing. The covenant that Moses received was like that. It was a picture of what was to come, a representation of the way Adonai would make things right. Ever since this contract was made with Moses, the priests have ministered day after day, offering sacrifices again and again. Those sacrifices were Adonai's provision until His perfect plan was completed, a picture of the atonement sacrifice that would one day have to be made. Now the new covenant has happened. I have offered one sacrifice, my body, for sin. My blood alone has the power to atone once, for all—the power to forgive sins and transgressions so that Adonai remembers them no more. The question then becomes, why is my blood so different? I am Adonai's Messiah, His servant yet I am no earthly king. Why can Adonai's Messiah forgive sins?"

Jesus directed his attention to John. "You were one of my first disciples. Do you remember what happened after John the Immerser baptized me?"

John thought briefly then said, "Yes, the sky opened and we saw the Spirit of Adonai descend like a dove and hover over you. We heard a voice from the heavens say, 'This is my beloved Son. My favour rests on him.'"[12]

Jesus smiled and nodded, acknowledging John's answer.

"And Peter," Jesus continued, "tell everyone what happened on the mountain at Cesarea Philippi when you, John, James and I spent the day together."

"You told us not to tell anyone about that," Peter whispered.

"I said not until I rose from the dead," returned Jesus.

Peter swallowed hard as he remembered the command and for the first time understood the strange instruction. He related the story.

"We walked up the mountain together. Suddenly your face became dazzling like the sun and your clothes radiated with light. There were two men with you. Somehow I knew that they were Moses and Elijah! They talked to you. I was shocked and said that I thought we should make a temple for each of you, one for Jesus, one for Elijah and one for Moses." He paused to blush, embarrassed, by the ridiculousness of his suggestion. "While I was babbling away about my ideas, a bright cloud overshadowed the three of you. Out of the cloud came a voice which said, 'This is my beloved Son, on whom my favour rests. Listen to him.' When we heard the voice, James, John and I fell onto the ground, terrified. Then I felt your hand on my back. When I looked around it was all gone, only you and the three of us remained."[13]

"I want you to think about these experiences, the prophesies of old and my time with you. Talk to my mother, Mary, ask her about the circumstances surrounding my birth. Finally, talk to the priest Hassi who was in the temple the day that I was crucified. He is in Dyadd. After you have learned and thought about all these things, I will see you again."

Then he was gone once more.

Bartholomew and Matthew said that Hassi used to serve as a rabbi in their hometown of Kadesh. Although it had been years since they had seen him, they described him as a good and honest man who loved to gossip, 'singing like a morning songbird' if given the opportunity. While the rest of the apostles disassembled the campsite and prepared to go to Nazareth to speak with Jesus's mother, Bartholomew and Matthew went to Dyadd to speak with Hassi. Peter spent the better part of an hour making contingency plans should Bartholomew and Matthew be caught and cautioned the two of them for we were all still wanted men. Bartholomew kept reassuring Peter that Hassi was not a man of political ambition and he was confident that the priest would not turn them in.

Thankfully, Bartholomew was right. As I finished stuffing my blanket into the pack and pulled it onto my back, Bartholomew and Matthew returned from Dyadd. We immediately set out for Nazareth.

"He seemed pretty nervous when we first broached the subject of the temple," Bartholomew began, sharing what he had learned from Hassi as we walked. "We eventually convinced him that he had nothing to fear from us and that we already knew that he was part of the major event that had happened in Jerusalem. Then he told us that during the Passover he had been chosen to be stationed at the Holy of Holies. He had been very excited to serve at the most sacred place of the temple, so close to the presence of Adonai. On the Friday when Jesus was crucified, while Hassi was helping the High priest, the sacred heavy curtain protecting the inner sanctuary of Adonai was suddenly torn in two from top to bottom!"[14]

Shock jolted the group of apostles. Everyone stopped walking, encircling Bartholomew to give him our full attention. This curtain was no mere drape hung for decoration; it was the very barrier between mortal man and his transcendent Creator, the chamber behind this veil was the epicentre around which the entire temple was constructed. Few men had ever seen the Holy of Holies for only a specially selected priest chosen at specific times of the year was allowed to enter the room. When this priest passed to the other side of the veil he had to have a rope tied around his waist for, should he die in the presence of Adonai, it was the only way to pull him out. I knew of the room's appearance only from the scriptures as described by its designer, King Solomon. The room was said to be overlaid with pure gold, having at its centre two sculpted cherubim whose wingspan filled the room. Under their wings was the ark of the covenant of the Lord. The ark, constructed under the direction of Moses, was made of acacia wood and overlaid with gold. The cherubim were mounted on either end of the lid. The wings of these cherubim pointed upward while their faces looked down upon the mercy seat of Adonai. It was as if invisible circles—beginning in Jerusalem and receding inwards towards the temple, then the Holy of Holies, the ark and finally Adonai's mercy seat—concentrated our need for Adonai and His passion for us to this focal point of Adonai's mercy. Inside the ark were the stone tablets of the ten commandments given to Moses. The veil used to conceal this chamber, now ripped asunder, was regal violet and crimson, made of seamless, choice linen.[15]

"When did this happen?" asked Peter.

"Hassi told us it was at noon, the exact time of Jesus's death!" exclaimed Bartholomew.

"Hassi said," added Matthew, "that it was as if invisible, mighty hands took the thick curtain and ripped it as easily as someone tearing a rag."

"What does it mean when the very barrier that separates Adonai from man is split?" I asked.

"What did Hassi say about it?" inquired Andrew.

"He was horrified, of course," continued Matthew. "He said the High Priest went white. Hassi feared the man would die on the spot. They both ran out of the inner room and assembled all the priests they could find in the temple as quickly as possible. Hassi said they discussed many possible reasons for the event. Some thought Adonai was angry with them, others believed that an evil spirit was in their midst and one or two suggested that it was a sign of the end of the priests' unique place as chosen men to bridge Jews to Adonai's holiness. After hours of discussion, it was decided that evil sought to deceive them. Only those in the room knew of the abominable occurrence so they vowed to keep the secret."

"Then Hassi asked how we had heard about the ripped curtain," Bartholomew broke in.

"And what did you tell him?" asked Peter.

Bartholomew and Matthew looked at one another, smiling, and shrugged.

"We said that the risen Messiah, Jesus, had told us that something significant had happened in the temple and that we were to talk to Hassi about it."

We all started laughing, realizing how ludicrous the truth sounded.

"The question still remains," Peter interjected, "what does it mean? Jesus specifically asked us to talk to Hassi."

"Maybe it is about our access to Adonai, just as some of the priests suggested," John pondered. "Perhaps it is that the priests no longer need to intercede for us with Adonai."

"That would be quite revolutionary," responded Matthew. "It does away with sacrifices, the temple and our whole way of living."

"Jesus did talk about a new covenant," John countered. "Maybe that's part of it." Then, as if not truly committed to anything he was saying, he turned to continue walking and added lamely, "I don't know. Let's talk to Mary and see what she has to tell us."

We followed him quietly, deep in thought. None of us knew where this quest that Jesus had sent us on would lead. It was new and different. I had spent two-and-a-half years with a man whom I had believed would be king, working to make it happen. During that time I had come to believe that my king was the Messiah prophesied by the prophets, Adonai's specially chosen servant, the bringer of a majestic reign for Israel. Now, however, I did not know what the future held or what was being asked of me. My mind felt like a balled-up knot of string that needed to be untangled. My Messiah had been killed then resurrected. He appeared to us. Although I was convinced that he was flesh and blood, he had the ability to appear and disappear at will; he was not subject to the laws of nature like the rest of us. Further, he seemed to have no desire to operate under those restrictions again.

What did Jesus want? What was he going to do? What was *I* supposed to do?

Mary was grinding grain outside her door when we arrived. She welcomed us graciously, despite the fact that eleven men had shown up at her home unannounced. She brought us a basin of water to wash in, water to drink and invited us to sit with her in the shade. I wondered what she thought as she sat with her back against the house's east wall, for when she did, we immediately surrounded her to form a semi-circle and waited intently for her to speak. Peter wasted no time telling her why we had come.

"Jesus has been resurrected from the dead," he blurted out.

A smile broadened across Mary's face as tears welled in her eyes. She inhaled slowly, deeply, and closed her eyes for a moment, tears trickling down her cheeks. She looked relieved yet not shocked.

"He has appeared to us twice and Magdala has spoken to him, too," Peter continued, as if trying to convince her of something he knew sounded crazy.

"I'm not surprised," she reassured him. "I cannot tell you the pain I felt watching my son suffer as he died on that cross. But I believed that death could never hold onto him."

"He told us to come and see you," Peter said, explaining our presence. "He said we were to ask you about the circumstances surrounding his birth."

All was quiet as we looked expectantly at Mary. Jesus had sent us here, she must know something which would help give us direction.

Mary took another deep breath, leaning her head back against the wall to tilt her face towards the sky. "So now it is finally time for me to tell my story, is it?" Turning her face towards us again she cleared her throat and leaned forward, returning our hopeful looks as she began. "Jesus's birth was quite scandalous, you know. I was betrothed to be married to Joseph but was pregnant with Jesus before we were married. Probably almost everyone in Nazareth knows this—but only Joseph, Jesus and I knew that Joseph was not Jesus's father."

I stared at her in disbelief. I heard Matthew and Andrew start to whisper to each other. Peter and James wiggled nervously where they sat and Bartholomew joined in a muted conversation. A confession by Jesus's mother concerning her illegitimate son was the last thing I had expected to hear! Was this really why Jesus had sent us?

"Wait, wait," Mary said over the mumbling, raising her hands. "Wait. You must hear the whole story." Everyone quieted. I was not sure if I even wanted to hear any more.

"One evening after supper," she continued, "I went for a walk. As I walked alone beside a stream, someone suddenly appeared in front of me. I knew at once it was no man. He was tall and broad in stature like a great soldier but he looked radiant, his clothes glowed like white fire. He was an angel! He told me his name was Gabriel and that I was highly favoured and blessed among women.

"Terrified, I asked him what he meant, what he wanted with me. He said, 'Do not fear, Mary. You have found favour with God. You will conceive and bear a son and give him the name Jesus. Great will be his dignity and he will be called Son of the Most High. The Lord God will give him the throne of David his father. He will rule over the house of Jacob forever and his reign will be without end.'"[16]

She quoted the angel as though reading from a parchment laid out before her.

"His words are embedded in my mind," she explained. "You do not meet an angel bearing such news and easily forget it. I did not understand how this would come to be for I did not have a husband and had never been with a man. This I told to the angel. But he said, 'The Holy Spirit will come upon you and the power of the Most High will overshadow you. Therefore, the holy offspring to be born will be called the Son of God.' And then I knew I was with child, I don't know how I knew, I just did. And it was true. I gave birth to Jesus nine months later. Everyone assumed that Joseph had disobeyed Adonai's laws about marriage, but that was not the case. Joseph bore the lies and condemnation gallantly."

My mind swam with what she was saying. How could this be? Was Jesus the literal Son of Adonai? The times Jesus had called Adonai his father flooded my thoughts. A man and a woman come together to create new life, each contributing half of themselves to make a new person. Had Adonai, the Creator of the universe, truly joined half of His God-ness to a human? Had the Most High joined His immortality to humanity's finiteness, His power to our frailty? Could Adonai's purity, holiness and wisdom really be combined with our imperfection, pride, and arrogance? I bristled at the thought. It seemed repulsive, repugnant and sacrilegious.

Mary continued her story.

"When I told Joseph that I was pregnant he wanted to nullify the engagement. Who could blame him? Would you believe your betrothed if she told you that she was still a virgin and yet was pregnant? Oh, he felt so hurt and betrayed. But Joseph was a good and upright man. He knew that I could be stoned for becoming pregnant outside of marriage so, not wanting to expose me, he was going to nullify our marriage quietly. That night an angel appeared to Joseph, this time in a dream. The angel said, 'Joseph, son of David, have no fear about taking Mary as your wife. It is by the Holy Spirit that she has conceived this child. She will have a son and you are to name him Jesus because he will save his people from their sins. It had to happen this way to fulfill the prophesy that Adonai gave to Isaiah, 'The virgin will be with child and will give birth to a son, and they shall call him Emanuel.' Then Joseph awoke and did exactly as the angel had told him.[17] I was so thankful to Adonai for giving me Joseph as my husband and father of our family, relieved that Adonai had confirmed to him the miracle that had happened to me. What a wonderful father he was to Jesus. They loved each other as if Jesus was Joseph's own flesh and blood. No one knew the truth except the three of us, not until now."

Mary paused for a moment to let all she had told us sink in. Then softly but with great purpose, she stated, "I am sure you know that Emanuel means 'Adonai is with us.' Offspring of any kind is, by necessity, the same as its parent. An ox can only give birth to an ox. You are human because you were born of humans. You are Jewish because of your ancestry to Abraham. Jesus is Adonai. It is his ancestry, his heritage."

"But," interrupted John, "he is your son, as well. He has human heritage and ancestry."

"Yes," smiled Mary, contemplating how to explain it so that we would better understand. "He is fully human and fully Adonai at the same time. Think of a coin. Both sides of a coin are completely different yet they make the same coin. If either of the uniquely different sides were gone the coin would cease to be a coin. It would lose its purpose."

We sat quietly, churning and working through what we had just heard, what it meant and the implications to our beliefs, our lives.

"I can see you need some time to think about what I have told you," she said, rising slowly. "I will leave you for a while. I have some errands to run at the market anyway. I have contemplated this secret for years now, you have much considering to do."

She left us to our thoughts.

"Have we just spent the last three years walking and talking face to face with the Most High?" James asked, aghast, his voice tense and full of fear.

"It can't be," said Thomas, shaking his head back and forth.

We all glared at him, remembering Thomas's adamant denials of the previous day. He shrank, realizing how his comment mirrored his recent doubts.

"I-I just meant," Thomas defended himself, "that it is an incredible thought. Could we have been living daily with Adonai?"

"Would Adonai do that?" I asked. "Would he want to walk on earth as a human?"

"Well, he walked with Adam and Eve in the garden," commented John, reasoning more with himself than convincing us of his position.

"Yes, I guess so," I returned thoughtfully.

Thinking about Adam, Eve and the beginning of creation, I wondered further at the implications of the Creator and Jesus being one. Did that mean that Jesus was present at the creation of time?

Words from the first book of the Torah filtered through my mind. "In the beginning Adonai said, "Let there be an expanse between the waters to separate the water under the expanse from the water above it," And it was so. And God saw that it was good." Had those been Jesus's words?

Months ago when we had been engulfed by waves while sailing across the Sea of Galilee, Jesus had calmed the storm by simply saying, "Be still." Had nature heard the familiar voice that had spoken it into existence and recognized its Master?

"Why wouldn't he have told us?" asked Matthew, interrupting my reverie. "Why let us believe that he was something that he was not?"

"I wonder how many times he did he tell us but we just weren't listening, hearing only what we wanted to hear," answered Bartholomew.

"He said that he was the way, the truth and the life. The only way to come to the Father," Philip recalled.[18]

"He told Nicodemus that Adonai sent His only Son into the world, so that whoever believed in the Son would have eternal life," added Peter.[19]

Then came a smattering of recollections as apostles recalled the words of Jesus with a new insight.

"He told the Pharisees that he came in His Father's name." [20]

"He said that we are from this world, but that he was from above and not of this world."[21]

"He said that he and the Father were one." [22]

"He said that we had known him and so we had known the Father. And that from now on we have known the Father because we have seen him." [23]

"He said 'Believe me that I am in the Father and that the Father is in me.'"[24]

"He said that he came from the Father and came into the world." [25]

"He said, every one who confesses Jesus before men, Jesus would confess before his Father, who is in heaven."[26]

Each of us retreated again into our own thoughts.

"The Creator of the universe lived with us. And I betrayed him," Peter said quietly into the silence.

"Think of the times I questioned him," commented James, seeming to not even hear Peter's dismay.

"And the times I joked with him," added Andrew.

"Does Adonai really play with children?" I pondered aloud. "Or spend his days with fishermen, merchants, tax collectors and prostitutes? Does the Creator of all we see choose to be born to a peasant woman? Doesn't that diminish Adonai?"

Even as I voiced my words aloud, my grandson Caleb's words

whispered in my ear, "See, Grandpa, I knew Jesus was big enough."

I realized that I confined and restricted Adonai by thinking He was too great and powerful to pour himself into a human shell. It seemed strangely ironic that I believed Adonai too powerful to become as finite as His creation. Did it not take more power to bond with creation than to merely create it?

"The Sabbath will soon be upon us," Peter finally spoke. "Let's prepare for it and hope we can sort through all this over the next few days."

Peter and the rest of the apostles went to set up camp outside of Nazareth, asking me to find Mary in the marketplace to let her know of our plans and that we would see her at the service in the morning. This I did.

On the way to the campsite, I noticed a large knotted tree in a field beside the road and decided to sit under it for a while to think, free of distraction. Pushing my back into the trunk, I began replaying all that I had seen and heard over the past days: the news of Jesus's resurrection, his appearances, the torn veil, the supernatural circumstances around Jesus's conception.

Suddenly the teachings of my rabbi came to mind. As a youth I had memorized many of the prophet's scriptures concerning the Messiah. As the words flashed in my mind I said them aloud.

"His servant grew up like a tender young plant. He grew like a root coming up out of dry ground. He didn't have any beauty or majesty that made us notice him. There wasn't anything special about the way he looked that drew us to him. Men looked down on him. They didn't accept him. He knew all about sorrow and suffering. He was like someone people turn their faces away from. We looked down on him. We didn't have any respect for him.

He suffered the things we should have suffered. He took on himself the pain that should have been ours. But we thought God was wounding him and making him suffer.

But the servant was pierced because we had sinned. He was punished to make us whole again. His wounds have healed us. All of us are like sheep. We have wandered away from God. All of us have turned to our own way.

And the Lord has placed on his servant the sins of us all.

He was beaten down and made to suffer. But he didn't open his mouth. He was led away like a sheep to be killed. Lambs are silent while their wool is being cut off. In the same way, he didn't open his mouth. He was arrested and sentenced to death. Then he was taken away. He was cut off from this life. He was punished for the sins of my people.

Who among those who were living at that time could have understood those things?

He was given a grave with those who were evil. But his body was buried in the tomb of a rich man. He was killed even though he hadn't harmed anyone. And he had never lied to anyone.

The Lord says, 'It was my plan to crush him and cause him to suffer. I made his life a guilt offering to pay for sin. But he will see all of his children after him. In fact, he will continue to live. My plan will be brought about through him. After he suffers, he will see the light that leads to life. And he will be satisfied. My godly servant will make many people godly because of what he will accomplish. He will be punished for their sins.

So I will give him a place of honour among those who are great. He will be rewarded just like others who win the battle. That is because he was willing to give his life as a sacrifice. He was counted among those who had committed crimes. He took the sins of many people on himself. And he gave his life for those who had done what is wrong.'" [27]

It read like a biography of Jesus's life, death and resurrection but it was written by Isaiah hundreds of years ago. I shivered, marveling at the clarity of the scripture and struck by their eerie, familiar chord.

A second recitation came to mind, this time from the prophet Jeremiah.

> "'Behold, the days are coming,' declares the Lord, 'when I will make a new covenant with the house of Israel and with the house of Judea, not like the covenant which I made with their fathers in the day I took them by the hand to bring them out of the land of Egypt, My covenant which they broke, although I was a husband to them,' declares the Lord.
>
> 'But this is the covenant which I will make with the house of Israel after those days,' declares the Lord, 'I will put My law within them, and on their heart I will write it; and I will be their God, and they shall be My people. And they shall not teach again, each man his neighbour and each man his brother, saying, "Know the Lord," for they shall all know Me, from the least of them to the greatest of them,' declares the Lord, 'for I will forgive their iniquity, and their sin I will remember no more.'" [28]

I sat in a daze, remembering the ancient scriptures which I had heard countless times yet never fully comprehended. I closed my eyes, falling instantly into a deep sleep.

I had a dream. All was black. Although I was not able to see, I sensed that I was in a dark hall surrounded by a vast emptiness. Then I heard the voice of Jesus say, "I am the way, the truth and the light." As he spoke a flame lit. He spoke again, saying, "I am Adonai's only son." Another flame sparked. Jesus's proclamations continued, statements he had made about who he was during the past two-and-half years, each one bringing a new light to share and brighten the previous flame. Gradually I realized that I stood in the centre of a grand palace.

The floors of the palace were made with cypress boards, the high ceilings constructed with cedar beams and timbers. The foundation was sure, forged of solid rock. Cedar walls engraved with carved cherubim, palm trees and open flowers were overlaid with pure gold.

Through the tall stately windows, some made of coloured mosaic stained glass and others of crystal-clear jasper, I could see dawn's first light. Soon the sun would illuminate the halls and rooms.

I understood that I had been living in this regal place since I had met Jesus but had not realized it because of the darkness. The splendour, I knew, was solely because Jesus had been there to touch it with his presence.

Then I awoke. Excited by my discoveries in the scripture, I ran to the camp.

When I reached the tents, only three apostles, James, Andrew and Matthew, were sitting by the fire. The rest, I presumed, were taking time to sift through all they had heard. As I approached the fire to join the three men deep in conversation, they smiled, nodding for me to sit.

"How could we be so blind?" James was saying. "I never dreamt that Jesus was saying that Adonai was his actual father. I don't know why, it just never occurred to me."

"But the Pharisees knew who Jesus was proclaiming to be," commented Andrew. "Think of the times they took great offense to his words."

"Yes, but the religious leaders were always getting their robes tied in knots over words and expressions, nonchalant comments and inconsequential rules," replied James. "You know, no possible loopholes left open."

"But what does it all mean?" Matthew asked, repeating the same question for which an answer had been sought for days.

"It means that we are all in really big trouble," James moaned. "Think about how we've acted. The stupid things we've said. The times we questioned him. I say we are all doomed."

"Well, I don't think he has given up on us yet," encouraged Andrew. "After all, he has appeared to us twice since his death and has sent us on this mission. I hope he didn't do all that just to condemn us."

"Have any of you thought about the passages in Jeremiah and Isaiah about the Messiah?" I asked, trying to change the subject to something I was a bit more sure about.

"As I was walking here," answered Andrew, "I was thinking of the prophesy of Isaiah and his use of the word 'pierced.' He knew that Jesus would be crucified."

"I was remembering the same passage," said James, "and was amazed that it said the Messiah would be considered a criminal but buried in a rich man's grave. That is just what happened when Joseph of Aramethea gave up his own tomb for Jesus."

"Those scriptures also say that the Messiah would continue to live after he had suffered," added Matthew.

"Isn't it strange," I asked, astounded that all three had recalled the same passage as me, "that looking back on Jesus's life the prophesies seem so clear yet without his life as perspective the same words are confusing and hard to understand?"

"Why have our religious leaders, who study the scripture daily, not clued into all this?" asked Matthew. "Why are a bunch of working men the ones who have unlocked the secrets of the prophets?"

"Perhaps they are just like us," offered James, "seeing only what they want to see, interpreting things in ways that are convenient, instead of in terms of Adonai's plan."

"We can guess and speculate all day," said Andrew. "As you say, we are just common men. I don't think we will fully understand what it means until we see Jesus again and speak to him about it."

We accepted this assessment.

We spent the Sabbath in Nazareth then traveled north to Capernaum. Having done all that Jesus had asked and with no further direction, we headed to the northern city to see Peter and Andrew's family. Although we continued to exchange ideas, we came no closer to any conclusions; we needed Jesus to plainly tell us his plans.

One afternoon, as we discussed and argued among ourselves as to what our next action should be, I was surprised by a visit from Jonathan. Throwing a cloak over my shoulders, we headed towards the rolling hills east of the city to talk. I was glad to be out.

"I have been worried about you, Father," Jonathan began. "You committed yourself so completely to Jesus and he was killed. Now

The Other Judas
229

there is talk of him having come back to life! I have not even seen you since the crucifixion in Jerusalem. What do you think of it all?"

Since the Sunday that Magdala had told us of Jesus's empty tomb, events had transpired so quickly that I now shamefully realized that I had not considered contacting my family.

"He is alive, Jonathan," I said with certainty. "I have seen him myself on two occasions."

"What!?" he exclaimed. He grabbed the sleeve of my tunic to stop me.

"Yes. Once just outside of Jerusalem and then again here in Galilee." As we continued walking to the outskirts of Capernaum I told him about the conversations with Joseph and Nicodemus, my encounter with the Roman guards and Jesus's appearances.

Reaching open field, Jonathan slowly lowered himself onto a large rock, propped his elbows on his knees and rubbed his forehead with both hands.

"It's so hard to believe," he said. "Why would any of this happen to Jesus? If he is Adonai's chosen one, why would Adonai let it happen?"

"I don't know," I said honestly after thinking over his questions. "But I believe that I may finally be looking for Adonai's plan instead of my own interpretation of what Adonai wants. It is as if I am seeing Adonai as the 'I AM' who spoke to Moses in the burning bush. He is not an entity created in my mind whose traits and actions are defined by me. He acts as He wants, not as I think He should."

I paused, scanning the horizon and trying to think of how to explain myself. Verbalizing my own muddled thoughts helped me sort out some of what I had experienced.

"It's as if I have been sailing in a boat over the ocean, seeing only what is on the surface and clueless to the world that exists below me. The boat has defined my perception of the sea. Every time that Jesus has appeared to us, he has challenged our understanding of who Adonai's Messiah is. I feel like I have been thrown out of my boat and am drowning in the ocean."

I caught Jonathan's confused gaze and smiled, continuing.

"There is a miraculous world that exists under the surface of the water, yet only when I am out of the boat can I hope to see it. Adonai has always been there, just below the surface, but to experience Him I have had to give up my impressions of who He is and understand that He acts of His own free will."

Thinking back over my misconceptions about the Messiah before the events of the Passover, I realized how short-sighted, paltry, and trifling my views were compared to Adonai's opulent plans for the King of the Jews. Thank Adonai Himself, that He did not satisfy Himself with my bland, mediocre notions!

"You seem so sure," Jonathan said, breaking my reverie.

"What can you be truly sure of?" I asked. "Are you sure of what you see? A magician relies on such a certainty for his illusions. If you eat healthily and are a kind and generous person are you guaranteed a long life? No, I think that faith and belief are the true realities. They are what is left when you cannot trust your eyes or when the world does not act like it should. When you distill down the complexity of life, everyone has faith in something."

We sat quietly and listened to the birds sing to each other.

"Faith requires a choice to believe," Jonathan said contemplatively. "It demands that you take a step towards what you hope is true with no guarantee that you have made a correct decision."

"Yes, it is a risk. But I believe that Adonai has shown us how much He loves us by sending His son Jesus to our world and that if we choose to believe in Him our lives will be made right with Adonai. I think if you take that leap of faith, that conviction will not be proven wrong."

"I will think about what you have said, Father," Jonathan promised, standing and looking like he was ready to head back to Capernaum.

He stayed for two more days in the city before returning home, spending his time talking to me and the other disciples about the discoveries we had made over the past few weeks. He did not confide in me whether or not he chose to believe in Jesus as the Messiah so, I, too, had to rely on my belief that Adonai's love and pursuit of him was real.

We were still waiting for direction ourselves.

chapter twenty-three

I 've had enough! I'm going fishing," Peter's frustration resonated in the room and reflected the anxiety we all felt. We had been in Capernaum three days after having accomplished everything that Jesus had asked of us, doing nothing but waiting. It was an unsettled feeling, constantly looking for Jesus to appear, like knowing that an important guest might arrive at your home at any moment. It kept us edgy with no sense of control. Besides the anxiety, I was tired of analyzing and second guessing my thoughts—yet there seemed to be nothing else to do until Jesus decided to join us.

"Any one want to join me?" Peter called over his shoulder as he left the room. It was already late, the sun about to disappear from the sky and anyone following Peter knew that he would be spending the night in the boat, working nets and gathering fish by moonlight. Only six of us collected our cloaks to head out the door after Peter.

By the time the boat was ready to launch, it was dark. We set out on the calm water and rowed towards the middle of the lake.

With each jerk of the boat as I dipped and pulled my oar through the water, I felt better. This fishing expedition was what I needed, something tangible, a procedure which required no contemplation, only action. I knew what to do and what to expect. We throw out the net, we capture the fish.

When we were far enough out, the seven of us gathered the nets into our hands and heaved them over the side of the boat before sitting back to listen to the gentle waves bump against the boat's hull.

"Let's see how we did," Peter said after about half an hour.

We pulled on the lines, peering over the edge at the approaching nets which felt strangely light. When they were beside the boat, we rummaged through the ropes discovering nothing. Not one fish.

Not yet discouraged, we threw them out again and waited. Again we pulled them in and found nothing. We repeated this worthless process over and over throughout the night, drifting with the current towards the north shore of the sea.

When the sun finally showed itself behind the looming land ahead of us, we were completely discouraged, the night had been an ugly reminder of our wait for Jesus. Just as we had eagerly hoped that our nets would be laden with fish only to find them empty, so for days we had been anticipating that we would see Jesus only to be disappointed at each day's end, deprived again of his presence.

As we approaching the shore, exhausted, I saw a lone man standing on the beach.

"Have you caught anything?" he called to us.

"No, it has been a long, disappointing night," Peter yelled back across the water.

"Throw your nets on the right hand side of the boat," the man called. "I have a feeling you'll find quite a catch there."

The seven of us regarded one another, shrugged and did as the man suggested. What did we have to lose?

As soon as we threw the nets into the water the ropes went taut, straining under an immense weight.

We started to whoop and holler at our good fortune.

I heard John say with a gasp, "It is the Lord!"

My eyes followed his pointing finger to the man on the beach. The current had pulled our boat closer to shore. It was indeed Jesus!

I heard a splash and felt a spray of cold water as Peter jumped from the boat and began swimming to shore. The fish in the net began flipping violently, trying to escape their captivity. Working diligently we brought the net and the boat to the beach before our catch pulled us into the water.

By the time we got the boat to shore, Peter was already sitting at a crackling fire with Jesus and had fish cooking on spigots and flat bread cooling on sticks.

Despite the inviting scene and enticing smells, the six of us stayed by the boat. I had anticipated Jesus's arrival for days but now I was afraid. My hands were cold and clammy, my pumping heart beat loudly in my ears and I shivered despite the morning's warmth. I had learned that Jesus was the Son of Almighty Adonai.

I remembered the first time I saw Jesus at the synagogue in Nazareth, recalled the voice in my head telling me to run. Now I felt stuck in the sand.

"I have spent years seeing Jesus's tenderness and compassion," I thought, "yet now I cower in fear."

He is the very Son of Adonai, your Creator. It was the truth.

"Come and have some breakfast," Jesus called. "And bring some of the fish you caught."

He sounded the same as always. Why not? It was not Jesus who had discovered his heritage and purpose. He had known it all along. It was we, his followers, who now truly understood for the first time.

Gathering enough courage to follow my five friends, I cautiously approached the fire. We sat while Jesus served us. We had learned that He was of Adonai yet He served us just as He had done throughout His life. Had I been valiant at all, I would have protested but I was too shocked, too apprehensive and unsure of how to act to have any boldness. Quietly, reverently, I waited, taking the fish, bread and my cues from the only One who knew the answers to my countless questions.

For years I had laughed, worked and lived with Jesus, now I ate in silence, awkward. Peter seemed particularly uncomfortable and shifted back and forth while playing absently with his food, staring at the ground and avoiding Jesus's eyes.

When we had finished breakfast, Jesus said to Peter, "Simon Peter, son of John, do you love me?"

A breath of air caught in Peter's chest as he continued to examine the sand in front of his feet. He said quietly, "Yes, Lord. You know that I love You."

"Then, tend my lambs," Jesus returned. He did not berate Peter for his past denial, instead, He asked again, "Simon Peter, son of John, do you love me?"

"Yes, Lord. You know that I love You," Peter replied, a bit more emphatically, desperate for Jesus to hear his true feelings despite his human failures.

"Then, shepherd my sheep," Jesus said.

A third time Jesus asked, "Simon Peter, son of John, do you love me?"

Peter was quiet for a moment, trying to control his emotions. His body quivered; still he stared at the sand. When he spoke it was but a whisper that shook with sadness and regret.

"Lord, You know all things. You know that I love You."

Jesus reached out and touched Peter's shoulder, speaking with the same kindness as when He had spoken to the adulterous woman whom the people had wanted to stone, "Tend my sheep." [1]

The waves of the Sea of Galilee washed rhythmically onto the shore. The fire crackled and spit. No one spoke. Every now and then Peter sucked in a great gulp of air while Jesus sat beside him with His hand on Peter's shoulder. Although I felt like I was intruding on a private moment, I could not stop watching. Adonai was touching man, forgiving and granting wholeness. I had seen Jesus heal physical imperfections and frailties. Now, with new eyes, I watched Adonai reach out to restore a hurting heart, to heal humanity's spiritual ache.

"You are forgiven, Peter," Jesus spoke again after a time of quiet.

He then reaffirmed the aspirations He had given Peter years before. "You are Peter and upon this rock I will build my church and the gates of Hades shall not overpower it!"[2]

Turning to the rest of us, Jesus abruptly changed the subject and asked, "What have you discovered about the new covenant?"

I was a little taken aback but John answered quickly.

"You told us that the old covenant was an image of the new one.

Jeremiah said that the new covenant would forgive sins and that Adonai would remember them no more."

"Yes, that is part of the new covenant. The sacrifices of animals are no longer required. I have become the sacrifice for humanity so that sins can be forgiven. That was the reason that the curtain was ripped in the inner sanctuary of the temple. But that is only part of the new covenant. There is more. What else did Jeremiah say would happen with the new covenant?"

I thought through the passage.

"That God would write His law on their hearts," I answered.

"Yes, Judas, you are correct. I have another question for you. When you married your wife, the partner that your father had arranged, why did you care for her and take her into your home?"

"Because the law required it of me," I answered. "I did not want to let my family down so I did what was expected of me."

"Was it always like that?" Jesus continued. "When your wife was sick and dying, did you care for her out of obligation then?"

I thought of my beloved wife for a few moments before replying, "No, we had lived together for so long by then that somewhere along the way it went beyond doing it because I should. When she was sick, I cared for her because I wanted to, not because it was required of me. I loved her."

"Yes. Exactly. Your motivation changed. In the beginning you acted based on the law but later you acted because of love. It is the same with the new covenant. The covenant given to Moses was law, requirements for right living, but the new covenant is from the heart, written on your heart. I desire love, not obligation, to motivate you. You thought that my kingdom would be an earthly kingdom, a political reign, but I want so much more. Politics are still rules, outward motivation. Even if the regulations are admirable, they are imposed by outward force. I want nothing less than your very heart, for you to obey because of love. I want you to act because you are loved. Just as it was with your wife, Judas. You may have performed the same actions at the beginning of your marriage as at the end. I am sure that if she were sick at the start of your life together that you would have looked after her just as diligently, yet the motivation would have been different. Law would have dictated your actions, not love. That is a fundamental difference in the new covenant. Adonai loved the world so much that He sent His only Son so that whoever believes in Him would have eternal life. Adonai took the initiative in demonstrating this love. He loved humanity first."[3]

Jesus's eyes sparkled with excitement in His eagerness for us to know that the acceptance and kindness He had demonstrated was from Adonai.

"Go and do the same," Jesus instructed. "As you have seen me love, I want you to love others. You have known and lived with Adonai's love, now love one another. If you love Adonai, you must love your brother also."

He paused a moment to allow us to think on this challenge before continuing.

"The life I call you to is not a life without cost. Adonai is Holy and Righteous. Never forget it! I did not come to nullify the Law but to fulfill it, enrich it. Think of it like a human body. The Law is like the body's bones, hard and rigid, giving strength and structure. Love is like the soft tissue that surrounds the bones. Without the bones the tissue and skin would have no form. It would be a mass of mush. Yet bones without muscle and flesh are just as useless. The law and love must be entwined together to work as a cohesive unit in order to be truly beautiful and purposeful. Likewise, I came not to destroy the Law but to fulfill it, giving it muscle, flesh and skin."[4]

Then He added with a chuckle, "Both figuratively and literally."

"Mary told us that she was a virgin yet she was pregnant with You. She said it was by the Holy Spirit that she conceived," I admired John's bravery in asking about Jesus's divine lineage.

"I have not always been known by the name Jesus as you have known me. Before time was created, I was 'the Word.' For a time, 'the Word' has become human and lived here on earth with you. This glory, which you have seen, I received from the Father. Before the beginning, 'the Word' already existed. 'The Word' was with God, and 'the Word' was God. Everything that was created was made through 'the Word.' Nothing that has been made was made without Him. Life was in 'the Word' and that Life is the light for all people. The light shines in the darkness, but the darkness has not understood it."[5]

I knew that Jesus's words communicated a wisdom beyond earthly comprehension. It was like being given a thick, sinewy chunk of meat, food too substantial for my teeth to tear. The flavour of the meat could trickle down my throat but my mouth was hopeless to process the food. In the end, I would have to choose to swallow and accept the food offered or remove and reject it. Chewing and breaking the food into smaller manageable pieces was outside my ability.

Yet, I thought, *what kind of God can be completely understood?* A God who can be analyzed and figured out is not worthy of adoration and praise. He is a fraud, no God at all.

Adonai's admonition to Job thousands of years ago resounded in my mind. The supremacy and authority of Adonai revealed as He asked,

Where were you when I laid the earth's foundation?
Who measured it? Who stretched a measuring line across it?

Who created the ocean? Who caused it to be born?
I put clouds over it as if they were its clothes.
I wrapped it in thick darkness. I set limits for it.
I put its doors and metal bars in place.
I said, "You can come this far. But you cannot come any farther.
Here is where your proud waves have to stop."

Have the gates of death been shown to you?
Have you seen the gates of darkness?
Do you understand how big the earth is?
Tell me if you know all these things.

Can you tie up the beautiful Pleiades?
Can you untie the ropes that hold Orion together?

Can you bring out all the stars in their seasons?
Can you lead out the Big Dipper and the Little Dipper?
Do know the laws that govern the heavens?
Can you rule over the earth the way I do?

Who put wisdom in people's hearts?
Who gave understanding to their minds?

I am the Mighty One.
Will the man who argues with me, correct me?[6]

Oh, Lord, I prayed silently to Adonai, my ears had heard about You but now my eyes have seen You. How wrong I was to judge how You, Adonai, should act and love Your creation. I will be satisfied to live in Your love, content to accept Your ways. I have seen great things that I do not understand, talked about things too wonderful for me to know. I will be happy to rest in the fact that Adonai has touched the earth, touched my life and chosen a way to be with me. That way is Jesus, my King.

"Lord," I asked, "Why have You shown Yourself only to us? Why not to the whole world?"[7]

"The prophesies about the Messiah talk about far-reaching influence," Jesus answered. "Isaiah wrote,

I will put my Spirit on him. He will make everything right among the nations. He will be faithful and make everything right. I, the Lord, have chosen you, my servant, to do what is right. I will take hold of your hand. I will keep you safe. You will put my covenant with the people of Israel into effect. And you will be a light for the other nations.[8]

This prophesy will be fulfilled. Israel's covenant is now in place, it is time for you to bring this light to the other nations."

A gasp escaped my lips. This was our future direction? What a huge responsibility! We were but ordinary men. I was a merchant, the men with me, fishermen. Was it to fall on *us* to share Adonai's plan with Israel and the surrounding nations?

"Do not fear," Jesus soothed, "you will not do this alone. The Father has a gift for you. You have heard me talk about it before. John the Immerser baptized with water, but in a few days you will be immersed with the Holy Spirit. You will receive power when the Holy Spirit comes on you. Then you will be my witnesses in Jerusalem, Judea and Samaria. You will even be my witness from one end of the earth to the other!⁹

"Trust me," Jesus continued with a knowing smile. "If you believe in me, the works that I have done you will do also. In fact, you will do greater works than these because I am going to the Father. If you love me, you will keep my commandments."¹⁰

Jesus spent the day with us on the deserted beach. As we talked with Jesus He strolled barefoot with us over the hot sand, cooling His feet now and then in the surf. It was a day of encouragement and building us up; it felt like a sparkling treasure.

By the end of the day we were sure of the hope to which we were called, convinced that nothing could separate us from the love of Adonai, which was in Christ Jesus our Lord, neither death, nor life, nor angels, nor principalities, nor things present, nor things to come, nor powers, nor height, nor depth, nor any other created thing.¹¹

chapter twenty-four

uring the next forty days Jesus talked with us often. Once He even appeared to more than five hundred believers at the same time.[1] Jonathon and Caleb were there. We were His witnesses to the people. The Torah instructs that the time between the Passover and the Feast of Weeks is a time of harvest. During the seven weeks between these events, scripture tells us to harvest crops and then, during the celebration, to bring an offering to Adonai from the blessings He has bestowed upon us.[2]

The seven weeks following Jesus's crucifixion were for me a time of harvest. Jesus had spent close to three years planting seeds of truth and understanding, coaxing my spirit to grow and weeding out misconceptions. Following His resurrection it seemed as if Jesus was on a threshing floor, tossing up his newly cut crop, watching the chaff blow away while the desired kernels remained.

Jesus clarified my own perceptions, pulling them out of an earthly context and placing them into an eternal one. He emphasized truths that He had shown during His sojourn on earth, equipping His disciples for our future work.

As my understanding was pulled into an eternal perspective, I often laughed to recall my mundane ideas about the king of the Jews. My presumptuous, grandiose plans were like a single drop of water splattering on a sun-baked brick while Adonai's plans were a drenching, soaking rain. My ideas were like the empty nets we pulled into the boat during our night of fishing three weeks ago while Adonai's designs were nets teeming with fish.

I had sought an earthly king, Adonai had provided a heavenly

Saviour. I had hoped that the Messiah would be Adonai's servant but Jesus was His very Son. I sought Israel's restoration but Jesus was a light to the nations, reaching to the ends of the earth. I saw the temporal, Jesus saw the eternal. I wanted a rescuer for Israel, He wanted to be a redeemer for the ages.

How much higher are Adonai's ways than my ways, His thoughts above my thoughts. Jesus came to remove sins from us, as far as the east is from the west. He came to show that Adonai's loving kindness is from everlasting to everlasting, as high as the heavens are above the earth.[3] He proved that we are not forgotten, nay, we are written on the very palm of Adonai's hand.[4]

I wanted people healed, Jesus wanted their strength to be renewed so that they would soar with the wings of eagles. I wanted to restore Israel's glory, He wanted to be a refuge to the poor, a shelter from the rain and a shade from the heat. Jesus desired to provide for all people a feast of juicy, rich food and pure, choice wines.

He was a stalwart defender of the poor in spirit, the comforter of those who mourn. He was merciful and pure of heart, a righteous measuring rod, fair, honest and persuasive.

Jesus was a visionary coming alongside His people and loving them. He is my Saviour. My Redeemer. My King.

My dream of the palace was ever present in my mind. Each day that I spent with Jesus, more lamps joined the chorus of light to reveal the beautiful palace touched by Adonai. The dawn had indeed arrived. Oh, what a glorious day it was!

Whenever Jesus appeared to us, however, we were keenly aware that we were on borrowed time. Jesus had told us that He would soon be leaving to go back to His Father in heaven. This time we understood.

He always added a caveat to this knowledge and promised something better, telling us that we needed to trust Him, that His Father's house had many rooms, that He was going there to prepare a place for us and that He would come back to take us to be with Him.

Vicki Clarke
242

The Feast of Weeks was ten days away and we had returned to Jerusalem for the celebrations. I was walking with my fellow apostles on the Mount of Olives when suddenly Jesus walked with us.

As always, it was glorious when He appeared. We anticipated it constantly, hoped for it incessantly, and reveled in His presence whenever we saw Him.

This time Jesus was different. He seemed both sad and excited. Gathering us together, He said, "Do not leave Jerusalem, but wait here for the Holy Spirit which the Father has promised."[5]

As He spoke, I was distracted by the sky behind Jesus. It was as if it moved towards us. It did not look like the clouds were blowing but rather as if the entire expanse was shifting. First there was a single, thin shaft of light that shone above us then the sky's bold blue-ness separated like two doors being slowly swung open.

The brilliance concealed behind the doors was riveting.

I was awestruck.

A great host of saints stood amassed in a vast, open field. They were adorned in shimmering clothes that moved like water glistening on a warm summer's day. They stood on either side of the space, creating an aisle that led to a great throne.

The place was surrounded by mighty, peaked mountains. There was no need for the sun or the moon to shine for the glory of Adonai illuminated it.

Jesus turned towards this throne room and began to ascend the steps before Him. Each step was made of a different precious stone. The majority were a translucent colour, mostly blues, greens and yellow with opaque or lustrous quartz dispersed between the hues. One stone was clear and veined with colour. The first gem was jasper, then sapphire, chalcedony, emerald, sardonyx, sardius, chrysolite, beryl, topaz chrysoprase and jacinth. The final stone, amethyst, was a brilliant violet.[6]

When Jesus's foot touched it, I heard music. I cannot say the number of instruments that played, for many were tones I had never heard before, but the musicians played in precise unison, the notes strong and distinct, music to herald the King. The sound resonated in my soul and I wanted to sing. I wondered how long my frail skin could contain my bursting spirit. I viewed the coronation of my King in the place where earthly flesh cannot survive.

As Jesus entered the room, he was surrounded by four winged seraphim. Two flew in front of him and two behind, draping a robe over His shoulders. The material of the garment danced, enticing my eyes, the hem cascaded behind Him to cover four of the jewel steps.

The seraphim had six wings. With two they covered their faces, with two they covered their feet and with two they flew.[7]

I do not know how I knew what the creatures were, only that my mind knew, just as it had known the type of stone each step was made of.

One seraphim called out to another as they swooped about Jesus,

"Holy, Holy, Holy is the Lord of hosts.
The whole earth is full of his glory."[8]

The next Seraphim responded with the same proclamation.

As Jesus began to walk toward His throne, the saints fell prostrate before Him in reverence. With each step that He took the place shook. The mountains cracked then melted as if, unable to stand in the presence of their Creator, they had no choice but to lay prostrate with the saints.

Suddenly there appeared angels, a multitude of heavenly hosts, standing regimented on either side of the throne. They were beautiful yet frighteningly powerful. They were as tall as two men with broad shoulders; an elite, mighty army, swords sheathed at their sides. Heaven's guard stood ready to defend the King.

The soldiers welcomed their Supreme Commander proclaiming,

"Glory to God in the highest,
And on earth, peace among men with whom He is pleased."[9]

When Jesus reached His throne He turned to face us and the opened door of heaven.

Then a great light shone, encompassing Jesus, embracing Him. I could not bear it, I covered my eyes, fell to the ground and put my head in the dirt. I heard a Voice exuberant with joy,

"Welcome home, my good and faithful servant!
My beloved Son, in whom I am well pleased!"[10]

Then came a jubilant cheer, one so powerful that I thought it would split the earth in two, as all of heaven rejoiced at the return of their King.

epilogue

here are many other things which Jesus did which, if they were written in detail, I suppose that even the world itself would not have room for the books that would be written.[1]

Tradition holds that most of the apostles were executed in torturous ways. Their lives after Jesus's ascension were not easy. They were often imprisoned and flogged, endured beatings and ridicule. They nurtured fledgling churches and believers, settled disputes and guided people in the teachings of Jesus. Their earthly rewards were small but they knew that they laboured for something eternal.

They were convinced that Jesus was raised from the dead, that He is Adonai's son and that He is the only way to Adonai.

Jesus's apostles were true witnesses. They lived with Jesus, walked and talked with Him, saw His revelations done in publicly observable ways. These men knew them as fact, not belief, because they witnessed it themselves. They knew Jesus was resurrected. They knew Him to be the Son of Adonai and preached this to their deaths. They allowed themselves to be tortured to death proclaiming it.

Their faith was absolute!

SOURCES

Drucher, Malka. *The Family Treasury of Jewish Holidays* Boston: Little Brown, 1994.

Gift, Joseph. *Life and Customs in Jesus's Times*, Cincinnati, Ohio: The Standard Publishing Foundation, 1957.

Schwartz, Lynne. *The Four Questions*, New York: Dial Books, 1989.

Wight, Fred. *Manners and Customs of Bible Times*, Chicago, Illinois: Moody Press, 1953.
www.holidays.net

ENDNOTES

CHAPTER TWO
[1]Matthew 13:44—46
[2]Lawhead, Stephen, *Avalon* (New York: Avon Books, 1999) p.253.

CHAPTER FOUR
[1]Deuteronomy 14:21
[2]Exodus 20:8
[3]Gift, Joseph, *Life and Customs in Jesus's Time* (Cincinnati, Ohio: Standard Publishing Foundation, 1957), p.101.
[4]Matthew 11:28, 30, *The Open Bible* (La Habra, California, 1979) p. 924.
[5]Luke 6:6-11

CHAPTER FIVE
[1]Exodus 18:17—23
[2]Luke 6:16
[3]Matthew 4:21, 22
[4]Luke 5:27, 28
[5]Luke 5:10

CHAPTER SIX
[1]Luke 19:1—10
[2]Leviticus 13

CHAPTER SEVEN
[1]Luke 7:40-50, *The Open Bible* p.985; John 11:2

CHAPTER EIGHT
[1]Luke 5:17—26
[2]Smith, James, *Rich Mullins His Life and Legacy* (Nashville: Broadman and Holman, 2000), p.72.

[3]Luke 10:38—42
[4]Ecclesiastes 3:3—8

CHAPTER NINE
[1]previous three paragraphs, Smith, p. 50, 54.
[2]Luke 8:1—3
[3]Revelation 1:14,15, *The Open Bible* p.1210,1211.
[4]Ephesians 6:12

CHAPTER TEN
[1]Gift, Joseph, p.49.
[2]John 4:32, *The Open Bible,* p.1017.
[3]Luke 9:3—5

CHAPTER ELEVEN
[1]Luke 9:10—17, Mark 6:52

CHAPTER TWELVE
[1]Luke 10:1
[2]John 8:1—11
[3]John 12:6
[4]Luke 8:22—25
[5]Isaiah 11:1, 2, 4
[6]Isaiah 42:1
[7]Isaiah 9:4
[8]Isaiah 9:3

CHAPTER THIRTEEN
[1]Matthew 20:20—28
[2]Luke 6:41
[3]John 11:32, *The Open Bible* p.1027.
[4]John 11:39, *The Open Bible* p.1028.
[5]Luke 7:11—17
[6]Luke 8:53—56

[7]Ezekiel 37:5, 6, 9, *The Open Bible*, p.790.
[8]John 11:1—46

CHAPTER FOURTEEN
[1]John 12:1—11

CHAPTER FIFTEEN
[1]Mark 11:1—10
[2]Luke 19:40

CHAPTER SIXTEEN
[1]Luke 21:5—6
[2]Luke 21:10—19
[3]Matthew 24:36—44
[4]Matthew 24:32—35

CHAPTER SEVENTEEN
[1]Luke 22:10—11
[2]John 13:5—15
[3]Matthew 26:28, *The Open Bible* p.944.
[4]Luke 22:21—34
[5]John 13:26
[6]Luke 22:35—38
[7]John 17:1—26
[8]Luke 22:48
[9]John 18:4—11

CHAPTER EIGHTEEN
[1]Revelation 8:6—13; 9:2
[2]Matthew 27:1—10

CHAPTER NINETEEN
[1]John 18:28
[2]Matthew 27:11—32; John 19:15

CHAPTER TWENTY
[1]John 19:19—30
[2]Leviticus 4
[3]Luke 23:35
[4]Isaiah 53:7
[5]Psalms 22
[6]Psalms 139
[7]Matthew 27:45, 46
[8]Exodus 33:21—23
[9]Luke 23:39—43
[10]John 19:31—36
[11]John 19:38—42
[12]Matthew 26:69—75
[13]Luke 2:41—52

CHAPTER TWENTY-ONE
[1]John 20:1—18
[2]Mark 15:44-46; Matthew 27:64
[3]Matthew 28:2—4
[4]Jeremiah 31:15
[5]Psalms 78:2
[6]Isaiah 53:5
[7]Luke 24:13—35

CHAPTER TWENTY-TWO
[1]Matthew 27:52—53
[2]Matthew 28:11—15
[3]Matthew 12:40
[4]Zechariah 13:7; Matthew 26:31, *The Open Bible*, p.944.
[5]Zechariah 11:12; Matthew 27:9, 10, *The Open Bible*, p.945, 946.
[6]Psalms 22:18, *New International Version* (Grand Rapids, Michigan: Zondervan, 1996), p. 467.
[7]Isaiah 9:5—7
[8]John 20:19—22

[9]John 20:24—29
[10]Isaiah 2:2—4
[11]Jeremiah 23:5 & 6,
[12]Matthew 3:16, 17
[13]Matthew 17:1—13
[14]Matthew 27:51
[15]2Chronicles 3:8-14; 5:2-7
[16]Luke 1:30-32, 35, *New American Bible* (New York: Catholic Book Publishing, 1970), p.68.
[17]Matthew 1:18—25
[18]John 14:6
[19]John 3:16
20John 5:43
[21]John 8:23
[22]John 10:30
[23]John 14:9, 10
[24]John 14:11
[25]John 16:28
[26]Matthew 10:32
[27]Isaiah 53, *NIV Super Heroes Bible* (Grand Rapids, Michigan: Zonderkidz, 1998), p.842,843.
[28]Jeremiah 31:33, 34 *The Open Bible,* p.720,721.

CHAPTER TWENTY-THREE
[1]John 21:1-17
[2]Matthew 16:18, *The Open Bible* p.193.
[3]John 4:19
[4]Brandt, Paul and Yancy, Philip, *Fearfully and Wonderfully Made* (Grand Rapids, Michigan: Zondervan, 1980), p.110,120.
[5]John1:1—18
[6]Job 38:4, 5, 8-11,17, 18, 31—33, 36, 40:2, *NIV Super Hero Bible* p.629-631.
[7]John 14:22
[8]Isaiah 42:2, 3, 6, *NIV Super Hero Bible* p.828.

[9]Acts 1:8
[10]John 14:12, 15
[11]Romans 8:38, 39, *The Open Bible* p.1089

CHAPTER TWENTY-FOUR
[1]1Corinthians 15:6
[2]Deuteronomy 16:1—10
[3]Psalms 103:8—18
[4]Isaiah 49:16
[5]Luke 24:49
[6]Revelation 21:19, 20
[7]Isaiah 6:2—4
[8]Isaiah 6:3, *The Open Bible* p. 632.
[9]Luke 2:14, *The Open Bible* p. 977.
[10]Matthew 3:17, *The Open Bible* p.915.

EPILOGUE
[1]John 21:25, *The Open Bible* p.1039.